THE DEVIL IN DISGUISE

Martin Edwards

Andrews UK Limited

Note from the author: In writing this book, I have been grateful for
the help of friends and colleagues expert on the Liverpool and legal
scenes. Nevertheless, this is a work of fiction and all the characters,
firms, organisations and incidents described are wholly imaginary.
So far as I know, they do not resemble any counterparts in the real
world; in the unlikely event that any similarity does exist, it is an
unintended coincidence.

Contents

Introduction

There is something mysterious, not to say suspicious, about Martin Edwards. How does he do so much? Leaving aside his highly successful legal career, which would be more than enough for most people, he's the author of the critically-acclaimed Lake District mysteries, one of which was shortlisted for the Theakston's Old Peculier Crime Novel of the Year. His other books include a perceptive re-examination of the Crippen case in the form of a novel, a true crime book and a collection of some of his 40-odd short stories, one of which won the Dagger award of the Crime Writers' Association. He has a third career as an editor and critic on the crime fiction genre. And then of course there are his legal books and more than a thousand articles, many of them concerning his professional speciality, which is employment law.

This crowded and nauseatingly distinguished curriculum vitae has one important omission: the Harry Devlin crime series, which features a Liverpool solicitor with a propensity for stumbling into murder cases. These were Martin Edwards' first published novels. On both sides of the Atlantic, there's a long tradition of lawyers moonlighting with crime fiction - and often writing novels with legal backgrounds. From the very start, however, Martin Edwards stood out among such lawyer-authors, even in a crowd that includes Erle Stanley Gardener and Michael Gilbert, Frances Fyfield and John Grisham.

Reviewers instantly recognised this - the first Harry Devlin novel, All The Lonely People, was shortlisted for the CWA's John Creasey Memorial Dagger for the best first crime novel in 1991. The book had three particular strengths: its lovingly knowledgeable portrait of Liverpool; Martin Edwards' quietly revolutionary refusal to follow the then-current trend for portraying overt violence in crime fiction; and the strength of the characterisation, in particular

Harry himself - damaged, endearing, intelligent and obstinately attached to the notion of justice.

Since then, the series has gone from strength to strength. The pop songs of the Sixties provide titles for all the books, giving them an added resonance for readers old enough to remember the songs when they were hit singles. After a gap of some years, the eighth novel in the series, Waterloo Sunset, appeared in 2008.

The series isn't frozen in time - both Harry and Liverpool have changed over the years. In the modern world it's not easy to create a credible amateur detective. But Harry is convincing, perhaps because he lacks the superheroic qualities of the amateur sleuths of the Golden Age crime fiction. He is a very British hero. It's a cause for celebration that he is still flourishing today.

Originally published in 1998, The Devil In Disguise is the sixth title in the series - though don't let this put you off reading it if you haven't yet read the earlier books; like all the Devlin novels, this works just as well as a standalone. The story focuses on the Kavanaugh Trust, a Liverpool arts charity, which hires Harry to deal with the vexed question of a benefactor's will - a will that unexpectedly does not benefit the Trust. Then Luke Dessaur, the chairman of the Trust, vanishes; and when he reappears, fallen from the third-floor window of a hotel, he is very dead indeed.

Martin Edwards draws his readers - and the unfortunate Harry - into a tangle of villainy. As ever, the novel is a cunning mix of contemporary and traditional ingredients. However dark the story, however, it is characteristic of Edwards' writing that an undercurrent of dry humour is often just perceptible. Watch out for the Liverpool's gentlemen's club, for example, the oldest in the country and equipped with the splendid collection of pornography in its members-only library. There's also a certain nostalgic pleasure in the Speckled Band, a bookshop devoted to crime fiction. In those days, London boasted three bookshops dedicated to crime fiction - indeed, Martin and I shared a book-launch in one of them when this novel was first published. Time and the internet has put paid to all three of them.

Still, time and the internet has its advantages too: thanks to their mysterious workings, The Devil In Disguise has become available again. When I reviewed the novel on first publication in 1998, I concluded that it was 'literate, quirky and intelligent... psychologically plausible and intelligently plotted.' Thirteen years later, I stand by the verdict but I'd like to add a rider to it: The Devil In Disguise reads even better the second time around than it did the first.

Andrew Taylor

Prologue

*H*e had dreamed of this.

Her parting words echoed around the cellar. 'Don't go away.'

As if he would. As if he could. Listening to her high heels click-click-click up the stone steps, he smiled to himself. He could have sworn he heard her choke back a grunt of pleasure at the prospect of what lay in store. The door closed behind her: was that a key turning in the lock, or just wishful thinking? He had always wanted to be her prisoner. And tonight his imagination was working overtime.

The steel handcuffs were cutting into his wrists, but for him the sensation was exquisite. At last she had consented to play the game. She seemed different, somehow, as if the fantasy excited her as much as he had ever hoped.

Waiting for her return, he stretched his limbs. She had snapped the other half of each pair of cuffs around the hooks set into the wall a little above head height. He let his mind wander. This was an old room; perhaps eighteenth-century merchants had once tethered their own slaves here. Those poor devils would not have chosen such a fate, but he luxuriated in it. He could move his trunk and legs, feel the warmth of the sheepskin rug against his feet. Presently she would release him and they would make love with wild passion.

Although he was in the heart of Liverpool, he might have been marooned on a Pacific atoll for all that he was aware of the world above ground. It was night-time in the city, but he could hear no voices or traffic noise, nothing but the faint buzz of an unseen fly. The air was damp and musty but he did not care. This was as close to heaven as he was ever likely to come.

The fly landed on his chest and he blew it off. She was taking her time, he thought. Impossible to understand: she had promised to be back within a minute, once she had checked that the front door was locked. *They did not want any unexpected callers, not tonight of all nights.*

He opened his eyes and tried adjusting to the gloom. An unshaded bulb glowed overhead, but most of the room was in deep shadow. Straight ahead, she had propped the dusty old mirror. All the better to see everything with, she had said. She had written something in lipstick on the splintered surface of the glass and he craned his neck so that he could read it.

YOU KILLED HIM, YOU BASTARD

It was as though a donkey had kicked him in the balls. He blinked once, twice, unable to believe the message in the words. Was his mind playing games of its own? He screwed up his eyes so hard that the muscles hurt and looked again.

YOU KILLED HIM, YOU BASTARD

It couldn't be true. She was teasing him. He sucked the moist air into his lungs and held his breath, telling himself that she was on her way back, that it was all some kind of joke. But in the end he had to exhale.

Slowly, experimentally, he tried to move his wrists. The handcuffs did not give. His skin was beginning to itch. The unseen fly was buzzing in the shadows, as if in mocking reminder that it was free.

Time passed. His breath was coming in short shallow gasps. He did not understand what was happening. Everything had seemed so perfect. Yet now he was limp and cold and afraid. And the heaven he had dreamed of had turned into his own private hell.

Part One

Chapter 1

A solitary candle lit the darkness, allowing Harry Devlin to see the man in crimson robes. The sickly smell of incense hung in the air. The high priest was standing in front of the altar, his arm raised. As the flame flickered, Harry caught sight of a gleaming blade.

'Blood is the sacred life-force in both man and beast,' a disembodied voice intoned. 'The rite of sacrifice enables gods to live and thus man and nature may survive.'

A small bundle lay trussed up on the altar. The whimper of a child cut through the silence. Harry's stomach lurched and instinctively he took a pace forward. Suddenly he remembered where he was. He halted, feeling foolish. Why did his imagination always run away with him? He was a grown man, a solicitor of the Supreme Court, supposed to be dispassionate and the master of his emotions. Yet he could not help shivering when he felt a touch upon his spine.

'Frightening, isn't it?'

He spun round. A woman was studying him intently, as if he were a specimen in a glass case. His cheeks felt hot and he said awkwardly, 'For a moment, I almost believed...'

'That's what we like to hear, Harry.' She bent her head towards his and added in a whisper, 'You know, the sign outside does make it clear that the exhibition isn't suitable for small children. Parents never cease to amaze me.'

A harassed teenage girl hurried past them, dragging a pushchair. Its occupant's whimper had matured into a wail. Harry always admired the fortitude of those who had children, but he kept quiet, guessing that Frances Silverwood would regard his reaction as another example of the inability of his head to rule his heart.

'Very lifelike,' he said. 'I know a judge who might be the twin of your high priest. Come to think of it, I'm not sure which one is the dummy.'

'Sorry to keep you waiting after I begged you to come over here,' she said, raising her voice to compete with the loudspeaker commentary. 'I had to take a call from my opposite number at the Smithsonian.'

'When they told me you were engaged I thought I'd take a look,' Harry said. He gestured to the sign by the entrance: *Understanding the Supernatural*. 'I wondered if it might give me a clue to the workings of the British legal system.'

'Bad day in court?' she asked over her shoulder as she led him through a door marked *Museum Staff Only*. He followed her down a long corridor so still that the slap of her flat-heeled shoes against the floor tiles sounded unnaturally loud.

He gave a rueful grin. 'The woman I was acting for was found guilty of *not* being a witch.'

She paused in mid-stride. 'You're teasing me.'

'Lawyer's honour. When witchcraft ceased to be a hanging offence, Parliament made it a crime to pretend to use sorcery. So being a *genuine* witch became a defence to the charge. My client was accused of casting a spell on her best friend's unfaithful husband, to make him love her again.'

'Good God. What happened?'

'The magic didn't work. To make matters worst, the friend found my client in bed with her man. There was a fight, the police were called and a prosecutor with time on his hands decided to test out the law on fraudulent mediums.'

'Only in Liverpool.'

Frances laughed, a rich deep sound. On a bad day, Harry thought, she might be mistaken for a witch herself. She was striking rather than beautiful in appearance, with a high forehead and sharp chin. As he had got to know her, he had begun to realise that her abrupt manner was a mask for shyness. He'd grown to like her and to believe it would do her good to laugh a little more often.

They arrived at a door whose sign bore her name and title: *Keeper of Ethnographical Artefacts*. She waved him inside and as he took a seat on a hard plastic chair, his eye caught a ghastly face staring at him from a display cabinet on the wall. It was a shrunken brown head with flowing black locks and its ravaged features had formed into the expression of a soul in torment. Harry's flesh prickled. With an effort he tore his eyes away and focused his gaze on the Native American portrait calendar on the wall behind Frances's desk.

'Sorry to startle you,' she said briskly. 'I should have given you advance warning. I'm very fond of Uncle Joe, but I tend to take him for granted nowadays.'

Trying to make light of it, he said, 'I ought to expect something out of the ordinary in a place like this. But why isn't he out on display?'

'Preservation is a problem with human remains,' she said crisply. 'Many of them were brought over from the colonies in the nineteenth century. We had to inter a number of Uncle Joe's colleagues in the local cemetery when the smell became too much to bear.'

Harry shuddered and glanced again at the shrunken head. Once it had belonged to a human being who lived and breathed. He felt his gorge rising.

Frances said, 'You don't approve?'

'Perhaps I'm too squeamish.'

'He keeps me company,' she said with a shrug.

Forcing a smile, he said, 'He looks even sterner than Luke Dessaur when a trustee turns up late for a meeting.'

To his surprise, she flushed. 'Strange you should say that. Luke is the reason why I asked you to come over here at such short notice.'

'I assumed that it was in connection with the meeting tonight.'

'It is. You see, Luke's told me that he's unable to come. The first time he's ever missed since he became chairman. I'm worried about him, Harry.'

He stared. 'Why's that?'

'I think – he's afraid of something.'

'*Afraid?*

Harry did not try to hide his incredulity. Could she be joking? Her earnest face gave no hint of it: no smile, no twinkle in the deep-set eyes. She was leaning forward, chin cradled in her hands, elbows touching her overflowing in-tray. Her whole body was rigid and he could sense the tension in her shoulder blades, almost taste the dryness of her lips.

Yet the thought of the chairman of the Kavanaugh Trust experiencing fear was comic in its absurdity. In Luke's presence, Harry always found himself fretting about the shine on his shoes or the length of his hair. Luke was the sort who had a fetish about punctuality and never took the minutes of the last trustees' meeting as read. He was capable of great personal kindness, but Harry had never heard him split an infinitive and suspected that he would rather face torture than surrender the crease in his trousers. What could perturb such a man – other than, perhaps, the prospect of having to act on Harry's advice?

'What exactly is the problem?'

Harry noticed a tear in the corner of Frances's eye. Hot with embarrassment, he studied his palms whilst she dabbed at her face with a tissue.

'I wish I knew. Last week he and I went to a rehearsal of a musical the Trust is subsidising. He seemed preoccupied, but then, he's hardly an extrovert. After a quick drink, I left him in the bar having a chat with the producer. I had to be up early for a train trip to London the next morning. When I arrived back, I gave him a ring at home. He was out, so I left a message on his answering machine. He didn't call back the next day, which puzzled me. It was so unlike him.'

Harry nodded. Luke always returned calls and responded to letters without delay. Something of a paragon. And as a client, therefore, something of a pain as well. Most of the people Harry acted for were consistent only in their incompetence. The previous day he'd been called out to advise a burglar arrested after being spotted by a woman whose house he had robbed the night before. She had recognised him because he was wearing her husband's clothes.

'I called again. Same thing. This time he did ring back. He sounded agitated and I asked if he was all right, but he assured me everything was fine. I thought he might be ill and not looking after himself properly. That night I dialled his home at around ten thirty, but again I could only get the answering machine. The day after, I bumped into him in the street as I was coming back from a meeting at the Albert Dock.'

'How did he seem?'

'His face was like chalk and he'd been gnawing at his fingernails. He looked as though he hadn't slept a wink since I'd last seen him. His hands kept trembling and his manner was twitchy. Suddenly I realised that he wasn't ill. He was worried sick.' She let out a breath. 'I said as much and he bit my head off. Told me not to interfere in his private business, said he could look after himself perfectly well. He'd never felt better. I was dumbstruck.'

'I bet.' Harry began to realise why Frances was concerned. Luke being rude? The Archbishop of Canterbury was more likely to let rip with a string of obscenities.

'After a couple of minutes, he calmed down and apologised. He did admit he had things on his mind, but said I shouldn't trouble myself about them. He would be fine. And that was that. There was nothing more I could do. Luke's lived alone ever since Gwendoline died. And he's proud, too. He wouldn't seek help even if he really needed it.'

'He's no fool.'

'But people don't always behave rationally, do they?' Frances said.

Don't I know it? thought Harry. Yet Luke Dessaur was one person who had always struck him as supremely rational. He had been personnel director for an arts and heritage charity before taking early retirement at fifty, weary of the endless round of redundancies and budget cuts, and devoting himself to the Kavanaugh Trust. 'So what did you do?'

'I called round at his house this lunch-time. I rang his bell and rapped on the door until my knuckles were sore, but there was no answer. Then a woman passed by. His next-door neighbour. She said that if I was hoping to find Luke, I was out of luck. She'd seen him driving off a few minutes earlier. He'd put an overnight case into his car.'

'Observant lady.'

'She's an old gossip with too much time on her hands,' Frances said. 'Though who am I to talk? I suppose you think I'm overreacting.'

'Not at all.'

What he really thought was that Frances's dismay revealed how sweet she was on Luke. He'd suspected it for a while. Looking round her office, he saw no evidence of a private life. No photographs, nothing unconnected with her work, although he knew that in her spare time she was a keen singer. He had heard her once at a private party, singing about the loss of love and loneliness. For his part, Luke had been a widower for years. Maybe she thought it time they both had a change of status.

'When I arrived back from Luke's house, there was a message from him on my voicemail. He asked me to present his apologies to the meeting tonight. He spoke in a jerky way, as if his nerves were in pieces. I called his mobile this time and managed to catch him. Though I guessed that he regretted answering as soon as he heard it was me on the line. It was as if he'd been hoping to hear from someone else.'

'What did you say?'

'I said he needn't try to bluff me. I knew him too well not to realise he was sick with worry. I asked him to talk to me, to trust me with the problem, whatever it was. He didn't bother to deny the truth of what I was saying, but he said there was nothing I could do, nothing anyone could do. He was desperate to get off the line. Finally he said a quick goodbye and put down the phone before I could utter another word.' She groaned, put her head in her hands. 'This must all sound ridiculous to you. Am I being silly?'

'You're bound to be anxious. And confused.' Harry paused. He thought about telling her of his own last conversation with Luke Dessaur, but something held him back. 'What's the explanation for the overnight case? Is there anyone he might be visiting? What about his godson?'

'You know Ashley Whitaker?'

'Yes, I often buy books from him. I first met Luke through Ashley, as it happens – years before Crusoe and Devlin started to act for the Kavanaugh Trust.'

'Luke can't be staying with him. Ashley and his wife are attending a book fair in Canada. I remember Luke mentioning it that night at the theatre.'

'Any other lines of inquiry?'

'You sound like a policeman,' she said. 'I know you have been involved in a number of – unusual cases, but I would hate to think...'

Harry loosened his tie. The room was warmed by twin radiators and poorly ventilated. Perhaps that, and the watchful presence of Uncle Joe, explained why he felt so uncomfortable. 'Luke's behaviour is a mystery.'

'Yes, but it's not...'

Again, she allowed her voice to trail away. Harry could guess the reason. She had meant to say: *it's not a* murder *mystery.* He said gently, 'Anyone else who might be worth contacting?'

She pushed a hand through her thick black hair. 'He's a good man, as you well know, but I wouldn't say that he has many friends. He and Gwendoline lived for each other. Since she died, I think he has led a solitary life. But I would have expected him to let me know if anything was amiss.'

Harry caught the eye of the shrunken head and quickly glanced away again. How could Frances concentrate on her work with that face staring down at her? 'Has he seemed out of sorts before?'

'As you might expect, this business with Vera Blackhurst has appalled him. He is very suspicious of her. He's even said that the Trust's survival might depend on the outcome of her claim. The Trust means a great deal to him – and we are desperate for money. But I can't believe there is any reason for him simply to... well, to act as though he is personally under threat.'

'Have you discussed this with the other trustees?'

'Only with Matthew Cullinan and even with him I was rather circumspect. He oozed charm as usual, but he obviously thought I was making a mountain out of a molehill. Perhaps I am. Even so, I wanted to have a word with you before tonight's meeting. I was sure that you would listen to me patiently. As you have. Sorry to come crying on your shoulder.'

She smiled ruefully and Harry found himself having to fight the urge to give her hand a comforting squeeze.

She wasn't his type, but he had a lot of time for Frances Silverwood.

'I'm sure Luke will be fine,' he said. But he wasn't sure that he really believed it.

She stood up. 'Thank you for hearing me out, Harry. I expect this will probably all blow over and I'll have made a complete fool of myself in Matthew Cullinan's eyes. Worrying over nothing.'

Harry stood up and took a last glance at the shrunken head. It stared back, as if to say: *You know it's right to fear the worst.*

Chapter 2

A gale was blowing the litter down Dale Street as Harry headed back towards his office. Empty burger cartons, chip papers and hot-dog wrappers were strewn along the pavement. He'd read that nutritionists believed there was a link between junk food and delinquency. If they were right, Liverpool was in for a crime wave.

He turned up his coat collar. Whoever said that April is the cruellest month had never spent January in Merseyside. It was one of the harshest winters he could remember and the forecasters promised worse to come. As his partner Jim Crusoe pointed out, it was perfect weather for probate lawyers. A cold snap that carried off a few elderly clients was always good for a solicitor's cashflow. Harry's sympathy was with the old people. After the warmth of the museum, the bitterness of the wind was hard to bear.

Yet the chill in his bones owed less to the weather than to his recollection of his last meeting with Luke Dessaur and the conversation which he had decided against mentioning to Frances Silverwood. A week earlier, Luke had called at Crusoe and Devlin's office in Fenwick Court. He had brought a letter from Geoffrey Willatt, the lawyer acting for Vera Blackhurst. Harry had been surprised to see him; the letter could have been sent by post or fax and a busy man would usually prefer a quick word over the telephone.

Luke was worried, that was obvious. In his early fifties, he was still a handsome man, tall and erect in his three-

piece pinstripe with exquisitely coiffured grey hair. He

had, Harry always thought, the confidence and charm of a leading counsel as well as the same small vanities: the fob-watch, the gleaming gold crowns, the natural assumption that every considered view he expressed was right. Frances was not, Harry felt sure, the only woman Luke left weak at the knees. Yet for once he looked his age. His brow was furrowed and he kept breaking off his sentences to rub tired eyes.

'Well,' he said, 'if you are absolutely sure...'

'Don't worry,' Harry said, not for the first time. 'Vera Blackhurst can't take the money and run. Even though she's flourishing a will made in her favour and appointing her as executor of Charles Kavanaugh's estate, remember we've lodged a caveat with the court. So she isn't allowed to obtain probate and make off with all his money until the dispute has been resolved.'

Luke sighed. 'In that case, I suppose we can do nothing more until the trustees meet.'

'Right. Everything's under control.'

It was a bold claim for any lawyer, let alone Harry, to make but it prompted Luke to nod his thanks before climbing to his feet and picking up his coat. At the door he paused.

'There is one other thing that I suppose I ought to mention.'

Harry had years of experience in dealing with people who had difficulty in coming to the point, but he would never have expected Luke to be one of them. 'What's the matter?'

'It's rather embarrassing. You see, I'm concerned by the behaviour of one of the trustees. It seems to me that the person in question may – may have been deceiving me.'

'Can you tell me more?'

'I'd rather not at this stage, if you don't mind. I need to think things through, perhaps speak to the individual concerned before I take matters any further. But to be frank, I've been having a few sleepless nights. And – I'm not making excuses – I may have been slightly indiscreet.'

'I doubt it,' Harry said. It wasn't flattery. He knew few people less likely to talk out of turn than Luke.

'Kind of you to say so, but I did mention that I was concerned about the Trust to – to someone the other day. Of course, I didn't mention any names and he said at once that I ought to seek legal advice.'

Harry thought for a moment. 'Was it Ashley Whitaker, by any chance?'

A rare smile flitted across Luke Dessaur's face. 'It's true what people say, Harry. You have missed your vocation as a detective. How did you guess?'

'The explanation's always a let-down,' Harry said. 'It's simply that I know you would only discuss something like this with someone you could trust.'

'You're right, as it happens. I value his judgment – and of course he was right. So I may need to consult you soon, for advice on the removal of one of the trustees.'

'Ah.'

'It is a very delicate matter.' Luke hunched his shoulders. 'Most distressing. Perhaps either you or your partner would care to refresh your minds about the precise terms of the trust deed. Unless I am very much mistaken, we will have to speak about this again.'

'Call me any time.'

But Luke had not been in touch again after that strange, unsatisfactory conversation – and now, if Frances was to be believed, his concern had turned into fear.

As soon as he was back in his own room, Harry hunted around for the lever arch files which contained the bulk of the Kavanaugh Trust papers. One came to light under his desk; another was propping up the unsteady table on which stood his new (or more precisely, reconditioned) computer. The revolution in information technology had touched even Crusoe and Devlin, but where Harry was concerned, there would always be scope for the lowest of low tech. The screen was blank: he reminded himself to switch the machine on before Jim Crusoe looked round the door and upbraided him for Luddism.

He opened the current file and a couple of dozen sheets spilled through his hands and on to the floor. As he scrambled around picking them up, he reflected that for all the computer salesman's honeyed words, the paperless office was as much a pipe-dream as the paperless toilet. When the documentation was back in its proper order, he began to sift through it in preparation for the evening. At least if the chairman did not turn up, the other trustees were less likely to put penetrating questions or to realise that he was practically innumerate. He gazed at the mass of dividend payment request forms and wondered why charity had to go hand in hand with bureaucracy. Surely that was not what Gervase Kavanaugh had intended?

A large figure loomed in the doorway. Jim Crusoe lifted his thick eyebrows in mock astonishment. 'Harry Devlin studying a file? What next?'

'The Kavanaugh Trust papers. I thought I'd better brush up for this evening. Why did I let you talk me into becoming involved?'

'We agreed, remember?' Jim eased himself down in the client's chair and Harry fancied that he heard it creak under the strain. His partner had put on weight recently: the result of too much home cooking as he tried to make up to his wife for a relationship with another woman of which Heather Crusoe was so far unaware. 'I would handle the money side. You'd deal with the litigation.'

It was true. When Crusoe and Devlin had acquired the business of Tweats and Company, they had taken over the files of a handful of estimable clients, including the Kavanaugh Trust. A surprising number of otherwise sensible people had never rumbled the fact that Cyril Tweats, for all that he modelled his bedside manner on Dr Finlay, knew rather less about the law than the average reader of John Grisham. Harry had been content to let Jim handle the work and his partner's offer had seemed like a good deal at the time.

When did a local charity ever become embroiled in courtroom battles?

Certainly, there was no reason to expect the Trust to engage in disputes. It had been founded by an elderly composer whose music had enjoyed a brief vogue in the thirties. Shortly before his death, Gervase Kavanaugh had set up a charitable trust with a view to distributing largesse to worthy causes in the arts in Liverpool. His son Charles, a lifelong bachelor, had regarded himself as a discerning connoisseur of art, although in truth he had as much aesthetic sensibility as a bullfrog (a creature to which he had borne a disconcerting physical resemblance). He had made a will years back leaving his estate to the Trust. A fortnight ago he had died in a nursing home following a short illness. After expressing their sorrow and paying tribute to his support, the trustees had turned their minds to the pleasant dilemma of how to spend all the money. The injection of new funds would be welcome since little was left of the original endowment. Charles's demise could not have been more timely. And then they had learned he had left his fortune to his housekeeper-companion, Vera Blackhurst.

'We can't fight her claim all the way to court. Our case isn't strong enough and the trustees can't afford the risk. Though I think we ought to check Vera out.'

Jim's eyes narrowed. 'Listen, I don't want you doing your Sexton Blake bit on behalf of the Trust. They aren't the kind of clients to mess around with. If there's any inquiry work to be done, we play it by the book, okay? Get them to instruct Jonah Deegan.'

'All right, all right. But there's something else you should know.'

He reported his conversation with Frances Silverwood and Jim shook his head. 'Luke afraid? I don't believe a word of it.'

'He came to see me the other day. I was waiting for him to come back to me before I mentioned it to you. He reckoned one of the trustees was deceiving him.'

'Good God. Who was he pointing the finger at?'

'He wouldn't say. But he was obviously troubled. Talked about losing sleep. He'd even mentioned it to Ashley Whitaker, who quite rightly told him to have a word with us.'

'But why should he be afraid? It's not like Luke to go over the top.'

'It's not like Frances to exaggerate, either,' Harry said grimly. 'Maybe I'll learn more at tonight's meeting. Matthew Cullinan's hired a room at the Piquet Club.'

'My God, you are moving in exalted circles. Don't they say that's the oldest gentlemen's club in England?'

'From what I've heard, that's because it caters for the oldest gentlemen. Matthew's probably the youngest member they've ever had. He's just been elected, apparently.'

Jim whistled. 'So soon? I heard there was a five-year waiting list.'

'Not if you're an offspring of Lord Gralam. He's even arranged for an outside caterer to come in to make sure that we are fed and watered.'

'All the trustees' meetings I've attended,' Jim grumbled, 'I've never done better than soup and sandwiches.'

Harry patted his partner on the shoulder. 'Sorry, mate. I've learned this much from rubbing shoulders with the nobility. It's not what you do that matters. It's who you know.'

The streets had been dark for a couple of hours by the time Harry found himself outside the entrance to the Piquet Club. A uniformed commissionaire who bore a marked resemblance to Sir John Gielgud opened the door eighteen inches and examined Harry's Marks and Spencer suit and Hush Puppies with disdain.

'May I help you?' The plummy tones made Sir John sound like a bingo caller.

Harry conquered the temptation to tug a forelock and said tentatively, 'Kavanaugh Trust?'

'Ah yes' – the commissionaire paused – 'sir. Take the stairs and it's on your left on the second landing.'

As he climbed the wide curving staircase, Harry studied the sepia-tinted pictures of eminent past members. Bewhiskered men with stern faces, proud Liverpudlians who had lived in an age when the city was great. The club was legendary for its wealth, derived from endowments established by merchants who had taken time off from slave trading to play cards with each other. He paused on the first landing, opposite a door marked *Strictly Private* and guarded by a security camera and alarm. Presumably that was where they kept their etchings: the Piquet Club's other claim to fame was that it boasted one of the finest collections of erotica in private hands. The stuff was supposed to make the Kama Sutra look as racy as *Teach Yourself Origami*.

On the second landing, he glanced through an open door to his right. A couple of white-haired men with hearing aids were playing piquet at a small table. The room had a domed ceiling which emphasised the atmosphere of religious solemnity. It was hard to imagine that they were in the heart of the city of football and pop music, of stand-up comics and stevedores.

Harry was seized by the sudden urge to shout, 'All right, lads! Let's have a look at the filthy pictures, shall we?' But he thought better of it. Even if the old fellers could be persuaded to unveil their stock of superannuated porn, their hearts would probably split under the strain once they took a look at it.

Suddenly he heard a woman's giggle from behind the opposite door. It was a sound as unlikely as rap music in

a monastery. From the doorknob hung a placard saying: *Kavanaugh Trust – Private Meeting*. Harry knocked and, without waiting for a reply, pushed open the door and walked inside.

Matthew Cullinan was facing him. He had his arms round the waist of a woman in a gingham overall and he was squeezing her ample buttocks.

Harry groaned inwardly. Why did he always rush in where others feared to tread? If only he had stayed outside and waited for a summons he might have been spared the spectacle of a scion of the aristocracy sexually harassing a serving wench. And wasn't Matthew reputed to be something of a shrinking violet, anxious to avoid any hint of publicity or breath of scandal? Perhaps he thought that goosing a caterer didn't count, that waving his cheque book around gave him some from of *droit de seigneur.*

Matthew winked at Harry and whispered in the woman's ear, 'We have company, darling.'

She looked over her shoulder and blushed. Plump, with a plain but pleasant face, she reminded Harry of a farmer's wife. He estimated that she was in her mid-thirties, rather older than Matthew. 'I did warn you that we shouldn't mix business with pleasure.'

To his surprise, she spoke with a slight German accent. Well, a Bavarian farmer's wife, then. Harry was flummoxed: he would have guessed that Matthew's taste was for leggy Sloane Rangers. Matthew disentangled himself from her and strode forward to offer Harry his hand. A half-forgotten phrase sprang to Harry's mind: *the tranquil consciousness of effortless superiority.* This fellow made the average cucumber look hot and bothered.

'Sorry to barge in on you.'

'No harm done. Inge is quite right. I should have allowed her to carry on sorting out the eats. May I introduce the two of you, by the way? Darling, this is the Trust's solicitor, Harry Devlin. Harry, meet my girlfriend, Inge Frontzeck.'

'Oh.' Okay, so he'd misjudged the scene. But why did her surname sound familiar?

The woman smiled. 'Hello. I do hope you weren't offended a moment ago.'

'No, no. Really. Not at all.'

Matthew grinned. With his floppy fair hair and amiable manner, it was easy to picture him in a straw boater and striped blazer, punting a girl in a summer frock down the Isis. He was an investment consultant and, having met him at some cocktail party for the great and the good, Luke had persuaded him to become a trustee. He was the younger son of Lord Gralam, but although the family home was in Surrey, he had moved up North the previous summer. Luke had assured Harry that Matthew was anxious to shun the limelight, to the point of being almost a recluse. But just at the moment there were no signs that he was easily embarrassed in the presence of others.

'We're the ones who should apologise. You must have thought we were enacting a scene taken from the club's private collection. I have been a bit naughty, I suppose. I told Luke that I felt it would be a good idea for us to bring caterers in since the club's facilities are, frankly, rather limited. Inge is in the business and I asked her if she wouldn't mind helping us out. A bit incestuous, perhaps, but it wasn't exactly a big enough contract to be put out to tender.'

'I quite understand,' Harry said hastily. 'Very good idea. Excellent.'

Inge beamed. 'I suppose I'd better leave you two to it, then.' She wagged a finger at Matthew. 'And no more distractions!'

She disappeared through a door into an anteroom and Matthew motioned Harry into a deep leather armchair. 'I don't think you'll be disappointed in the service or the food, Harry. Of course, this is only a sideline. Inge doesn't need to work. But it keeps her out of mischief. Or at least it does if I'm not around.'

'Frances has spoken to you about Luke, I gather,' Harry said.

'Ye-es,' Matthew drawled. 'I must admit, I wasn't quite sure why she was getting so steamed up.' He yawned and started to take papers out of a leather briefcase which bore his initials in gold. 'Oh well, what have we got on the agenda tonight? The usual begging

21

letters from gay and lesbian watercolourists, another approach from that docker who re-wrote *Hamlet* in Scouse dialect?'

'Vera Blackhurst is the main item on the agenda.'

Matthew's face darkened but before he could speak, the door was flung open and a breezy voice said, 'Evening, folks.'

Roy Milburn's dark hair was tousled and his tie askew. His cheeks were flushed and, as usual, he was accompanied by a whiff of alcohol. He walked with a noticeable limp, the legacy of a recent crash when he'd driven his old banger into a lamp-post after a night on the ale. Although he was only in his early thirties, the broken blood vessels on his nose and the dark rings under his eyes made him look ten years older. Yet despite that and his developing paunch, he always reminded Harry of an impish schoolboy.

Roy looked around the room. 'Nice place, even if it is a bit spooky. I'm sure I saw two corpses playing whist downstairs. Any chance of a squint at the dirty books after we've finished? After all, we're famous for being dedicated to the cause of the arts in Merseyside.'

Matthew's eyes gleamed. 'The collection is reserved for the eyes of members and bona fide students only, I'm afraid.'

'Very unfair, when you remember we're all donating our valuable time out of the goodness of our hearts. There's no bloody money in it for us, so surely there ought to be some perks.' He turned to Harry and grinned. 'And how's my favourite legal eagle? Did I ever tell you why they bury lawyers under twenty feet of dirt?'

'Go on,' Harry said gloomily. Roy had an inexhaustible supply of lawyer jokes.

'Because deep down, they're really good people.'

Matthew raised his eyebrows as Roy belly-laughed at his own wit but merely said, 'Do I hear footsteps on the floor? Yes, here are Frances and Tim.'

A large heavily built man in an ill-fitting tweed jacket and shapeless trousers held the door open, ushering Frances through before him. 'Sorry I'm late,' Tim Aldred said as he shambled towards a vacant chair. His tone was defensive, as though he had an excuse ready to deflect any criticism of his tardiness. 'Where's the chairman?'

'A very good question,' Frances said grimly.

'He's otherwise engaged,' Matthew said. 'No matter. The catering is all laid on.'

Harry was tempted to say that if he hadn't butted in, the caterer might have been laid, but he thought better of it.

'Well, that's the important thing,' Roy said. 'Let's not worry about the Dinosaur, eh?'

'But where *is* he?' Tim asked. 'I've never known him miss a meeting before.'

Matthew gave a dismissive wave. 'Just one of those things. Now, if you don't mind, I might as well ask Inge to serve as we talk. Agreed, everyone? Splendid. Are you sitting comfortably? Then let's begin.'

Chapter 3

As the clock in the corner struck eight, Matthew Cullinan leaned back in his chair and said, 'If you want my opinion, she is a greedy, mischievous, dishonest, scheming bitch.'

For a few moments, there was a hush. Harry thought that he could hear a faint snoring from the card players downstairs. Then Roy sniggered and said, 'You really must stop beating about the bush, Matthew. Come right out with it. Why don't you speak your mind?'

Tim Aldred cleared his throat. As usual, his demeanour was so hesitant that Harry found it hard to believe that his role on the board was to represent the performing arts. The average church mouse was a foul-mouthed dissident by comparison. 'But can we be absolutely sure you are right, Matthew? I only met Vera Blackhurst once, but she struck me as genuinely fond of Charles.'

Matthew expelled a sigh worthy of a long-suffering schoolmaster confronted by the irrational stubbornness of the classroom dunce. 'Oh really, Tim.'

Tim went pink but said doggedly, 'I realise this is inconvenient for us, but perhaps Vera swept Charles off his feet.'

'But what did she see in *him*?' Roy asked.

'Money,' Frances said drily.

Roy feigned amazement. 'You're suggesting it wasn't a love-match?'

'Surely her motives don't matter,' Tim said. 'If he left the money to her, then there is very little that we can or should do about it.'

'I think you are missing the point,' Matthew said. 'It is not just a question of money. With all due respect, Tim, a matter of principle is involved here.'

Tim bowed his head, his resistance crushed. Frances contented herself with studying the papers in front of her. Roy Milburn glanced in Harry's direction and winked.

'Careful, Matthew. This must be music to Harry's ears. When clients start talking about the importance of principles, I guess Crusoe and Devlin's bank manager starts to sleep a little more easily.'

Frances said, 'Well, Harry, how do you see things?'

He wiped his brow with his palm. The room was as stuffy as Frances's office but that wasn't the reason he was sweating. It was one thing to advise a recidivist in a remand centre; offering words of wisdom to trustees in a tight corner was more of a challenge. He remembered, too, that Luke believed that one of the people round the table was deceiving him. But who – and why?

'First,' he began carefully, 'we need to remember the kind of man Charles Kavanaugh was.'

Matthew grunted and Roy chortled. 'Exactly,' Harry said in his briskest tone. 'No-one could deny that Charles was an eccentric. And I suspect that none of us shared his taste in *objets d'art...*'

'You can say that again,' Roy broke in. 'Forget about never speaking ill of the dead. Now we aren't beholden to him, let's call a spade a spade. He knew less about art than this chair I'm sitting on. And as for his so-called treasures – let's face it, they are utter crap.'

There was a short embarrassed silence. Harry reflected that Roy had done nothing more than voice the opinion shared privately by all the trustees. Charles Kavanaugh had fancied himself as something of a connoisseur of the arts; he described the substantial Victorian villa in which he lived as his studio and had not only collected pictures and antiques, but also tried his own hand at sketching and painting. Everyone who had ever seen his collection dismissed it as worthless stuff which would give bric-à-brac a bad name. His own pictures were especially deplorable: splodgy landscapes and misshapen nudes composed with a lack of skill that was truly breathtaking. Yet there had always been a tacit understanding that to ridicule them was unthinkable. But now Charles was dead and he had gifted his fortune to a blowsy gold-digger whilst the trustees were left with a house full of junk.

'You wouldn't be saying that if Luke was here,' Tim said reproachfully. 'He's always a stickler for the proprieties. And Charles is barely cold in his grave. I rather think the chairman would want us to show our respect.'

Roy said, 'But the Dinosaur isn't here, so we can all have our say. And frankly, the one thing that has always baffled me is this. How did Charles manage to accumulate so much stuff without even stumbling on anything of the remotest merit?' He laughed. 'I mean, whatever happened to the law of averages?'

Frances gave him a fierce look and said, 'Harry, you were interrupted.'

Roy gave an elaborate sigh and picked up his pencil again. He always doodled his way through trustees' meetings, covertly sketching caricatures of his fellow board members. Luke had once caught sight of Roy's portrayal of him as an immaculately groomed Tyrannosaurus Rex and had not been amused. These days he eked out a precarious living as a cartoonist for one of the local free sheets, although he'd trained as an accountant after university before spectacularly failing his exams. On that slender basis, he'd been asked to act as honorary treasurer to the Trust. After glancing at the last balance sheet, Jim had said it was like appointing a train robber as Lord Chief Justice.

Harry said, 'We've always known that Charles intended to donate his collection of artistic ephemera...'

'Crap,' Roy murmured, directing a provocative wink at Tim.

'...or whatever you may like to call it, to the Trust, in the fond belief that the sale proceeds would generate substantial funds. Obviously a fantasy. But he always led everyone to believe that was merely the icing on the cake. He never married, there were no children, nothing but the Trust to carry on the Kavanaugh name. There was every reason for him to leave his estate to the Trust to make sure that it was able to keep up its good work. Until he met Vera Blackhurst.'

'I still say she's on the make,' Matthew burst in. He thrust out his lower lip, as if daring anyone to disagree. 'She was a housekeeper, nothing more, the latest in a long line.'

'A housekeeper with peroxide hair and tits that Juno would die for,' Roy said. 'Don't underestimate her. She's as tough as a Birkenhead barmaid. Let's face it, she had to be. Living with Charles for forty-eight hours would be enough to send most people off their head.'

'He wasn't so bad,' Tim said defensively. 'Granted, he had his funny little ways, but most of us do.'

Roy gave him a withering look but Harry said quickly, 'Miss Blackhurst's story is absolutely clear. I've discussed the position at length with her solicitor. She's instructed my old boss, Geoffrey Willatt, of Maher and Malcolm.'

'A very prestigious firm,' Frances said grudgingly.

Harry nodded. Like Jim Crusoe, he'd been recruited by Maher and Malcolm at a time when the demand for trainee solicitors had far exceeded the supply. It had been rather like a couple of kids from Toxteth being offered a scholarship to Eton. 'And correspondingly pricey. She means business, all right. Geoffrey tells me he's convinced she would make a first class witness, should it ever come to that. Besides, the will is crystal clear.'

'She made sure of that,' Matthew muttered.

'Are you suggesting she forged it?' Frances asked.

'Why not? Charles was a sick man. He'd scarcely had a chance to get to know this Blackhurst woman before he fell ill. Soon he was in a nursing home and never left it again. What had she ever done for him? Yet we're supposed to accept that two days before he died he wrote out a will in her favour in his own fair hand.'

'It was properly witnessed,' Harry said. 'There is no question of its being a forgery.'

'And who were the supposed witnesses? Two part-time care workers who didn't have a clue what they were signing. How can we be sure it was the so-called will that they put their names to? It could have been any scrap of paper.'

Harry shook his head. 'Sorry, Matthew. Charles told them it was his last will and testament. He even mentioned that he meant to be generous to Vera – because she had been very good to him'.

Roy paused in his doodling to roar with merriment.

'Hey – you don't think they were lovers, do you? The mind boggles. Perhaps they did it with paper bags over their heads.'

Harry saw Tim Aldred turn crimson again and glanced over Roy's shoulder to see the latest work-in-progress. It was a lewd sketch of a bullfrog mounting a busty blonde. The assurance he had given to Luke that everything was under control looked increasingly like wishful thinking.

He said hastily, 'As some of you probably know, Charles's original will was drawn up years ago by a lawyer named Cyril Tweats, who also acted for the Trust. My firm took over his practice and we have the will in safe keeping. Apart from a few minor bequests, Charles gave everything to the Trust. So far, so good. The snag is this: the act of making a new will destroys the old one.'

'In other words,' Frances said, 'unless we can discredit the new will, the Trust will get nothing.'

'Appalling,' Matthew said. 'And wholly unacceptable. Look at how much we've been spending, especially in view of the blank cheque that the chairman gave to the Waterfront Players when they wanted to put on *Promises, Promises*. I did warn him against it. Musicals always cost the earth.'

'It was a reasonable decision at the time,' Frances said. 'Luke was confident he could persuade Charles to give the Trust a loan to alleviate any short-term financial problems.'

'To think,' Roy murmured, 'that we spent so many years toadying to Charles – and it may all have been in vain. I never thought he had any sense of irony. Maybe I was wrong.'

A gloomy silence settled upon the gathering. 'I do wish Luke were here,' Frances said.

Harry said, 'The real question is whether there are any grounds for contesting Vera's claim.'

'What was Charles's mental state towards the end?' Matthew asked. 'Everyone realised that he had been doolally for years. Including, I'm sure, the Blackhurst woman. She was obviously prepared to take advantage of a mentally infirm man. I simply can't believe that the law will allow her to get away with it.'

Harry had practised his most impassive expression before coming out here. Just as well: it was having to work overtime. 'There's no evidence that Charles was certifiable. But that isn't the end of the matter. I have told Geoffrey Willatt the trustees may contest the will.'

'Good for you!' Matthew said. 'Hit 'em hard. That's what my father always says to the family lawyers whenever we have a spot of legal trouble.' During their brief acquaintance, Harry had heard Matthew make passing reference more than once to Lord Gralam's solicitors; it seemed that they were Mayfair-based rottweilers who made even Maher and Malcolm's fees seem like an unmissable bargain.

'What exactly can we hit them with?' Tim asked.

Harry shrugged. 'For starters, we might say that she exercised undue influence over her employer when he was seriously ill. She was in the same room when Charles and the witnesses signed it.'

'Is that legal?'

'Sure. You can have the Household Cavalry present at the same time as you execute your will as long as you adhere to the proper formalities. But it's unsatisfactory, all the same. My guess is that she was determined to make sure that there was no hitch. She didn't trust Charles to get it right.'

'Who can blame her?' Roy said.

'Let's be realistic,' Harry said. 'Suppose we are right and Vera Blackhurst was a woman on the make. She didn't invest too much time in cuddling up to Charles. I guess she will want to sort this out sooner rather than later. Her solicitor said she sympathised with the Trust's predicament.'

Matthew grunted. 'As I said, she's a lying bitch.'

'Was any offer made?' Tim asked.

'Oh no,' Harry said. 'I don't wish to raise your hopes. Geoffrey Willatt did say that at least the Trust would benefit from Charles's collection of treasures.'

'I hope his tongue was firmly in his cheek,' Roy said.

'Geoffrey has no sense of humour whatsoever. It's part of the person specification for partners in Maher and Malcolm. All I can say is that there is a small chink of light. We must make something of it. So I have a proposal.'

'Take out a contract on Vera Blackhurst?' Roy suggested. He stretched his arms and emitted a comfortable belch. Harry reflected that it was just as well that Luke, that model of decorum, was not present.

'A bit late for that. No, we need a few bargaining chips. It would help to have a little background about Vera. Anything that we might use to strike a deal that leaves the Trust with a share – however modest – of the Kavanaugh estate.'

The trustees digested this in silence for a few moments. Harry watched them closely. Matthew's face was dark with anger. Tim and Frances looked tired and miserable. Even Roy had lapsed into silence. Finally Frances spoke.

'Didn't Ambrose Bierce say a litigant is someone who gives up his flesh in the hope of saving his bones? I take it you don't believe we should see her in court?'

Harry shook his head. 'Too risky. Too time-consuming. And above all, too expensive. Jim and I recommend the Trust to hire a private investigator to check her out. I can instruct a reliable local man if you wish.'

Matthew frowned and opened his mouth again but Frances intervened before he could speak. 'That seems like sound advice to me. I'm sure that Luke would be in favour. Are we all agreed? Very well, Harry, you have your go-ahead. Now, any other business? No? Excellent. I propose then that we all adjourn to the pub.'

As the others drifted towards the door, Harry joined Roy Milburn, who was putting the finishing touches to his latest sketch on the back of the minutes of the last meeting. He looked up and grinned. 'Well, well. Who would have thought it, the Kavanaugh Trust hiring a gumshoe?'

Harry looked over his shoulder and studied the cartoon of a Humphrey Bogart look-alike in trilby and mackintosh. He pictured Jonah Deegan in his mind and shook his head. 'Sorry, but you're way off the mark. A flat cap and a duffel coat is more our man's style.'

'Must you shatter my illusions?' Roy put his pencil back in his pocket. 'By the way, what you said about the lawyers' fees reminded me of something. Know why the Law Society prevents solicitors from having sex with their clients?'

'I'm sure you're about to tell me.'

Roy chortled. 'Because it stops them charging twice for essentially the same service.'

***

'It's been a long evening.'

Tim Aldred leaned back on the bar stool and gave an elaborate yawn. Harry had a curious sensation that Tim was waiting for him to react to something. He glanced at his wrist to check the time, then gasped.

His watch had disappeared.

Panic gripped him. He looked around frantically, uttering a silent prayer that he would find the watch. It was Swiss, a good make, but what mattered was that it had been a present to him from his wife Liz, in the days before their marriage had gone wrong, long before she had finished up on a mortuary slab, victim of a callous murderer. It kept good time, but even if one day it stopped for ever he would never give up wearing it. It was part of his life, a reminder of lost innocence as well as one of the few tangible things he had to remember her by.

'What's wrong?' Tim asked.

Harry sucked air into his cheeks. Was it possible that for the very first time since Liz's death he had forgotten to put the watch on? Or had he drunk more than he'd realised and taken it off in an absent-minded moment?

Tim grinned, showing large uneven teeth. 'Is this what you are looking for?

Casually, he stretched an arm around Frances Silverwood, who was sitting between them, and fished the watch out of her jacket pocket, handing it to Harry with a little bow.

'So I can answer my own question. It's ten o'clock.'

'Tim!' Frances cried. 'That's amazing!'

Fastening the watch back on to his wrist, Harry said ruefully, 'Talk about the quickness of the hand deceiving the eye. I never even realised it was missing. How on earth did you manage that?'

Tim opened his hands in an easy-when-you-know-how gesture. 'Magic.'

'Pity you never took up the law. I have plenty of clients who could do with a conjuror rather than a solicitor. I long ago ran out of rabbits to pull out of my hat.'

'You're extraordinarily clever, Tim,' Frances said with an encouraging smile. 'I've said it before. You're too good an act to spend all your time performing at parties for children or old age pensioners.'

Tim coloured. 'Oh, it's nothing.' His moment on centre stage having passed, he again became the awkward introvert familiar to Harry from the trustees' meetings. He finished his pint of beer and mumbled, 'Well, I suppose I really must be going.'

'Thanks for the drink,' Harry said. 'As soon as there is any news from Jonah Deegan, I'll let you know.' Tim responded with a non-committal grunt and Frances gave him a penetrating look. 'Look here. Am I right in thinking that you're not entirely happy with the tactics we agreed tonight? Keep it between the three of us if you like.'

Matthew Cullinan had declined to join them here, since he had to take his girlfriend home. Roy had consumed a swift pint at Harry's expense and then disappeared before there was any danger that he might have to put his own hand in his pocket.

'It's just that I'm not sure I like the idea of disputing the will. No offence, Harry, but a charity like the Trust should be concentrating on its clients, not on legal argument. For God's sake, tonight we spent five minutes discussing applications for funding and the rest of the time the possibility of going to law. We had no right to expect anything from Charles Kavanaugh. If he chose to leave his money elsewhere, that's his prerogative. We should respect it.'

'The Trust needs the money,' Frances said quietly. 'That's Luke's view, he told me so the last time we spoke. And you know he would never be a party to anything underhand. We should follow Harry's advice.'

Tim sighed. 'Maybe you're right. I suppose I've always had an old-fashioned outlook.'

'I'd call it honourable,' Frances said. 'And I'll go further. If I really believed that Charles had made a rational decision to disinherit the

Trust and give everything to his lady friend, I'd defend to the death his right to do so. But I can't accept her story at face value. It stinks, frankly, and we owe it to the Trust to test it out. If it survives close scrutiny, I'm inclined to say good luck to her. We might solicit a donation, but that's all. Because what you say is right. And it does you credit.'

'Thanks.' He was mumbling again, plainly embarrassed. 'I'll be off then.'

'Good night,' Harry said. He watched the man go, bumbling through the crowded room in the vague direction of the exit and speculated whether, just as Frances was evidently attracted to Luke, so Tim might carry a torch for Frances.

Harry's route back to his flat took him through the city centre. As he walked, he wondered again about Frances's claim that Luke was afraid. The Blackhurst problem alone could not, surely, account for it. Perhaps it was something to do with the supposed deception by one of the other trustees. Frances, Matthew, Tim or Roy? The meeting had offered no clues. He resolved to give Luke a ring the next morning, to see if he had returned home.

Fifty yards ahead, he caught sight of a woman emerging from the Ensenada, a restaurant famed equally for cuisine and cost. As he watched, she stepped under a streetlamp and flagged down a taxi. He had only met her once before, but he would have recognised that shocking blonde hair anywhere. Talk of the devil. Vera Blackhurst was living it up already.

He ducked into a doorway as a tall grey-haired man in an overcoat followed her out of the restaurant. His coat collar was turned up and, although his build and walk seemed familiar, it was impossible to identify him. As Harry peered through the darkness, the man held the cab door open for Vera and was rewarded for his courtesy by a peck on the cheek. He put his hand on her arm and it seemed to Harry that it lingered there before they said their goodbyes and the man waved her off.

What was going on?

The man strode across the road and disappeared down an alleyway on the other side. Harry hesitated, then remembered how his hackles had risen when Jim had scoffed at his habit of poking his nose into other people's business. He took a deep breath, then hurried off in pursuit of Vera's companion. The alley led to Lord Street but when he arrived there, his quarry had disappeared.

'Shit!' he exclaimed.

A drunk who was leaning against a litter bin said, 'You never spoke a truer word pal,' and promptly threw up over the pavement.

Harry groaned. Perhaps Jim was right after all. The man had probably parked in one of the multi-storeys – but which? He opted for the NCP in Paradise Street and raced to the main exit.

After five minutes he realised he had chosen wrongly. None of the cars which emerged contained anyone who remotely resembled Vera Blackhurst's companion. He sighed and told himself that probably it didn't matter. It was a free country. She couldn't be expected to mourn her late employer for ever. Let's face it, there was no harm in going out for dinner with someone.

And her companion couldn't possibly have been Luke Dessaur – could it?

Chapter 4

Jonah Deegan had acquired an answering machine. It was akin to an Ancient Briton investing in a microwave oven. As Harry listened to the taped message the morning after the trustees' meeting, he found it difficult to suppress a burst of laughter. At last he had come across someone less at ease with technological advance than himself.

'There... uh, there's no-one here at present. I mean to say, there won't be at the time you hear this recording. I know it's a real pain when you hear one of these things, anyhow, don't hang up without letting me know who's called. Start talking after you've heard the whatsit – yes, I know, the tone. We'll get back to you as soon as possible. All being well.'

Jonah's parents had named him wisely. In the unlikely event that he had ever had a shred of optimism in his make-up, a career in the CID followed by long years operating on his own account had served to rob him of it. What puzzled Harry was Jonah's use of the royal we. The old man was usually as careful in his choice of phrase as a Chancery lawyer and since leaving the force he had operated as a one-man band. Surely at his time of life he was not about to turn over a new leaf?

'This is Harry Devlin. I have new instructions for you. Can we meet at one o'clock for a bite of lunch on board the *Queer Fish*?'

He felt pleased at having couched his request in terms that Jonah would find difficult to resist. Provided he picked up the message during the morning, the prospect of a paying job coupled with a free lunch and a trip to his beloved waterfront should ensure the old man's presence at the appointed time.

He still couldn't make up his mind whether the man with Vera had been Luke Dessaur. He rang Luke's home number but there was no reply. A metallic voice on Luke's mobile number told him that the phone was switched off and please to try later. He put the receiver down and told himself that he'd run out of excuses to delay sifting through his correspondence. He was wondering why, whenever he received a particularly stupid letter from another solicitor, it came on letterhead festooned with quality assurance logos when his receptionist rang.

'Kim Lawrence for you.' Suzanne had an extraordinary gift for uttering the four words with the aural equivalent of a knowing wink and a nudge in the ribs. Harry's involvement with the solicitor from Mersey Chambers was now widely known, although he still found difficulty himself in defining their relationship. He felt himself blushing even as he asked for her to be put through.

'Sorry to bother you,' Kim began before pausing. He was struck by her tentative tone. Outside the office she could be a mass of contradictions and uncertainties, but during working hours she adopted the persona of the cool, decisive lawyer with such skill that very few realised that it was no more than a disguise.

'Glad you rang. I was wondering if you would be interested in seeing *Vertigo* again? It's on at the Philharmonic Picture Palace.'

'Thanks – but is there any chance I can see you before then? Tonight, for instance?'

'Sure.' He was surprised by the urgency of her tone, but gratified by it. 'What would you like to do?'

'Tonight is the annual general meeting of the Liverpool Legal Group. I haven't been for years, I thought I might show my face this time. Shall I perhaps see you there?'

Harry knitted his brow. From anyone else, the suggestion would have been a patent leg-pull. He loathed the politics of their profession. For him, attending a lawyers' talking shop held as much appeal as undergoing a colonic irrigation. Yet her question was not satiric, but rather anxious – almost pleading. Quite out of character. He would need to feel his way through this conversation. 'I hadn't planned...' he began.

'Sorry,' she said quickly. 'I should have realised. Silly idea. Forget it.'

'No, no. Jim reckons I ought to take an interest in the future of the profession. I say the Legal Group has no more influence over it than a bunch of fortune tellers. But if you're going, perhaps I should break the habit of a lifetime.'

'Fine,' she breathed. 'And thanks.'

'No problem. I can moan about diminishing profits with the best of them. And it'll be good to see you again.'

'You too,' she said quietly.

Suzanne rang to say that Jonah had called back to confirm their lunch meeting. Things were beginning to move. On his way out to court, he looked round Jim's door. His partner looked up from the glossy brochure he was studying and said, 'We need to sharpen up our corporate image.'

Harry groaned. This was old ground. 'Don't tell me. Another public relations consultancy has got its claws into you. Remember the salesman who wanted us to sponsor a Formula One racing car? With our luck, it would have crashed at the first bend and incinerated the driver.'

'You're prejudiced. Old-fashioned. We need to move with the times, keep up with the competition. The woman who phoned me is full of ideas. We could hold a season of seminars for regular clients, mailshot them with news of changes in the law.'

'Wonderful. Do you think the governor of Walton Jail might let us circulate our clients with details of how to lodge an appeal against conviction?'

Jim scowled. 'Your idea of practice development is buying a round for the villains who hang out at the Dock Brief.'

'Don't knock it. It works. And I'm quite willing to raise my blood-alcohol level in the line of duty.'

'We need to be proactive.' A thought evidently struck Jim and he tossed the brochure across the desk. 'I've talked to her on the phone and she's offered to come in for an hour to talk things through. Are you interested?'

Harry glanced at the photograph on the front cover. 'Juliet May Communications? And this is Juliet May, I presume?'

'Uh-huh.'

She was a striking redhead with large brown eyes. Harry gazed at the picture for a few seconds and said, 'Obviously, it would be wrong for me to pre-judge matters. I suppose in fairness I ought to give her a hearing.'

Jim grinned. 'I thought that on reflection you'd be willing to reconsider. Leave it with me, I'll fix something up. I warned her you'd be a challenge – to say the least – but she was quite relaxed about that, said a one-to-one session with you would suit her fine.'

'She obviously has good taste.'

'She'll learn. So how was your meeting at the Piquet Club?'

'I didn't get to look at the naughty books. Must be slipping. The trustees spent most of their time bitching about Blackhurst. And guess what? She was out on the town herself last night.'

He described his sighting of her outside the Ensenada. 'I even wondered if the man with her was Luke. But quite apart from the fact he can't stand the sight of her, he's not as solidly built as the chap I saw. All the same, I'll mention it to Jonah. The trustees were happy to instruct him and I'm seeing him for lunch. If anyone can dig the dirt on Vera, he can.'

'You think there is dirt to be dug?'

'Why not? How many people do you know without a skeleton in their cupboard?'

Only as he left the office did Harry reflect on his partner's pained expression and wonder if his careless final remark had been misinterpreted. Jim was an uxorious man, married with two children, but last year he had wandered from the straight and narrow with an attractive girl, a woman police officer much younger than his wife. Harry was the only other person who knew about the relationship: he'd once barged in on them at the most delicate moment imaginable. So far as he knew, Jim had now stopped seeing the other woman. He certainly hoped so; he cared for the Crusoes and did not want to see any of them hurt. But he sensed that even if Jim managed never to be found out, his conscience would continue to trouble him.

He headed through the city streets under a sky that threatened rain. Charles Kavanaugh had been buried on just such a day. Harry had been required to represent the firm at the funeral because Jim was involved in a heavy property deal; it had given him the opportunity to meet Vera Blackhurst for the one and only time. She had been dressed from head to toe in black and kept wiping away tears from her heavily made-up cheeks. Harry had taken an instant dislike to her. Perhaps it was unfair, perhaps she had worshipped the ground that the dead man had walked on. But somehow he could not believe it. When he had muttered a few words of condolence to her at the graveside, she had burst into uncontrollable weeping. Grief took different people in different ways, but when she put her handkerchief away, he noticed that her small dark eyes were as hard and unemotional as pieces of coal.

Outside the magistrates' court, the wild-eyed vagrant the local lawyers called Davey Damnation was in full cry. He was a cadaverous figure who had been hanging around the city for months and his knowledge of the Book of Revelation surpassed even Harry's familiarity with *The Big Sleep*.

'And the city had no need of the sun!'

'Thought you were a prophet of doom, not a weather forecaster,' Harry murmured. But out of a strange mixture of habit and superstition, he tossed a few coins into the battered hat which Davey kept at his feet. The response was less than euphoric.

'He that is unjust, let him be unjust still!'

Harry grinned. 'That's no way to talk about the chairman of the bench.'

Davey glared. If he had ever possessed a sense of humour, it must have been worn away by years of living rough. His age was unguessable: perhaps early forties, but he had the weathered flesh of a man twenty years older. He drew in his breath, but before he could launch into another diatribe, Harry hurried into the building. When he emerged a couple of hours later, he had secured an acquittal for one client and a paltry fine with time to pay for another. The clouds had rolled away, too. Perhaps it was going to be his day.

Davey thought otherwise. He jabbed his forefinger at Harry as if pointing out a bag thief on an identity parade.

'And the smoke of their torment ascendeth up for ever and ever: and they have no rest day nor night.'

The prophet's understanding of the difficulties faced by the local legal profession was remarkably acute, Harry decided. He strolled down Dale Street in the direction of the waterfront. The river was quiet, as usual these days. More freight was put through the Port of Liverpool now than at any time in its history, but the supertankers lacked the romance of the old days, when the world's ships had sailed here. He sighed and turned into the Albert Dock complex. The *Queer Fish* was a small restaurant boat moored outside Gladstone Pavilion that offered snacks and meals to tourists and a wealth of gossip to locals. As Harry stepped on board, the proprietor hailed him like a returning prodigal.

'If it isn't Harry Devlin! How super to see you again. Where have you been hiding yourself?'

What would be an effusive greeting from anyone else was par for the course with the rubicund matelot standing by the kitchen door. Harry knew that the warmth of his welcome was genuine. Dusty Rhodes loved people and good food in equal measure. He had once been a cook in the Royal Navy, but nowadays running the *Queer Fish* was as close as he came to a life on the ocean waves. His affectionate nature had led to an incident resulting in his dishonourable discharge, but in the safer waters of the Albert Dock he was able to indulge his passions to his heart's content.

'Yeah, long time no see. I've invited Jonah Deegan along.' Dusty knew the detective, who was always happy to have lunch here if a client could be found to foot the bill. 'Any chance of a quiet table for two?'

'Your wish is my command. Follow me.' Dusty looked back over his shoulder. 'Old Jonah, eh? So is the game afoot, as Sherlock would say?'

Harry took a seat. 'Ask no questions and I'll tell you no lies.'

Dusty pouted. 'Spoilsport. Ah, here's the man himself.'

Harry glanced towards the door. Jonah Deegan was hobbling towards him. The old man suffered badly from arthritis and was in the queue for a hip replacement. But Jonah on one leg was still more effective than most inquiry agents on two: he had the priceless gift of being able to accept nothing at face value. In response to Dusty's cheery greeting, he simply scowled. Old habits died hard and Jonah had never had any time for shirtlifters. But Dusty was a detective's dream, a mine of information about goings-on in the city who simply loved to be quarried. With Jonah, the job mattered more than anything and he just about managed to keep his prejudices in check. Harry suspected that the old fellow might even entertain a sneaking regard for Dusty, but knew he would sooner die than admit to it.

'Glad you got my message. Pull up a chair and after we've had a bite I'll explain what I'm looking for.'

'I've got company,' the old man said with his habitual truculence.

Harry had noticed a bespectacled young woman in dungarees threading her way through the tables behind Jonah, but he had not imagined they were together. She stepped forward and offered her hand. 'Stephanie Hall. Pleased to meet you, Mr Devlin. I've heard a lot about you.'

As they shook hands, Harry tried to weigh her up. She had a fresh face, a mop of unruly fair hair and a grip that would not have shamed a prison warder. There was something about her cast of features that reminded Harry of someone, but he could not place it. He was too busy wondering why Jonah had brought her along.

'I never realised I was famous.'

'Your detective exploits, of course. Jonah here has told me all about the cases you've been involved with. He doesn't have much time for amateurs but I bet that, if pushed, he might make an exception for you.'

Harry was bemused by the fond, almost proprietorial way in which she referred to the old man, who was shifting uncomfortably in his chair. 'You work together?' he asked cautiously.

'Partners,' Stephanie beamed.

He gaped at her. Female private eyes were nothing new, but *Jonah* teaming up with a girl less than half his age? It was less likely than a joint venture between the Law Society and a troupe of morris dancers. 'Oh. Right. And since when...?'

'Well, I'm jumping the gun slightly. Officially the partnership commencement date is the first of next month. But I'm on board now and we've made a few small changes already.'

'Ah. The answering machine?'

'For example. Though I'm having some trouble persuading Jonah to switch it on. But as I've said to him, we have to move with the times. Clients' expectations have changed since he first hung up his nameplate. We have to offer a quality service. Customer care. Value for money.'

To judge by the crimsoning of his leathery cheeks, Jonah had experienced increasing difficulty in keeping quiet throughout these exchanges. Finally the old curmudgeon could bear it no more.

'Stephanie's my sister's daughter, you see.' Harry had never heard him sound so defensive. 'She's always been keen on the idea of coming into the business.'

43

'And you've said no for the past two years, haven't you?' she said with an amused glint in her eye. 'But in the end you saw it made sense.'

'We'll have to wait and see, won't we?' he said grumpily.

Stephanie winked at Harry. 'He's expecting me to fall flat on my face. But the fact is, Mr Devlin, he isn't getting any younger. He has all the experience and contacts, but he needs another pair of hands. I may not be an ex-copper, but I'm brimming with enthusiasm and I'm full of ideas.'

Harry organised the food and as they ate he learned a little more about the odd couple's plans. Stephanie was a geography graduate, but since her teens she had always had a yearning to follow in her uncle's footsteps. It offered, she said, a perfect opportunity to satisfy her natural curiosity about people and to be paid for the privilege.

By the time he was pouring out the tea, Harry decided that he liked Stephanie very much. She had the same square jaw as her uncle and he guessed that she would be as resolute in the pursuit of an inquiry, although she might not take such pains to make her clients aware that she was doing them a favour by taking on their case.

As he told the story of Vera Blackhurst, Stephanie asked frequent questions. 'What do we know about her?'

'Very little. Until Charles's death, I was scarcely aware of her existence. I met her once, at the funeral. She was about as inconspicuous as Sharon Stone in widow's weeds. And her hat was the ugliest I've ever seen. Like a rejected exhibit from the Tate.'

Stephanie grinned. 'Can't say anything about that. The Deegans are hardly famed for their sartorial elegance. Tell me – was there anything suspicious about his death?'

Jonah had become a little restive and now he could contain himself no longer. 'Stephanie has this idea that she'd like to help solve a murder mystery.'

'It's a weakness we have in common,' Harry said.

'One of the reasons I asked her along,' Jonah said gloomily. 'I thought you two would get on like a house on fire.'

'Unfortunately, the answer to her question is no. Charles never enjoyed good health. Miriam, his mother, pampered him from infancy. He was always overweight and he suffered from diabetes as well as a variety of other ailments. During the last few years, he ate to excess and it put a heavy strain on his constitution. He had a heart attack a little while ago. But in the end the diabetes did for him. He had a couple of toes amputated, but it was too late to prevent gangrene setting in. Even if he hadn't suffered a second and fatal coronary, he wasn't likely to have survived. No possibility of foul play.'

Stephanie rubbed her chin. 'And the will was found amongst Charles's effects at the nursing home after his death?'

'Correct. Vera was present when he died. Holding his hand, by all accounts. Of course, his death was not unexpected. There is no doubt that it was a case of natural causes.' Harry's eyes narrowed. 'Apparently the body had no sooner been wheeled away than Vera was asking the matron to look through Charles's effects to make sure that his important papers were looked after. By which she meant, of course, the will. He'd kept it in his bedside cabinet during the last forty-eight hours of his life. Vera said that Charles would have wanted the trustees to be informed of his passing. Luke Dessaur had called in to see him several times and I gather that most, if not all, of the trustees had visited to pay their respects.'

Jonah grunted. 'Hypocrites.'

'Vera said she was too upset to ring round herself, but she asked the matron to let Luke have the news. And it was the matron who told him about the new will. She said she'd caught sight of its contents. By accident, of course. She hadn't meant to pry.'

'Oh yeah?' Jonah said. 'I expect she was hoping for a mention.'

'If so, she was disappointed. She told Luke that Charles had left the Trust his treasures – I suppose she assumed they were valuable

– and that the rest was going to Vera. You can imagine Luke's reaction. He was appalled and consulted Jim Crusoe right away. Jim advised the trustees to lodge a caveat. Which was duly done.'

'And what's the effect of that?'

'I won't bore you with all the legal technicalities,' Harry said. In truth, he was far from sure that he could remember them. 'But it prevents Vera from sealing a grant of probate for up to six months. So she can't pay herself a large slice of Charles's fortune and then skedaddle. Even if she wants to. It slows everything down.'

'Sounds like every other legal process I ever heard of,' Jonah grumbled.

'Useful for the trustees, though. Charles was a wealthy man with a wide variety of assets. Stocks and shares, property and so on. Sorting out a complex estate always takes time. Even so, we won't be able to hold off Geoffrey Willatt for ever.'

'Fascinating,' Stephanie breathed. 'Vera sounds like a mystery woman.'

'Something else happened last night.' He described seeing her leave the restaurant and his fruitless chase after her companion. 'I did wonder if the man with her was the chairman of the Kavanaugh trustees. It seems unlikely, even though there was a resemblance. But it prompted me to looking through the file again and I've started wondering about the language used in the will. Geoffrey Willatt has given me a copy. It's written out in shaky longhand but it's simple and legally sound. In other words, very suspicious.'

'Why?'

Harry grinned. 'Any lawyer will tell you, do-it-yourself wills are almost always badly drafted.'

Jonah coughed. 'You just want to drum up more business.'

Stephanie shushed him. 'Are you saying Charles was too stupid to draft a will properly?'

'Not exactly. What I am saying is that I wouldn't have expected him to use the briefest valid attestation clause. That is, the bit before the signatures. He used the phrase: *signed by the testator in our presence and by us in his.* Very neat. But it's not a form of words that would spring naturally to the mind of a dying man.'

She opened her eyes very wide. 'Could he have copied it from his old will?'

'No. His lawyer, Cyril Tweats, had many qualities, but brevity was never one of them. He always used a more verbose formula. It was part of his style. My guess is that Vera checked out the wording in a book and dictated the terms of the will to Charles.'

'I agree,' Stephanie said eagerly. 'I'm sure you're on to something.'

Harry chuckled. Jonah was quite right: Stephanie was a woman after his own heart. 'So it's over to you two. If you can give the trustees any information which will help them to drive a suitable bargain with Vera, they will be delighted.'

'We'll do our best,' she said, reaching for her bag. 'Thanks for the instructions. We'll report back as soon as possible. Just one more thing I ought to mention.'

'Yes?'

'We've had to increase our fees. Forced on us by the level of overheads. I've often told Jonah, he's been selling himself short for years. Don't think of it as a price rise so much as a long-overdue correction. See you.'

Jonah winked at Harry, who mouthed at him, 'Bloody answering machine.' Whatever her qualities as an investigator, it looked as though Stephanie was intent on becoming the acceptable face of her uncle's brand of capitalism.

Ten minutes later he was walking back into Fenwick Court. As he stepped into reception Suzanne hailed him. The pleasurable alarm on her face filled him with foreboding: she loved nothing better than to be the breaker of bad news.

'Mr Crusoe wanted to see you. Urgently.'

'Any idea what it's about?'

She shook her blonde locks. 'All he said was that he wanted me to make sure you got the message. At once. He doesn't trust you to check your e-mail.'

Harry made straight for his partner's room. 'A problem? Or is Suzanne simply enlivening her afternoon by turning on her best shock-horror manner?'

Jim looked up from the pile of title deeds in front of him. 'I think you would call it a problem. Luke Dessaur has been found dead.'

Chapter 5

He called Frances Silverwood right away. It was evident from her muffled tone that she was choking back tears as she gave him the brief details of which she was aware.

'Luke had booked into the Hawthorne Hotel down on the Strand. God knows why. He had a single room on the third floor and he fell from the window about half past midnight. As far as I can gather, it's not clear whether it was an accident – or suicide.'

'*Suicide*?' Harry's head was spinning. 'Surely that's not possible?'

'That – that's what I would have said. But apparently it is a strong possibility.'

'Why? Did he leave a note?'

'I don't think so. It's just unbelievable, Harry.' He heard her taking a deep breath at the other end of the line. 'Sorry. I'll pull myself together soon, but this has come – as rather a shock, to say the least.'

'If there's anything I can do.'

'I – I don't like to ask this,' she said.

'Go ahead.'

'I realise you're a busy man. I trespassed on your time yesterday and I don't want to make a nuisance of myself. But I wonder – could we have a word about this, once I've had a chance to collect my thoughts? I'd like to talk to someone. If that doesn't sound foolish in a grown woman.'

'Of course it doesn't. Are you free later this afternoon? I have a meeting at Empire Dock after work.'

'I could be at your office for five thirty, is that all right?'

After ringing off, he felt a twinge of conscience, aware that his motives were not purely altruistic. The news of Luke Dessaur's death was not merely startling. It saddened him. They had never been close, but he had always respected the older man. The waste of a good human life always made him feel dismay. Yet he had the honesty to admit to himself that he was also intrigued. It was impossible to understand what had happened to Luke, to think of a reason why he should have left home for a hotel and then finished up dead. But he needed to make sense of the mystery. It was a feeling with which he was familiar, one that perhaps he should resist – but could not. Even if he did not give in straight away, it would continue to tease him like a seductive woman, nibbling away at him until he had no choice but to surrender to his instincts.

When Frances arrived, Harry was shocked by the change in her. Her shoulders were hunched and her voice croaky. He'd never seen her eyes so red and she kept blowing her nose. Although she gave the excuse that she was going down with a cold, he did not believe her. Luke's death had left her desolate.

Darkness had fallen and it was cold outside, but she suggested that they walk for a little while along the waterfront. Harry was quick to say yes. He loved the river and in times of trouble often sought to calm himself by watching the waves as they lapped against the shore. They paused in their stroll near the ferry terminal and stood by the rail, looking out towards the straggling lights of the Wirral peninsula. For a while neither of them spoke.

'Thank you for sparing me your time,' she said at last.

'It's the least I could do.' After a pause he said gently, 'Would you like to take me through what happened, as far as you know?'

'Yes, I must have sounded pretty incoherent when we talked earlier. Sorry. There isn't actually a great deal to tell. I tried ringing Luke's home number one more time today and a policewoman answered. She was tight-lipped at first. Needless to say, I was bewildered. But I was able to put a few pieces together partly through talking to her and partly through having a word with Don Ragovoy, the manager at the Hawthorne Hotel. He's been involved with the Museum as a sponsor and I know him slightly. I called there before coming round to your office.'

'And?'

'Don said there was no record that Luke had ever stayed there before and he had no idea why he should suddenly have decided to do so yesterday.' She frowned. 'It makes no sense. Why should he pay good money for a room in a hotel when he lives only a few miles away?'

'Had he been drinking?'

'So Don says. After picking up his suitcase, he seems to have driven into the city and left his Rover in the hotel's underground car park. If he was planning to meet someone in town and have a few drinks, why not simply take a taxi? He had an evening meal alone in the restaurant.'

'Ah.' So one mystery was solved. Luke had not been Vera's dinner companion at the Ensenada.

'Apparently the waitress who served him said he seemed tense and preoccupied. In his room they found an opened whisky bottle and an empty tumbler.' She swallowed. 'Nobody saw him fall. His room overlooked an inner courtyard, according to Don Ragovoy. A night porter whose cubby-hole is on the ground floor heard a thud outside and went to investigate. He found Luke's body stretched across the gravel.'

Harry flinched. More than once in his life he had seen the body of someone dead before their time. One corpse had belonged to his wife. The memory of his last sight of her always swamped him with nausea.

'An accident, perhaps?'

'Don Ragovoy claims it couldn't have been. Although Luke's room had a window opening out on to a tiny balcony, it would be very difficult for someone simply to slip to their death. The balcony isn't for everyday use, it's a design feature. Don showed me the corresponding room on the floor below. To get out, one would have to open the window to its fullest extent and then haul oneself over the railing. Not as difficult as Don made out, but far from easy.'

'You have to take what he says with a pinch of salt. He has the reputation of his hotel to protect and his own job to think about. If it turned out that the place he is running is a deathtrap, he would be finished.'

'Even so, he has a point. Why would Luke want to scramble out of his bedroom window in the early hours – unless he wanted to end it all?'

'Strange that he left no message.'

She sighed. 'I agree. He is – sorry, was – so precise, so well organised. And so considerate. That's why I refuse to believe that he can have meant to commit suicide. Mind you, he was only an occasional drinker. If he'd drunk more whisky than was good for him, perhaps he became confused. And there are other possibilities. I've even wondered if it was some form of – oh, I don't know – some form of a cry for help.'

'But think of the method he chose,' Harry said. 'Not an overdose. Not something where there was a chance someone might haul him back from the brink. You say his room was on the third floor. You don't get a second chance if you fall from that height.'

She gulped. 'I suppose you're right. It just seems so extraordinary. I can't understand why he would want to do such a thing.'

'One thing I've learned,' he said, 'is this. No matter how well you think you may know another person, you can never know everything about them. You can live with someone for years and yet they may have secrets you never begin to expect.'

She inclined her head and said softly, 'You know about sudden death, don't you? Your wife was murdered.'

'Yes,' he said. 'There was once a time when I reckoned I knew Liz inside out. Of course, I was deceiving myself. At least as badly as she deceived me.'

Still facing out across the river, she said, 'I cared for him, you know.'

'Yes, I know.'

'I'd known him slightly for years. He'd always been closely involved with the arts in Merseyside and at one time he was a non-executive director of the Museum. He knew about my singing and invited me on to the Trust board after he was appointed chairman. I don't pretend he was always an easy colleague. He had such integrity. Most people were in awe of him. But he didn't court popularity. Or ever compromise on his principles.'

A silence followed and Harry remembered his last conversation with Luke Dessaur. Luke had believed that one of his fellow trustees was deceiving him, perhaps even committing a crime. Surely such knowledge would not cause him to take his own life?

'The last time I saw him...' he began.

She turned towards him. 'Yes?'

'He did seem... to have something on his mind.' Even as he uttered the words, he realised how lame they sounded. He had been about to confide in her, but under her penetrating gaze he'd found himself faltering. It was inconceivable that Frances was the person Luke thought had been deceiving him – wasn't it? – but just as it had during their meeting at the Museum, something made him hold his tongue. Perhaps it was nothing more than a lawyer's inbred caution.

'I told you yesterday, he's seemed afraid recently. But – why?' There was a note of urgency in her voice, as if she sensed that he knew more than he was yet willing to reveal. He cursed himself for raising the subject on impulse.

Having abandoned candour, he had no choice but to obfuscate. At least legal training came in handy sometimes. 'I suppose none of us can tell what would drive a man to the depths of despair.'

Yet the thought slid into his mind that perhaps it was not a question of despair at all. A man of integrity would make enemies –

it was inevitable. And a man unwilling to compromise on personal standards might be a danger not only to himself, but also to others.

***

After saying goodbye to Frances, he headed along the waterfront towards Empire Dock. The Liverpool Legal Group often hired a room there for its meetings. Harry lived in the same complex, in one of the apartments that had been carved out of the old warehouse. He sometimes had to take care not to be spotted by professional colleagues when he was on his way home; he had no intention of spending his evening talking with other solicitors and barristers about their tribulations as well as their trials.

Thinking about Kim Lawrence distracted him from speculating about the death of Luke Dessaur. Why had she invited him to the Legal Group AGM, of all things? Kim was a sole practitioner, a lawyer with crusading zeal who specialised in family and criminal law. In Liverpool, there was no shortage of work in either discipline. She had little time for the establishment, which made her attendance at Empire Dock tonight all the more curious. He sighed. Compared to Kim, his wife Liz had been an open book. He knew he must be patient, but sometimes he despaired of ever being able to understand the way Kim thought, let alone to try to read her mind.

As he walked along the riverside pathway, he became aware of an emptiness in his stomach. Surely he was not nervous? It made no sense: he had nothing to fear from the hacks of the Legal Group. And he should be looking forward to the chance to see Kim. The wind whipped against his cheeks as he mulled it over. There had been something strange in the way she had spoken on the telephone. Was it possible that she had met someone else?

He was the last to arrive. Unpunctuality was one of his vices. It derived, he supposed, from a pathological fear of boredom, of arriving too early and having nothing to do. It seemed better to turn up just in time, but in practice he always left things to the last minute and found himself panicking about whether he would ever make his appointment. He always regretted it and kept vowing to mend his ways: one more resolution he never kept.

The penalty on this occasion was that he had lost his chance to sit next to Kim. She was always prompt and he noticed her blonde head at the front, facing the raised dais on which the Group's officers were arrayed. If she had tried to keep a seat free for him, there was no sign of it. He found a place in the back row, treading on a few toes and causing a bit of tutting as he did so. Geoffrey Willatt, sitting on the dais, caught his eye and frowned. Harry winked at him in the hope of provoking a scowl. The tease worked, as it always did. Then, as he craned his neck to see over the balding heads in front of him, he saw Kim deep in conversation with Quentin Pike, a partner in a firm called Windaybanks.

Odd, but comforting. As the proceedings began, he reflected that at least there was no chance of Quentin becoming a rival for her affections. Quentin's chubby exterior concealed – as callow police officers often discovered to their cost – an incisive defence lawyer's mind as well as a sly wit. But he was a devout Catholic with a charming wife and an ever-increasing number of children. Harry could not imagine him embarking on an affair with a professional rival noted for her earnestness and campaigning zeal.

Come to think of it, many people would have regarded Harry as an equally improbable partner for Kim. Although they shared an unswerving loyalty to the underdog as well as a passion for justice that even bitter experience of the real legal world could not dim, the ways in which they expressed their beliefs could scarcely have been more different. Kim favoured lobbying Parliament and candle-lit vigils. Harry preferred to search on his own for the truth in cases which fired his imagination. In contrast to her fierce sense of purpose, he had only a dogged unwillingness to leave any conundrum unresolved.

He was, despite himself, impressed that the meeting was so well attended. The economic climate was troubling and lawyers were feeling the pinch. The Group was trying to retrieve lost ground. They knew they could never expect public sympathy. They lived in an age when Roy Milburn's lawyer jokes always raised a laugh, a world in which audiences guffawed at the scene in *Jurassic Park* where a dinosaur eats a lawyer as he sits on the toilet. So to make up, they comforted each other. Litigators expressed dismay about the slump in income from conveyancing work. Property lawyers condemned the latest cuts in legal aid. Everyone united against those soulless accountants who were snatching so much of the work that should properly be handled by solicitors and barristers in private practice.

'All we ask,' one speaker insisted, 'is to be paid properly for what we do.'

This eminently reasonable sentiment received loud applause, but Harry kept his hands upon his knees. The man who was complaining possessed a Jaguar, a house on the Wirral and a mistress with a taste for designer clothes. Harry did not doubt that the fellow was strapped for cash, but reckoned that neither the Lord Chancellor nor the clients were likely to shed any tears for him.

The plastic chair was hard, the discussion short of intentional humour and Harry was relieved when Geoffrey Willatt concluded the formalities. As people began to rise and move in the direction of the bar, Kim turned and looked over her shoulder. Harry caught her eye and she waved. Yet she then turned back to talk to Quentin Pike. What were they debating – surely not the scope for charging more for a house sale and purchase?

Only one way to find out. He ambled over and perched on a chair in the row immediately behind them. Quentin was in the middle of a sentence when he glanced round and saw they had company. The words died on his lips and he gave Harry a nod of welcome whilst scanning his face, as if trying to discover something.

'Evening, Quentin. Kim. So what's your verdict – is there a future for the high street solicitor?'

Quentin beamed, as he often did in court when trying to glide over a serious flaw in his case. 'It's very worrying. For once I agree with dear old Geoffrey. We shall all have to tighten our belts.'

'I'm sure you're right.' Harry couldn't resist glancing at the other man's ample girth. Quentin's bathroom scales probably screamed for mercy every morning. 'But I expect we'll survive. I must admit I find the scare stories rather wearing, though I noticed you two found plenty to discuss.'

Kim's pale cheeks coloured. Quentin patted her on the shoulder. 'As you well know, Ms Lawrence is always worth listening to. And now, I'm afraid, I must leave you both.'

'Stay and have a drink.' Harry would normally have felt that two was company, three a crowd. But something was up and he could not be sure that Kim would confide in him. Maybe after a couple of rounds Quentin might be ready to talk.

'Sorry. I was on duty last night and it takes its toll.' He paused and added, 'Besides, I'm sure the two of you have enough to chat about together.'

Harry noticed Kim blush again and as Quentin made his way towards the exit, he asked, 'What was all that about?'

'Any chance of that drink?'

'My God, is it as bad as that?'

She gave him a thin smile. 'Not really.'

A couple of minutes later they had found the quietest corner of the room and Harry was savouring a pint of best. In the background, he could hear people grumbling about court delays and the cost of professional indemnity insurance. He said, 'This is the last place I expected you to suggest for an evening out.'

'I needed to talk to Quentin. And besides, there's something I want you to know.'

She put her glass down on a small table and fiddled with the copper bracelet on her wrist. Her eyes had the downward cast of a bringer of bad news.

It doesn't matter, Harry told himself. How could she hurt him? As a boy he'd had to listen to the news that his parents were dead. Years later, two policemen had called at his flat early one morning to tell him that his wife had been murdered in a dismal back street. Not too long ago he had discovered that someone he liked was a killer. He had risked his life then and Kim had saved him. She owed him nothing. Besides, anticipation was always worse than the event. Whatever she had to say, it was better to get it over and done with.

He touched her slender arm. 'Go on.'

She swallowed. Her hands were trembling slightly. It occurred to him that she had been dreading this moment, that she had rehearsed a little speech but now the right words were evading her.

'You know how much my work with MOJO means to me.'

Puzzled, he nodded. She was regional chair of the Miscarriages of Justice Organisation and she admitted herself that she devoted more time to it than was healthy for her own legal practice.

'Ever since I was a law student,' she continued hesitantly, 'it's seemed important to me to do everything possible to help people betrayed by the legal system.'

'God knows,' he said, 'there are plenty of them.'

She managed a faint smile. 'You understand, Harry. It's one of the things I've always liked about you.'

That sounded disturbingly like an epitaph. He ground his teeth, said nothing.

'So I'm hoping you'll also understand what I'm about to say. You see, I've been offered a job.'

He stared at her. 'But you have your own firm.'

'Yes.' She waved a hand dismissively in the direction of their colleagues, chattering over canapés. 'But I've never felt as though I truly belong to the profession. Filling in forms, charging by the hour. The more I think about it, the less it seems to have to do with justice.'

He grunted. 'I know what you mean.'

'And I've come to realise that my work for MOJO gives me much more satisfaction than anything else. We can make a difference, Harry. And if we can help to put right even a few of the travesties that the law inflicts, then I can't think of a more worthwhile way of spending my time.'

'So MOJO have offered to take you on the staff?' A wave of relief swept over him. What was all the fuss about? 'Wonderful news. Congratulations.'

'It's not as simple as that,' she said. 'As you know, the organisation runs on a shoestring. There's no way that the North West branch could afford to take someone on to the payroll. The money simply isn't there.'

'What, then?'

'The national headquarters is in London. The present chief executive has had a coronary and been offered ill-health retirement. They've asked me if I'd like to take the position in his place.'

He caught his breath, trying to take it in. 'So do you have to relocate?'

She nodded. 'I've discussed it with the Board. I wanted to know if it was possible for me to keep a base in Liverpool. The answer was no. Whether we like it or not, London is the centre of influence. The chief executive has to be there full-time. And it's not just a Monday to Friday job. If I want it, I have to move.'

'And – you do want the job?'

'Very much.' She paused. 'I've wrestled with it night and day ever since they put the offer to me. But if I don't seize the chance now, I'd always regret it. Even so, it's a frightening prospect, making

59

a fresh start in a strange city at the other end of the country. I'm settled here. Perhaps even in a rut. But I'm not like you, I'm not a native Scouser. All the same – it would be a wrench to leave Merseyside. And you.'

She stroked his hand. Her fingers were cool. He was absurdly conscious of the sweatiness of his own palms and coughed to hide his dismay.

'Thanks. But – what about your business?'

'As you saw, I've been talking to Quentin. The reason is that, coincidentally, Windaybanks approached me a couple of months back. They wanted to know if I'd like to join forces with them. I said no and didn't give it a second thought. I've no interest in being part of a big partnership. But when the MOJO job came up, I gave Quentin a ring, asked if he'd be interested in taking over my caseload without taking over me. They came straight back and made me an offer. He's just been answering a few of the questions I asked. And he's being very reasonable, he's not insisting on an immediate response. One thing's for sure. They are offering me the chance to walk away with cash in my pocket.'

'And will you take it?'

'I don't know, Harry. That's the truth. I simply don't know.' She paused. 'What do you think I should do?'

In another part of the room, someone guffawed. The mood of the legal luminaries had lightened. After a few gin and tonics, things never seemed so bad.

He made up his mind. 'You should have another drink, that's what you should do.' And draining his glass, he wandered over to the bar.

'Let me get those,' Geoffrey Willatt said as the barman rang up the price on the till. Harry turned and gaped at his old principal. It was rather as if Bumble had offered an extra helping of gruel to Oliver Twist.

'Thanks.'

'My pleasure. Glad you could spare the time to join us. We must all stick together, Harry.' Geoffrey absent-mindedly adjusted his old school tie. 'There are simply far too many people coming into the profession. We need to restrict the numbers. I like the idea of making would-be solicitors undertake a personality test to see if they are suited to the work.'

'Just as well that idea wasn't around in my day,' Harry said. 'They would never have allowed me to qualify.'

If Geoffrey Willatt privately agreed with him, he was too discreet to reveal it. He lifted his glass. 'Cheers. Oh – and by the way.'

'Yes?' Of course, there must be an ulterior motive for this unwonted generosity.

'This Kavanaugh business. The caveat the trustees have lodged. They surely aren't going to contest the will, are they? There are no grounds.'

So that was it. Harry pursed his lips and thought about having to fill in his income tax return. It was his foolproof method when he wanted to assume a sombre expression. 'They're not happy, Geoffrey. Not happy at all. There is a good deal of money at stake. Charles Kavanaugh had promised it all to them, then your client turns up and five minutes later she's copped for the lot.'

'I'm sure she would be happy to reach an accommodation with them,' Geoffrey said, smoothing down an errant strand of grey hair. 'I can assure you, she is a very reasonable person. Very reasonable indeed.'

'Well, I'll put it to my clients, but I can't make any promises. Now, if you'll excuse me.'

'Of course. I must let you get back to Ms Lawrence.' Geoffrey coughed. 'Perhaps I may expect to hear from you in early course?'

'Perhaps,' Harry said with a sweet smile and returned to Kim's side.

'What are you looking so cheerful about all of a sudden?' she asked.

'Oh, just solved a little puzzle, that's all.'

It was true. He did not yet know why Vera was so keen to do a deal when all the cards seemed to be stacked in her favour. But he had at least worked out the identity of the companion whom he had half-recognised following her out of the Ensenada. Of course, it hadn't been Luke Dessaur, but another distinguished member of the Liverpool establishment, the famously respectable Geoffrey Willatt. And to add to his amusement, he'd also remembered Roy Milburn's joke about lawyers who went around screwing their clients.

Chapter 6

The death of Luke Dessaur was a nine day wonder. For a while people in Harry's circle talked of little else and although he now had other things on his mind he noticed how quickly shock gave way to speculation. Some argued that Luke had simply been the luckless victim of a tragic accident. He'd had too much to drink and not realised the risk he was taking when he opened his bedroom window and leaned right out to get a breath of air. Others reckoned it must have been suicide. Why else would he have booked into the Hawthorne Hotel? Presumably he could not face ending it all in the house he had once shared with his late wife. On a cold winter's night, there would have been little reason for him to open the window, let alone lean out so far that he lost balance and fell to his death.

Yet why should a pillar of the community have killed himself? As Jim Crusoe said, the explanation must lie in Luke's own personality.

'He often seemed remote, but that may date back to the time when he lost his wife.'

'She died of leukaemia, didn't she?' Harry asked.

'That's right. It was years ago, but everyone agrees he was devoted to her. Nursed her all the way through a long final illness. After that, he threw himself into his work.'

'You think he never stopped grieving?'

'Sometimes it's impossible to forget.' Jim spoke in an uncharacteristically gentle tone and Harry realised that his partner was thinking of the scars left by Liz's death.

'If it was suicide, then he must have had a breakdown. Why else would he behave so oddly in the days leading up

to his death and finally leave home and check into the Hawthorne?'

'His mind must have been in turmoil.' Jim's face clouded. 'Frances said he'd seemed afraid. We know why now, don't we? He was summoning up the courage to kill himself.'

'Doesn't make sense to me.'

'Still looking for mysteries?' Jim considered him. 'Is everything all right?'

'Yes, any reason why it shouldn't be?'

A deliberately casual shrug of the big shoulders. 'It's just that for the past couple of days you haven't seemed yourself.'

'What makes you say that?'

'Don't take this the wrong way,' Jim said mildly, 'but you've been arriving early and leaving very late and not sparing anyone much more than a hello and a goodbye. Your secretary told me this morning she'd never known you be so up-to-date with your paperwork. There's even a filthy rumour that behind closed doors you're practising on the computer. Any minute now and you'll be surfing on the Internet.'

Despite himself, Harry smiled. 'So – there must be a problem? I can't win.'

'Dead right.'

It was difficult to keep a secret from a partner. Jim had found that out for himself the hard way. Why pretend? Harry sighed and explained that Kim might be about to leave Liverpool.

Jim grunted. 'Sorry to hear that. But you say she's still in two minds?'

'The job was made for her. She'd be crazy to turn it down.'

'You could be long-distance lovers.'

Jim's easy assumption that the affair had been consummated deepened Harry's melancholy. He could not bring himself to tell his partner why he and Kim had never slept together. The last time she had made love to a man, he had died in the act. She was still fighting to rid herself of the sense of guilt that she felt because of the death of someone who had been married to another woman.

Jim took a deep breath. 'You're not going to thank me for this.'

'Words of wisdom coming up,' Harry said gloomily. 'Go on.'

'If she did go – it could be for the best in the long run.'

'Thanks,' Harry said in his curtest tone. 'But right now, that feels unlikely.'

Jim was trying to choose his words with care, to make a point without causing pain. The effect was clumsy: he was like a bear trying to hold an eggshell in its paw. 'I mean, it has always seemed to me that the two of you are so – different.'

'That's why I like her,' Harry said. 'Because she is different.'

Jonah turned up later that day to report progress on the Vera Blackhurst inquiry. He was wearing a thick scarf and walking even more stiffly than usual. The thought passed through Harry's mind that the old man was himself a candidate for being carried off by the bad weather. And a hundred to one he hadn't made a will.

'She's a lady with a past, that's for sure,' Jonah wheezed. 'Only trouble is, it doesn't look as though it's the same past she told Charlie Kavanaugh about when she applied for the job with him.'

'I wonder if she's told Geoffrey Willatt that?'

Jonah shook his head. 'I'd have thought he'd have had more sense than to get involved with the likes of her.'

'Perhaps it's not so surprising. His wife left him eighteen months back. She ran off with a partner in Boycott Duff. I suppose that if Vera has turned on the charm...'

'There's no fool like an old fool,' Jonah said. 'Any road, I've had a scout round the house, rooted through a few of the old feller's things.'

Jonah was perhaps ten years older than both Geoffrey Willatt and the late Charles Kavanaugh, but Harry let it pass. 'How did you manage that?'

Jonah winked and tapped the side of his nose. 'You ought to know better than that, lad. Ask no questions and you'll get no lies. Let's just say that I did a bit of sniffing around.'

'Isn't Vera still living there?'

'Yeah, queening it for the time being. She's a lady who likes the sound of her own voice, from what the neighbours tell me. It's a posh area, the people there don't have much time for servants with ideas above their station. Which is how they see Lady Muck. Apparently, she's all set to take a long holiday abroad, calls it a pick-me-up. She's bragged about going on a cruise, maybe round the world. Reckons it's the only way to travel. Claims that she's travelled on the *QEII*, flown in Concorde. I'm told she cracks on she's some sort of distressed gentlewoman. You know, someone of good birth who fell on hard times and was forced to start working for a living. But one thing's for sure. She didn't work for the people she claimed to have done when she replied to old Charlie's advertisement.'

'You followed up her references?'

'It's more than Charlie ever did, stupid old bugger. They're phoney, of course. The names and addresses she gave simply don't exist.' Jonah began to cough and his eyes started watering. Presently he recovered his composure sufficiently to be able to say, 'Old age, Harry. That's my problem. It's a bastard. Don't let anyone tell you any different.'

Harry forbore to suggest that the cigarettes Jonah had spent a lifetime smoking might have had something to do with it. He'd given up smoking himself the day after Liz's death: he'd felt driven by an obscure urge to escape from the past. Now he regarded the weed with the smug disapproval of a late convert to healthy – or, at least, less unhealthy – living.

'Can I get you a drink? Coffee, tea?'

Jonah's gnarled hand waved in contemptuous dismissal. 'I'll have a pint of best later on and that'll see me right. Any road, back to Blackhurst. The next thing is to find out what she's really been up to all these years. Bear in mind, it may take some time. There isn't much for me to go on yet.'

Harry nodded. 'With Charles dead, I can't believe we could get enough evidence to make a criminal charge stick, even if she obtained the job by deception. She could come up with half a dozen stories to explain the references away. The CPS would never prosecute.'

A ferocious snort conveyed Jonah's opinion of the Crown Prosecution Service. 'CPS? Couldn't Prosecute Satan, more like. In my day, the police decided for themselves whether or not a charge could be made to stick. They weren't forced to leave it up to a bunch of pen-pushers who wouldn't recognise a criminal if he wore a mask and carried a swag-bag. I used to go by my nose. It never let me down.'

Jonah's nose, large and bulbous, was no thing of beauty, but it had served the old man well. Harry said, 'I'll get back to the trustees, warn them it may be a while before you turn up anything more.'

'They have other things to worry about anyway, don't they? I gather they've lost their chief. Sounds like a rum business.'

'Too right. There are plenty of questions to be answered. Maybe the inquest will cast some light.'

The old man grunted. 'If you believe that's what inquests are for,' he said, 'you'll believe anything.'

Jonah's scepticism, borne of long years of compulsory kow-towing to coroners, proved all too justified. Harry decided to attend the inquest, telling himself that it was a mark of respect for Luke, but knowing in his heart that it was no more than a manifestation of his insatiable curiosity. His hopes were quickly dashed. As soon as he learned the identity of the coroner seised of the death, he realised that there was no chance of enlightenment.

Seymour Cunis was a decent fellow who hated more than anything else the thought of hurting anyone's feelings. What would be a strength in most people – and was, Harry had to admit, a rare quality in a litigation lawyer – was a fatal flaw when it came to discharging the duty of his historic office. Seymour was addicted to holding public appointments. In addition to being a deputy coroner, he was vice-president

of the Liverpool Legal Group and an active member of innumerable committees devoted – at least according to their constitutions – to good works. Since even Seymour had never discovered how to expand the number of hours in a day beyond twenty-four, he found it necessary to spend as little time on each task as possible. His enthusiasm for prioritisation (a word he'd picked up at a seminar and subsequently used to justify his own brand of instant justice) coupled with his unwillingness to cause distress made the outcome of the proceedings a foregone conclusion.

'Open verdict,' Harry forecast in a whisper to Ashley Whitaker, who was sitting beside him at the back of the court.

Luke Dessaur's godson blinked, as he often did. He was an amiable fellow, but he always gave Harry the impression of living in a world of his own. Events in the here-and-now always seemed to catch him by surprise. 'Really? I expected an adjournment.'

'Forget it. Seymour won't want to record a verdict of suicide if there's even a smidgeon of doubt about Luke's intentions. He hates to upset relatives of the bereaved. Even though Luke had no family, he'll regard you as the next best thing. If it had been left to Seymour, he would have ruled that Roger Ackroyd was the victim of an unfortunate accident.'

Ashley said sharply, 'But what about searching out the truth?'

'Don't hold your breath for that. Seymour's a lawyer. He knows the truth comes out in court much less often than most people would like to believe. He won't want to prolong the agony.'

Ashley knitted his brow, as if trying to come to a difficult decision. He was an old friend of Roy Milburn's, but the two men could hardly have been more different. Ashley was always reluctant to give offence. If at times he seemed to be a dreamer, he could afford to be. He was married to a wealthy woman and their affluence had enabled him to turn his hobby into his work. He ran a second-hand mystery bookshop and enjoyed the rare good fortune of never needing to worry about the bottom line.

'I see. In that case, there is very little I can do today.'

'What did you want to do?'

Ashley seemed about to say something, before changing his mind. 'Never mind. It will keep.'

Seymour Cunis ran true to form. He let everyone have a say, but made sure that as soon as they said it, the case moved on. No-one ever had a chance for second thoughts in his court. And besides, the evidence was wholly inconclusive. Seymour called Don Ragovoy, the manager of the Hawthorne Hotel, an American whose statement was as bland as a can of diet cola. The police and medical evidence was equally low-key. Yes, Luke had been drinking on that last night. No, he hadn't been paralytic. Clearly, his judgment could not have been at its sharpest. There was nothing to suggest any breakdown in safety procedures. The police did not consider that further investigations were likely to be fruitful. The hotel was not at fault; Luke had just been unlucky.

Ashley was asked whether Luke had ever shown any inclination to end his own life. He denied it with unaccustomed vigour and Seymour clicked his tongue in genuine sympathy. Although there was no suicide note, the records revealed that, just before midnight UK time, Luke had telephoned the hotel in Toronto where Ashley and his wife were staying. The Whitakers had been out and Luke had simply left a message that he had rung. He'd said a return call was not necessary.

'According to the note the switchboard girl gave me, he simply said, "It doesn't matter",' Ashley said bitterly. 'I took that at face value and thought no more about it until I heard the news from home the next day. Fortunately, we had a flight booked for that very evening, but of course, we would have come straight back anyway – even though there was nothing we could do.'

'You mustn't reproach yourself,' Seymour said. It was a phrase he often uttered and, although Harry found his approach frustrating, there was no doubt that he uttered it with the best of intentions.

Seymour grasped the chance to sum up as soon as he could. 'It is all quite tragic. The late Mr Dessaur was a man of considerable distinction. There are, it is true, a number of circumstances in this case that are difficult to understand. But that is by no means unusual. The conclusion I am forced to reach is perhaps unsatisfactory. But I must not shirk it simply for that reason. I find myself constrained to record an open verdict.'

'Seymour's verdict was like his surname,' Harry said wryly that afternoon. 'Neither one thing nor the other.'

Jim grinned. 'Ah well. Not every mystery has a solution. Though I think I can guess why you're wearing your smartest suit today. And is that tie made of real silk?'

'It was a Christmas present,' Harry said defensively. 'I simply never got round to unwrapping it until now.'

'You're turning into a bit of a Beau Brummel. I never thought I'd see the day.' The phone buzzed. 'Yes, Suzanne? Fine, I'll tell Harry she's arrived.'

He turned to Harry and winked. 'She's all yours.'

Within a couple of minutes of the start of their meeting, Harry had decided that even the photograph in the brochure had not done Juliet May justice. He put her age somewhere in the late thirties and she had laughter lines around the eyes and the corners of her mouth, but that simply added to her appeal. Her perfume was discreet and, he guessed, very expensive. She was dressed simply in jacket, blouse and skirt but years of marriage to a woman who believed money was made to be spent had taught him a little about the cost of *haute couture*. He guessed that Juliet May spent as much in a week on clothes as Liz might have managed in a year. She didn't bother with jewellery except for a gold band on the third finger of her left hand. Mr May, he reflected, was a lucky fellow.

Suddenly he became aware that she had asked him a question. 'Sorry, I didn't quite catch that.'

She smiled. 'I hope I'm not boring you.'

'Oh no. Certainly not.'

'But I had the impression your mind was wandering.' Her tone was playful. No question: she was teasing him. 'I simply asked who you regarded as your key target clients.'

Harry pondered. 'Adulterous burglars who get injured at work, I suppose. Provided they qualify for legal aid.'

She laughed. 'At least you're honest.'

'I realise it's a disadvantage when it comes to marketing legal services. Or anything else, come to that.'

She pretended to wince. 'Your partner did warn me that you wouldn't be easily convinced of the benefits of engaging a consultant. So I didn't come here expecting an easy ride. But don't you think it's worth making more of an effort to sell your problem-solving skills?'

'Problem solving? I have enough trouble with the quick crossword in the morning paper.'

'That's not what I hear. You have quite a reputation for searching out the truth.'

'Believe me, most of my clients would regard that as a supreme disadvantage in any solicitor.'

'You don't do yourself justice,' she urged.

He gave her a sad smile. 'One thing I've learned in the law is this. Justice isn't as easily come by as most of us would like to believe.'

'You've unravelled one or two mysteries,' she persisted. 'And when it comes to achieving justice, I know that you've put right at least one notable miscarriage. The Edwin Smith case – the so-called Sefton Park Strangling.'

He was genuinely startled. 'How do you know about that? I once promised someone – closely involved – that I wouldn't spread the truth around, go shouting my mouth off from the rooftops.'

'I do my homework, Harry. I always advise my clients to research their potential targets and I practise what I preach. But what you say is right. You never seem to court publicity. Perhaps you ought to try it for a change.'

'I didn't get involved with the Sefton Park murder in order to get my name in the paper,' he said sharply.

'I appreciate that. And of course your attitude does you credit, I'm not seeking to persuade you otherwise. I'm simply saying that you obviously have skills that are marketable, perhaps in very different circumstances.'

He grunted. 'Cases like that don't crop up every day. Most of the people I act for are as guilty as Crippen.'

'Who says Crippen was guilty?' she asked, her eyes shining. 'My theory is that he was innocent. Where was the proof that the bones they found in Hilldrop Crescent were his wife's? She could have zipped off to America with a lover. The pathologist made too many assumptions, he was desperate to make a name for himself. If Crippen hadn't fled with Ethel Le Neve, the police might never have made the charge stick.'

He gaped at her. 'Don't tell me you're a true crime buff?'

'All mysteries fascinate me,' she said simply. 'In real life or in fiction. When I asked around about Crusoe and Devlin, I was intrigued by what I heard. It seems you're a man after my own heart. So when your partner offered me the chance of this meeting with you, I jumped at it.'

'I suppose I should be flattered.'

She smiled at him. 'I suppose you should.'

After she had departed, Jim wandered into his room and said, 'Well?'

'She was quite plausible,' Harry said carefully.

'She was in here for an hour and a half, for God's sake.' Jim grinned. 'I was beginning to wonder what the two of you were getting up to in here with the door closed. Just as well you were talking business. You do realise who she's married to, don't you?'

'No.'

'Casper May.'

Shit, Harry said to himself. And then – *How could she?* He'd had a narrow escape. For a few minutes he'd toyed

with the idea of inviting Juliet out for a drink one evening.

He wasn't being disloyal to Kim; he had no intention of propositioning a married woman. He would simply have liked to spend more time with someone he found appealing. Just as well he had resisted temptation. If Casper May got the wrong idea about you, you were dead meat.

Chapter 7

Harry hated funerals. He would never forget the first that he had attended, after the death of his parents whilst he was in his early teens. It had been a typical Liverpool day, cloudy and with spits of rain, the kind of day he had seen a thousand times before and even more often since. And yet it had been a day when a sick and empty feeling in his guts told him that life had changed for ever. Until then, like any boy, he'd believed that bad things happened to other people. Suddenly he knew better and nothing would be the same again.

Yet now he was attending his second funeral inside a month. Harry sat at the back of the church, sharing a pew with a couple of Americans, the manager of the Hawthorne and a tall young man who was evidently a colleague. He had attended the service for Charles Kavanaugh out of a sense of duty; this time, he was driven by a nagging sense of unfinished business. He needed to understand what had happened to Luke. That mattered to him: he'd lost his mother, father and wife for no good reason. He had to keep believing that life was not always so cruel, or so meaningless.

But the service offered little reassurance. There were no clues, no credible explanations. Much was said, by the vicar, by Frances Silverwood and by Ashley Whitaker about Luke's good works and his sense of duty to others. The hymns were sensitively chosen. For all that, the one word in everyone's mind was never spoken. *Why?*

He reflected that one of the terrible things about suicide was that it imbued everyone who had known the deceased with a desolate sense of failure. It was a feeling that was unavoidable, yet infinitely depressing: *we knew each other, we were friends, yet that wasn't enough to make him want to keep living.*

When the service was over, he joined Matthew Cullinan, Roy Milburn and Tim Aldred outside. The grey of the sky matched the trustees' mood; even Roy was subdued and from his grimace Harry guessed that his damaged leg must be hurting. They were waiting to say a few words of comfort to Frances when she emerged from the church and filling their time with the inevitable topic of conversation.

'Of course it's a tragic loss,' Matthew was saying. He was wearing a three-piece suit and had his thumbs in the pockets of his waistcoat. 'I have to say that, with hindsight, one or two things do become clear.'

'What do you mean?' Tim asked.

'Well, he was a born worrier. The way he used to fuss over the vetting of grant applications. Attention to detail is all very well, but it can get out of hand.'

Roy stretched his arms and Harry noticed a gold watch glinting from his wrist. 'Let's face it. The Dinosaur was always a bit of an old woman.'

Tim said angrily, 'You'd never have dared say that whilst he was alive.'

'I freely admit it. He liked to have his own way. He always had to be right. But I suppose even he had his Achilles' heel, or we wouldn't be here today.'

'So you believe he killed himself?' Harry asked.

'Don't you? The idea of an accident is just too far-fetched.'

'I agree,' Matthew said. 'The coroner wanted to spare people's feelings, that's all very commendable. But between ourselves, it's obvious, isn't it? Luke did away with himself.'

'I couldn't take it in when I first heard,' Tim said. 'Luke, of all people. He's the last person I would have expected to...'

'I've heard that said a good many times today,' a new voice said. It belonged to Ashley Whitaker. He was accompanied by his wife, a pale blonde with downcast eyes.

'I heard that Luke tried to telephone you on – the last night,' Tim said after condolences had been expressed.

Ashley blinked at the pebbles on the path, still glistening after overnight rain. 'Yes. I keep wondering what he wanted to say.'

Frances Silverwood joined them as he spoke. Under her overcoat, her shoulders were stooped and Harry sensed she had been struggling to hold back tears.

'I hope you're not torturing yourself, Ashley,' she said quietly. 'It must be tempting to take some of the responsibility on yourself, to imagine that if only you'd taken the call, things might have been different.'

'You've read his mind,' Melissa Whitaker murmured. A slender woman with high cheekbones, she had the sort of blue eyes that people wrote poems about. Harry knew that Ashley idolised her and he could understand why. Yet she was so quiet that it was surprisingly easy to overlook her. If Harry hadn't been watching her closely, he wouldn't have noticed her give her husband's hand a comforting squeeze as she spoke.

'It's human nature,' Frances said. 'You were always close to him, Ashley. It's significant that after he dialled your number and couldn't get through, he didn't try to call any of the rest of us.' She paused and Harry guessed that in her mind she was adding the words: *not even me*. 'But I'm sure there was nothing you could have done.'

'I've already told him that,' Melissa said. 'But he's been brooding ever since we heard the news.'

'Don't,' Frances said to him. 'God knows, if there is any blame, we should all take a share of it. Luke knew a great many people, but he was a lonely man. He never got over Gwendoline's death. I have this feeling that his death was a long time coming. He'll have thought it through in his rational way. My guess is that he was calling you simply to say goodbye.'

Ashley grunted and Harry said, 'In that case, surely it's odd that he didn't write to Ashley. Or anyone else, come to that.'

'Plenty of suicides don't leave a note,' Tim said.

'Are you an expert on the subject?' Roy asked.

The question seemed to shock Tim. He coloured and mumbled something unintelligible. There was a short uncomfortable silence. Harry found himself shivering and was not sure that the biting wind was entirely to blame. Finally Frances said, 'Have we heard any more from Vera's solicitors?'

'Not yet. I haven't yet revealed what we know about her false references. Meanwhile, I'm waiting for further revelations from our private investigator.'

'Let me know when there's news,' Frances said briskly. 'And now, everyone, if you'll excuse me, I must be going. It's been quite a draining day.'

As Matthew followed her down the path towards the lych gate, Ashley sighed and said, 'Good to see you again, Harry. I'm only sorry about the circumstances. As a matter of fact, I wondered if it would be possible for us to have a quiet word later? Do you have anything on this evening?'

'Nothing special.' Kim was duty solicitor tonight. He had seen her only briefly at court since the Legal Group's AGM. Anything was better than a television dinner and an evening alone spent watching unfunny sitcoms.

'Let me run Melissa home, then I'll come back to the shop. I've bought some new stock you might be interested in looking at.'

After the Whitakers had said their goodbyes and headed off towards the car park, Roy Milburn stared after them and said out of the corner of his mouth, 'Gorgeous, isn't she?'

'You fancy Melissa?' Harry asked.

'Why so surprised? She's rich and she looks as good as when I first knew her. Only trouble is, she's always been as neurotic as hell.'

'I've never noticed.'

'Look at her fingernails some time. She wears false ones because she chews them down to the quick. Believe me, she's a nervy one. Not someone to mess around with.'

Harry did not regard bitten fingernails as evidence of an unstable personality, but he let it pass. 'You've known her a long time, then?'

'We were all students together. Her daddy owned Grayson's Brewery. The ideal father-in-law, wouldn't you say? Ashley was the lucky one she fell for. He had this little-boy-lost manner that came over a treat.'

Tim had been shifting impatiently from foot to foot and Roy's mocking tone seemed to provoke him into saying abruptly, 'By the way, Roy, when does your case come up?'

Roy's smile faded. 'Next week, isn't that right, Harry?'

'Uh-huh.' Roy had been charged with drink-driving after the crash in which he'd been injured and had asked Crusoe and Devlin to take the case. At a cut price, he'd added, given the business they had from the Kavanaugh Trust.

'Will you lose your licence?' The note of *schadenfreude* in Tim's voice was unmistakable.

Recovering his usual cockiness, Roy put a hand on Harry's shoulder and said, 'Far from it. With Loophole Devlin on my side, I'm expecting a public apology and handsome compensation.'

'In that case,' Harry said, 'you need a magician rather than a solicitor. Have you thought about engaging Tim's services? He's the expert at pulling rabbits out of hats.'

Roy laughed. 'So how's it going, Tim? Still entertaining Merseyside's infants and geriatrics?'

'It's all work,' Tim said. 'And I need the money. Though I do have something different on next week. I've been hired by Jericho Lane Labour Club to perform at a fund-raising event for charity. Come along if you like, you two. And bring a friend.'

Roy chuckled so derisively that Tim reddened with anger.

'I'd love to come,' Harry said hastily. 'Though I'll be amazed if you're able to teach Liverpool politicians any new tricks.'

'Politicians? They're almost as bad as lawyers.' Roy paused. 'Which reminds me. Why don't lawyers go to the beach?'

Harry's heart began to sink. 'Break it to me gently.'

'Because cats keep trying to bury them.'

And Roy shattered the quiet of the graveyard with a belly laugh.

***

As he drove back to the city centre, Harry reflected that until now he had not appreciated how adroitly Luke had maintained peace within the Kavanaugh Trust. He had done it partly through force of character, partly through refined chairmanship skills. Every meeting had been meticulously prepared, with little scope for deviating from the agenda. In any group of people, there was potential for acrimony; the more so, perhaps, with those who might fancy that they had an artistic temperament. But in the past Harry had witnessed little backbiting; with Luke gone, people were daring to antagonise each other.

The prospect of a visit to the Speckled Band Bookshop cheered him up. He spent more time and money there than he should have done. It was a pastime rather than a business; Ashley was as happy to spend half an hour chatting with a fellow devotee about the novels of Agatha Christie or Dorothy L. Sayers as he was to sell any of his stock.

The shop was a stone's throw from the Bluecoat Centre. It occupied an old building that might have been elegant in Britain's imperial heyday but now bore the stains of centuries of unclean air. Harry glanced upwards as he approached and saw a trio of sooty gargoyles glaring down from the rooftop, as if they held him personally responsible for failing to sandblast them back to their original state. The sign on the door said *Closed*, but when Harry knocked, Ashley answered and let him in.

Ashley could have afforded the swishest interior design that money could buy, but Harry was glad he had resisted temptation. The Speckled Band was a dusty, rambling cavern with floor-to-ceiling shelves and creaking wooden floorboards, a world away from the sterile High Street chain stores that only stocked bestsellers, and all the better for that. Towards the back of the ground floor, an open log fire crackled. Never mind what the safety people might say, who knew what treasures might be found lurking in a place like this?

'Take a look in the boxes on the floor,' Ashley said, indicating a couple of huge cardboard containers. 'Stuff we brought back from Toronto. I've not marked prices, but if you see anything you fancy, just let me know. I'll make us a coffee in the meantime.'

The smell of old books was everywhere and Harry knew few sweeter perfumes. He dived into the boxes and spent a few happy minutes flicking through battered rarities. Murder stories where bodies were found in hermetically sealed chambers surrounded by snow that bore not a single footmark; crimes investigated by a blind detective with a super-sensitive auditory nerve; and one little gem he remembered borrowing from the library as a boy in which, it was true, the butler really did it.

When his host returned with two chipped mugs, he pointed to a small pile of books he had put to one side. 'Tell me how much I owe you.'

Ashley waved him into a shabby captain's chair by the side of the desk at the back of the ground floor. 'Don't worry. They lack their dustwrappers and the Philip Macdonald is no more than a reading copy.'

'Reading is what interests me. I've never understood why, in your trade, "reading copy" is practically a term of abuse. And as for the idea of putting all one's books in plastic jackets and never daring to open them...'

'You're like me,' Ashley said. 'A hoarder rather than a collector.'

'The one thing that worries me is that I'm running out of space in the flat. I may have to move before the floor gives way under the weight.'

Ashley took a sip of his drink. He'd changed out of his suit into more familiar garb, an old jacket with patches on the elbows and a pair of corduroy trousers. With his prematurely thinning hair and vague manner, he reminded Harry of an Oxford don. Or at least of what he imagined an Oxford don would be like if he ever met one.

'You're the same as me in another way, I think. When you come across a puzzle, whether it's in a book or in everyday life, you want to solve it.'

'Everyone tells me it's a character defect.'

Ashley chewed at his lower lip. 'It's the reason I asked you round this evening.'

'I thought you simply wanted to sell me a few books.'

'They were an excuse.'

'What's on your mind?'

Ashley leaned forward in his chair. 'It's about Luke. I was very fond of him, you know. I've known him all my life. He was an old friend of my mother. We've always been close.'

'I'm sure you miss him badly,' Harry said. He wondered what was coming.

'Although he lived a public life, he was a very private man. Difficult to get to know. Although I say it myself, since poor Gwendoline died, no-one knew him better than I did.'

Harry nodded. 'His death must have come as a terrible blow.'

'Yes, it did. It hasn't been easy to think coherently about it. But I've tried to understand how he might have arrived at a decision to kill himself.' Ashley swallowed. 'And I've come to a conclusion.'

'Which is?'

'It's impossible.' Ashley pointed at the locked room mystery at the top of Harry's pile. 'Not in the physical sense. I'm not talking about John Dickson Carr stuff. But psychologically. It's all wrong, Harry. Luke would never have done it.'

Harry coughed. 'I do realise it's difficult to come to terms with. When someone does something so – so shocking and out of character.'

'You think I'm rationalising my distress? Well, maybe. That's Melissa's view. But I wanted to speak to you because I felt you might listen with an open mind.'

'To what?'

Ashley blinked and said deliberately, 'To my theory that Luke was murdered.'

Part Two

Chapter 8

'But the evidence...' Harry began.

Ashley's expression showed what he thought about the evidence. 'I know that, as a lawyer, you're bound to say that there's nothing at all to suggest that someone else killed Luke. The police took the same attitude when I spoke to them.'

'So you've already raised this idea officially?'

'Oh yes. And it got me nowhere. Their minds were made up. It was a simple case, easily ticked off the list of things to deal with. I suppose I can't blame them. They are overworked and at first sight it does all seem very straightforward. Middle-aged, middle-class man going through his own kind of mid-life crisis. Well-respected, but with an empty private life. One day he flips and books into a hotel. He spends the evening drinking in his room and eventually he plucks up the courage to kill himself. The conclusion is obvious – unless you know the man as I did.'

Harry recalled his conversation with Frances. 'How well *can* we know anyone else?'

'I understand your point,' Ashley said. 'But bear with me. In my opinion, Luke wasn't the suicidal type – in fact, he was the last person in the world who was likely to do something like this. But suppose I'm wrong. I'm certain – absolutely certain – that if he did, he would leave behind a message, an explanation of some kind. Yet there was nothing.'

'There's no law that says a suicide has to explain himself to the people he leaves behind.'

'Yes, but in Luke's case, I find his supposed behaviour inconceivable. He was the most methodical man I ever met. You're well aware yourself that he hated loose ends.'

'He tried to call you in Toronto,' Harry pointed out.

'Yes, and he failed. The official assumption, as I understand it from reading between the lines at the inquest, is that he was planning to break the news to me on the telephone. Yet when he didn't manage to get through to me, he is supposed simply to have clambered through the window and jumped out. Sorry, but I just don't buy that.'

'I agree it seems extraordinary,' Harry said carefully. He did not wish to make the usual lawyer's mistake of putting words into someone else's mouth.

'Yes, I gathered that you were puzzled from your remarks at the inquest and at the church. That's one of the reasons why I thought I would have a chat with you about it all.'

'But what about the possibility that it was an accident?'

Ashley pulled a face. 'I realise the hotel manager has to protect his own back. But I've had a look at the hotel. I turned up there yesterday, pretending to be interested in booking rooms for a group of friends. I've seen the room in which – it happened.' He sighed. 'I take the man's point. It's unlikely that Luke died by accident.'

'Even if he'd had a skinful?'

'It's *physically* possible that it happened that way. But I simply don't believe it.'

'You prefer to think that someone else was responsible?'

'It's not a matter of preference,' Ashley said sharply. 'It's a question of trying to find out the truth.'

Harry looked at the overburdened shelves all around them. Titles such as *And Death Came Too*, *Murder Included* and *Ten Minute Alibi* spoke for themselves. 'Don't take this the wrong way, but isn't it possible that you're letting your imagination run away with itself?'

Ashley folded his arms. 'Melissa thinks so. The police were courteous, but obviously felt the same. They pointed out that there were no signs of a struggle in the hotel room, no evidence to suggest someone else had been present there, let alone that murder was done. I hoped you would have a more open mind.'

'Because I'm often accused of excessive imagination as well?'

A slow grin eased across Ashley's face. 'I suppose so. But the truth is that you've been proved right more than once where murder is concerned.' The grin disappeared. 'And I thought you'd be interested if I told you that whilst I was at the Hawthorne, I talked to as many members of the staff as I could. Guess what I found out?'

'Tell me.'

'There is a porter, a chap called Julio. He wasn't keen to talk, but I sensed he knew something and eventually I prised it out of him. The evening that Luke died, he passed his room, carrying a late arrival's luggage. He heard raised voices. Two people were in there, arguing about something.'

'Luke and who else?'

Ashley grimaced. 'He couldn't tell me. He was hurrying past, keen to finish his shift. If the man in the room hadn't died, he'd never have given the incident a second thought.'

'Was anyone seen around the place at the relevant time? An unauthorised visitor, someone hurrying away in a panic? Anything like that?'

Ashley shook his head. 'It's a big anonymous place, understaffed at night. The security struck me as rudimentary. As far as I can tell, anyone could have wandered in or out, with little risk of being challenged.'

'Why wasn't Julio's information mentioned at the inquest?'

'He told me he hadn't reported it to anyone. I sensed it was bothering him, but not enough for him to want to do anything about it, to call attention to himself. Don Ragovoy was keen to brush Luke's death under that carpet and that was fine by Julio.'

'You told the police about this?'

Ashley nodded. 'They said they would speak to Julio, but they made it clear they weren't really interested.'

'Of course, even if Luke met someone at the Hawthorne and had a quarrel with him – or her – it doesn't prove he was murdered by that someone.'

'True. But it makes it more likely. And remember that Luke had been drinking. He may have opened the window for a bit of air. Even if there was a struggle, he may not have been able to put up much of a fight. In any case, he may have been taken unawares and hit on the head before being pushed out. I gather – he was pretty smashed up by the fall. No way of tracing a prior head injury.'

'Plenty of ifs in that theory. But suppose you're right. What can you do about it?'

'Listen, Harry. My parents died a long time ago. Apart from Melissa, Luke was the person I was closest to in the world. Even though we didn't live in each other's pockets, could go weeks without seeing each other, he was someone I always respected, could always rely upon and turn to if ever there was a need. To think of him dying in the way he did makes me sadder than I can describe. If he didn't kill himself, I owe it to him to find out what happened. And to see justice done.'

Neither of them spoke for a few moments and then Harry said, 'Why would anyone want to kill Luke? And how did they manage it?'

'So,' Ashley said softly, 'you are prepared to humour me, to entertain the idea that this might be a case of murder?'

Harry chewed at a ragged fingernail. 'Tell you something. The thought had already crossed my mind.'

Ashley's eyes gleamed. 'Really?'

'I never mentioned it to anyone. I was sure they'd dismiss it as one of my idler fancies – you know the feeling? But my reasoning was much the same as yours. I could accept, with difficulty, that Luke might have wanted to do away with himself, that he might have concealed from the rest of us his deep unhappiness and dissatisfaction with life. But the absence of a note or message – particularly to yourself – that just didn't add up.'

Elated, Ashley clapped him on the shoulder. 'I was sure you were the man to talk to about this. So – what's the next step?'

Harry indicated the shelves of mysteries which surrounded them. 'If you and I can't come up with a few ideas, who can?'

They finished up having a meal together at the Ensenada. Ashley insisted on paying and Harry did not argue too strenuously. What was the point of knowing people with money if you did not help them to spend it?

'Would you like to talk to me about Luke?' he said as the soup arrived. 'It would be helpful for me to understand him better. Bear in mind I only ever saw him in a professional context. I couldn't claim that we were bosom buddies: it was a formal relationship.'

'He may have seemed austere, but the truth is that he was very shy. Painfully afraid of doing the wrong thing. Perhaps it was down to his upbringing. He was an only child of elderly parents. Father an actuary, mother a doting housewife. They weren't short of money. As a boy he suffered a lot of ill health and I think his mother over-protected him. He had a rather solitary adolescence and to the best of my knowledge, my own mother was the first girl he ever courted, at the age of twenty-one.'

'But they didn't marry.'

'No. My guess is that she was keen to settle down and grew tired of waiting for Luke to pop the question. Then she met my father at a dance. He rode a motor cycle, was a glamorous figure in comparison to Luke. She was swept off her feet. By the time they were married, three months later, I was already on the way.'

'And Luke kept in touch?'

'He told me more than once that he was heartbroken at losing her. And she did care for him, insisted on asking him to be my godfather. But she never admitted to any regrets about her choice, even when my father crashed on a bend when I was five and broke his neck.' Ashley sighed. 'It was a tough time. I've been poor and I've been rich, Harry and there's no doubt: rich is a lot better.'

'I suppose that if Luke hadn't married by that time...'

'It's crossed my mind that he and Mother might still have got together, yes. But who knows? It's history. In any case, she met my stepfather.' Ashley grimaced. 'Another likely lad. A bar owner this time.'

'Meanwhile, Luke lost his own wife.'

'It was a tragedy. To understand Luke, you have to bear in mind that Gwendoline's illness was diagnosed before they first became engaged. He'd met her after the break with my mother. Whether it was on the rebound or not, I have no idea, but no-one could have been more devoted. He proposed to Gwendoline and they were married only weeks after she was told about the cancer. Against all the odds, she recovered.'

'I didn't realise.'

'Oh yes, I've been told that it seemed like a miracle. Very romantic, you know, love conquering disaster. And by all accounts they had a happy married life. Until, out of the blue, the illness recurred. They had thought it was gone for ever, but really it was only sleeping. This time there was no happy ending. But Luke nursed her through it all. He took his obligations very seriously.'

Harry nodded. 'Even his worst enemy would have been forced to admit that.'

Ashley leaned across the little table. 'And it has crossed my mind that, if there was a motive for his murder, that particular characteristic may have provided it. If he came across something that was not right, he would have considered himself duty-bound to act. Luke was never a man to turn a blind eye to wrongdoing.'

'Have you any particular wrongdoing in mind?'

Ashley seemed to be on the verge of imparting a confidence, then blinked hard and kept his mouth shut after all. Harry was about to press him when he noticed a familiar couple being ushered to a table in the opposite corner of the restaurant. He couldn't help chuckling. So Geoffrey Willatt and Vera Blackhurst really had become an item.

As he sat down, Geoffrey caught Harry's eye. At once his cheeks turned pink, giving him the look of a bishop caught straying into a peep-show. Harry lifted a hand in greeting and then decided to seize the moment. After all, presented with a gift horse, it was a mistake to start looking it in the mouth.

He excused himself to Ashley and strolled over to the corner table. 'Evening, Geoffrey. Miss Blackhurst, we've met before. At Charles Kavanaugh's funeral.'

Her smile of greeting did not touch her eyes. 'Mr Devlin, isn't it? I remember. You act for the Trust, don't you?'

He had to admire her coolness. Vera Blackhurst was someone it would be a mistake to underestimate. Her hairstyle was pure sixties Myra Hindley, while her dress displayed a pair of breasts whose gravity-defying upward thrust was a miracle of science. 'That's right. I suppose we're on opposite sides of the legal fence at the moment.'

Geoffrey Willatt cleared his throat. 'I mentioned to Mr Devlin the other evening that I felt sure that our – little local difficulty could be amicably resolved.'

'I'm sure of it,' Vera said pleasantly. 'Charles often told me that he had a soft spot for the Trust. He was an artist himself, as you well know. I'd hate to see his favourite charity suffer.'

'Nice of you to say so,' Harry said with a sharp glance at Geoffrey, who was trying hard not to squirm.

'On the other hand,' she continued in an accent that Harry identified as broad Cheshire, 'I'm ever so disappointed by the trustees' reaction to Charles's will. I'd have hoped that they would have respected his last wishes. After all, I'm just an ordinary person.

The last thing I want is a legal dispute. I'm so fortunate I've found an understanding solicitor.'

There was nothing in the least bit ordinary about Vera Blackhurst, Harry was sure of that. He turned to the understanding solicitor, who looked as though he'd suddenly become afflicted by dyspepsia, and said, 'Combining business with pleasure, then, this evening?'

'We have one or two things to discuss,' Geoffrey said stiffly. 'The office isn't always the ideal setting for these meetings. Miss Blackhurst has had a very trying time lately. She was very attached to her late employer. I suggested that we chat over a bite to eat.'

'Better not let Pino hear you talk about his cuisine like that,' Harry teased. The loquacious proprietor of the Ensenada was fiercely protective of its reputation for fine food. 'You make it sound like a transport caff.'

'You know what I mean,' Geoffrey said through gritted teeth. 'Now, if you'll excuse us...'

'Of course. Good to see you both. I'm sure we'll be in touch.' He grinned and returned to his seat.

'Friends of yours?' Ashley asked.

'Not exactly.' Harry told him the story. 'But let's get back to Luke's death. Have you discussed your views with Frances Silverwood?'

'No.' Ashley gave him a searching glance. 'Any particular reason why I should?'

'Only that, apart from yourself, she seemed as close to Luke as anyone. And she obviously had a considerable affection for him. Was it reciprocated?'

'Listen, Luke felt Gwendoline was irreplaceable. He'd become accustomed to living on his own after her death. I don't think a second marriage was high on his agenda.'

'Maybe he liked to keep Frances dangling on a string.'

'You're doing him an injustice. It would be nearer the truth to say that he treated women with an old-fashioned courtesy and attentiveness. Even someone who is no doormat can find that very appealing.'

'I'd like to know what she thinks about your idea.'

'This is difficult for me to express in the right way,' Ashley began slowly. He fiddled with his napkin, not looking Harry in the eye. 'But I have some reservations about mentioning this to any of the Kavanaugh trustees.'

'And why is that?'

Ashley hesitated for a moment before replying. 'Well, you see, the last time I saw Luke, he told me that he was expecting trouble within the Trust. There was a serious problem with one of the trustees. He said he'd been agonising over it, but he felt he had no choice but to act.'

'Which trustee? And how was he going to act?'

Ashley seemed to be choosing his words with care. 'There was no point in asking for more information than he was prepared to disclose. Besides, it was none of my business. The only thing that bothered me was Luke's distress. He'd been sleeping badly. The whole affair, whatever it was, had been preying on his mind.'

'When was this?'

'Melissa and I invited him round for dinner just before we set off for Toronto. We talked while Melissa was out in the kitchen. I said the best thing would be to consult the Trust's solicitors.' He smiled. 'Doing my best to drum up business for you, as usual.'

'One of these days, I'll put you on commission. But don't hold your breath. As a matter of fact, Luke did speak to me.'

'He did?' Ashley was clearly relieved.

Harry recounted his last conversation with Luke Dessaur and Frances's belief that, in the days leading up to his death, Luke had been afraid of something. 'If only he'd given me a clearer idea about what was on his mind. Was it this problem with the unnamed trustee – or something else?'

'What else could it have been?' Ashley demanded. 'He wasn't rich but he didn't have money worries. He told me years ago that he'd left everything he had to cancer charities, in memory of Gwendoline. That shows you the sort of chap he was.'

Harry nodded. 'Like you, I didn't cross-examine him. I wish now that I had.'

Ashley closed his eyes for a moment. 'Of course, I'd like to believe that this business about an errant trustee was entirely unconnected with his death.'

Harry studied him. 'Have you been able to guess who Luke was talking about?'

After a pause, Ashley said, 'No, no. I haven't.'

But he was blinking nervously and Harry thought: *You may be a good book dealer, but you are a poor liar, my friend.*

As Ashley was settling the bill, Harry spotted Pino and waved him over. 'I see my old boss is still one of your most reliable customers. You know something? He was the first person who ever brought me here for a meal. It was when I qualified as a solicitor.'

'Ah, a great cause for celebration!'

'Tell you the truth, I think he was just ecstatic that I'd said I was planning to leave his firm. But do you know the lady he's with, by any chance?'

'I must be discreet!' Pino said, putting his finger to his lips. It was akin to Mae West taking a vow of celibacy.

'Of course,' Harry said. 'As you always are. I mustn't be nosey. Not that there's anything to be nosey about. Geoffrey's divorced, isn't he? He's every right to take a lady friend out for dinner.'

'Absolutely! And he and Miss Blackhurst have become regular customers these past two or three weeks, I'm glad to say.'

'Is that so?'

Pino beamed and said, 'I tell you one thing, Harry. In confidence, of course.'

'Naturally,' Harry said, crossing his fingers behind his back.

'I would not be surprised if Miss Blackhurst were to become the second Mrs Willatt one day.'

'You think so?'

'Believe me. I see the signs. It is a love-match, that one.'

Harry looked back at the couple in the corner. Geoffrey Willatt had recovered his composure and was holding forth, probably on the iniquities of the Lord Chancellor's treatment of the legal profession. Vera was gazing into his eyes, looking at him with the fondness of a butterfly collector studying a rare specimen. And for the first time in his life, Harry felt sorry for Geoffrey Willatt.

Back in his flat, Harry stayed up till the early hours, drinking more than was good for him and watching the late-night film. It was *Night Moves*, an old favourite not least because Gene Hackman played a long-suffering investigator by the name of Harry Moresby. Easy to identify with the character: he had a relentless need to know, an obsession with finding out things. Trouble was, it never did him any good.

Harry knew many of the scenes by heart. Eventually the detective would discover the truth about the disappearance of the wild child Delly, solve her murder and put a permanent end to her stepfather's criminal scheme. But still the outcome would be disastrous for him. As the credits rolled at the end of the film, he would lie injured and helpless in a motor boat which kept going round and round in ever-widening circles.

Harry took another draught from his can and reviewed the day's events. There were too many questions. What was Vera's game? Why had she needed to fake the references she had supplied to

Charles Kavanaugh? And was it possible that one of the trustees was also a murderer?

He toyed with the idea. Frances, Tim and Roy all lived alone and so, presumably, had no verifiable alibi for the time of Luke's death. Matthew shared a house with his girlfriend, but he too might have been able to get the chance to commit the crime. He was chilled by the thought that he had been in their company on the night of Luke's death and searched his memory for clues that might point him in the right direction. But there were none.

He sighed. What good would it do to try to learn if Ashley was right? Nothing could ever be proved. Turning up stones was usually a mistake. Yet he knew he would not be able to resist temptation even though, if Liz were still alive, she would surely be as cynical as Ellen Moresby, the errant wife who reproached her husband when he insisted he must go out on a case.

'Why?' she asked in a line that always haunted Harry. 'So you can pretend you're solving something?'

Chapter 9

Another morning, another murder. No doubt this time, no question of suicide or accident. A young woman had been found dead the previous evening in Upper Parliament Street, a pair of scissors driven into her back. According to the early bulletin on Radio City, the police were linking the case with a number of other killings.

As he shaved, Harry thought about the crime. So the Scissorman had struck again. For a couple of years now he had been stabbing prostitutes to death. All his crimes had been committed in northern cities; his last two victims had been Liverpool girls. The murder of a whore seldom made headline news but the media had finally seized on the Scissorman case after the trial of a suspect called Norman Morris had collapsed. An offender-profiling expert had declared himself confident that Morris was the guilty man and a woman detective working undercover had persuaded Morris to boast drunkenly that he was the man the police could not catch. The only snag was lack of evidence. And on the day of the Scissorman's first murder in Liverpool, Morris had been with his publisher in London discussing a book about his ordeal.

Pulling on his shirt, Harry reflected that for as long as miscarriages like the Morris case occurred, there would be plenty of work for MOJO – and for Kim. It was so easy to be deceived by appearances. Morris was odious but innocent: for all anyone knew, the real culprit could be perfectly respectable, a pillar of society. A professional man, perhaps even a lawyer. As far as Harry was aware, no solicitor had yet metamorphosed into a serial killer. But there was always a first time.

The Scissorman's latest killing was the talk of the Crown Court. Never before had two consecutive murders in the sequence been committed in the same city. In the robing room everyone was speculating about whether the murderer had settled in Liverpool. As Harry listened to the conversation, he could not help hearing in his mind the raucous cry of Davey Damnation.

'And I gave her space to repent of her fornication; and she repented not!'

Quentin Pike was sitting in a corner, a bundle of unopened files on his lap. Usually he was at the heart of any group of gossips, but this morning he seemed uncharacteristically quiet. Harry wandered over to him and was startled to see that the tubby lawyer's eyes were red and puffy.

'You all right?' As soon as the words left his lips, Harry realised it was a foolish question.

'The dead girl,' Quentin said in a voice barely audible above the buzz of conversation all around. 'A sergeant downstairs mentioned her name. Half-caste girl called Celine. She is a client of mine. Was a client of mine.'

'Ah.'

'The stupid little bitch,' Quentin said savagely. He was talking to himself rather than to Harry. 'She was hell-bent on destroying her life. Heroin, cocaine, you name it. And she was a pretty girl. Delicate features, despite the shit she pumped into her system. Of course, she had the usual whore's c.v. Parental abuse, taken into care, a long list of petty misdemeanours. She'd kept me busy since she first reached the age of criminal responsibility. I warned her, believe me, I warned her. I said she'd be dead before she was twenty-one.'

'And how old was she?'

'Sixteen the week before Christmas,' Quentin said. 'I overestimated her survival instinct.'

Harry put a hand on the other man's shoulder. 'We aren't our clients' keepers.'

Quentin Pike turned to face him. 'No, but I tell you one thing. If I don't mourn that silly girl, no-one else will.'

He clambered to his feet and, tucking the files under each arm, made his way unsteadily out of the room. Harry closed his eyes. Murder, he had learned, was like that. It was not a simple matter confined to the killer and the slain. So many lives were touched. The ripples kept spreading outwards.

Trying to rid his mind of the idea that had begun to form about Davey Damnation, he headed for the cafeteria and spotted Kim in the queue for service. He sidled up behind her and whispered, 'Will you let me put a little magic into your life?'

She jerked round; her cheeks were pink. 'My God, Harry, I wondered who it was.'

'Sorry if I startled you. But it's a serious proposition. A magician of my acquaintance is performing tonight at the Labour Club in Jericho Lane. He's invited me along and I wonder if you'd like to come. And by the way, would you like to get me a coffee?'

When they were seated at a table, she said, 'I had no idea you were into magic.'

'I'll try anything to make money out of the Legal Aid Board.'

'In your dreams. They long ago mastered the black arts themselves.'

'In that case, I may have to settle for entertainment. Can I tempt you?'

'It's a long time since I've been inside a Labour Club. At one time of day I was an active member of the Party. But it changed after it was taken over by the smarmy army. People who spent more time talking about justice, less in actually making it happen. Other things became more important to me than politics. Especially MOJO.'

Harry stirred his coffee with infinite care. 'Speaking of which,' he said without looking at her, 'are you any nearer to reaching a decision?'

'About what to do?' She sighed. 'I had a call from London last night. They're starting to push. I decided I ought at least to speak again to Quentin this morning. But he's not in the mood for business discussions today.'

'Yes, I was speaking to him a couple of minutes ago. He's taking the death of his client badly. You know, a strange thought crossed my mind...'

He hesitated. He'd been on the point of saying something about the Scissorman and Davey Damnation, but now did not seem the right moment. Besides, Kim had started to talk about Quentin.

'He cares about his work more than most people realise,' she said. 'That's something I have to weigh in the balance. If – if I did sell my business, I'd want the firm that took over to look after my clients. If they didn't, no-one else would. But I'd trust Quentin to fight for them.'

'So – you are thinking of making the move?'

She bent her head low over the coffee cup. 'God, Harry. It's one of the hardest decisions I've ever had to make. The job means so much to me. But I don't want to let you down.'

'London isn't the end of the world.'

'I mustn't be unfair. Being Chief Executive of MOJO isn't a nine-to-five job, any more than yours is. How often do you think we would see each other if we were two hundred miles apart? We need to be realistic. If I move, what sort of future is there for our relationship?'

He finished his drink. 'Do you want it to have a future?'

'I – oh, I just feel guilty, that's all. Since we started to go out together, it's as if I've messed you around all the time.'

He moved his head close to hers. 'I'm very fond of you, Kim. You know that. But I'd hate you to pass on the job, stay here and always resent me for it.'

'This magic show.' Her voice faltered slightly. 'When will you be picking me up?'

Walking through the city streets in a daze, he found himself on the other side of the road from the magistrates' court. Davey Damnation was in full flow, haranguing a couple of hapless trainee solicitors.

'And I will give unto every one of you according to your works!'

Harry had always had a soft spot for Davey. The man's sheer persistence, his determination to rant away come rain or shine seemed perversely admirable. But he knew nothing about him, neither where he lived nor where he came from. Nor whether he was capable of deeds to match his wild words. Harry stared at the scarecrow-like figure, trying to decide what – if anything – he should do when someone shouted his name. With a guilty start, he glanced over his shoulder, to see Matthew Cullinan hurrying down Dale Street towards him. He was accompanied by Inge Frontzeck.

'Just the man! Sorry for bellowing, but you were obviously miles away.'

Harry mustered a smile. 'Plenty to think about.'

'Tough morning in court, eh? Never mind. Win a few, lose a few. You remember Inge, do you?'

She blushed. 'How could he forget after our meeting at the Piquet Club?'

Harry surveyed her. She looked quite different when not dressed for work. Elegant make-up, expensive jewellery. Over her shoulder was slung a bag emblazoned with the logo of the city's most prestigious fashion store. She was hanging on to Matthew's arm as if afraid that if she let go she might never see him again. He felt a spasm of jealousy. If only Kim had been the proprietorial kind. But then she would have been a different woman and he would not have cared for her so much.

He indicated the bag. 'Shopping trip?'

Matthew grinned. 'Just as well we bumped into you. Another couple of hours and we'd both have been paupers.'

She brushed his cheek with a finger. 'I don't remember you breaking into your capital this morning, Matt.'

'You never gave me a chance. I'm surprised your plastic cards haven't melted after all their activity. You know what women are like, Harry.'

'Er – yes,' Harry said, although experience had taught him that he certainly didn't. But he was puzzling over a contradiction he sensed in Matthew Cullinan. Matthew liked to make a big thing out of his desire to shun the limelight, especially where his charitable works were concerned. But when you came to know him, his manner was hardly that of someone anxious to do good by stealth. Perhaps it was simply that Harry knew so few upper-class people of any description, let alone any who wished to do good by stealth.

'Look,' Matthew said to Inge, 'Since we've stocked up with enough food to feed an army, why don't we invite Harry here to dinner? Tomorrow evening, perhaps? Do come, if you don't have anything else on.'

'It's very kind of you...' Harry hesitated. In other circumstances he would have been rifling through his collection of excuses for avoiding tedious social engagements. But he wanted to seize any chance to find out a little more about the Kavanaugh trustees.

'You'll have to check with Mrs Devlin first, of course,' Inge said.

'Well, no. My wife – she died three years ago.'

'I'm sorry.' Inge paused. 'Is there someone you'd like to invite along as well? A friend?'

Harry thought about Kim's reaction. A magic show at a Labour Club, fine. But a posh evening with people whom she would dislike on sight would certainly put the kiss of death on their relationship. If it wasn't dead already. 'Actually, there isn't...'

'Doesn't matter,' Matthew said heartily. He fished in his wallet for a business card and scribbled on the back of it. 'This is where we live. Say eight o'clock?'

Harry cringed inwardly but managed to force a smile. 'I'll look forward to it,' he said.

The couple waved and were gone. And when he glanced back across the street, Davey Damnation too had disappeared.

Stephanie Hall was waiting in reception when he arrived back at New Commodities House. On the way, he had resolved to put Davey out of his mind, telling himself it was crazy to think that the pavement preacher could be capable of murder. Stephanie's shoulders were hunched and although she had a magazine in her lap, she was ignoring it. Harry could sympathise with that: the dog-eared copies of *Which New Multimedia System?* that Jim had left lying around hardly made compelling reading.

'This is a surprise,' he said. 'I've left a couple of messages for Jonah on the answering machine but he hasn't got back to me. I wondered if something was wrong.'

'There is,' she said, following him into his room. 'He's in the Royal.'

Harry's stomach lurched. 'What's happened?'

'Heart attack,' she said thickly, pulling a tissue from the pocket of her coat. 'Too many of those bloody cheap cigarettes. He complained of chest pains when we had a meal together at the weekend. Six hours later he was in intensive care.'

Harry swore. 'How is he?'

'Oh, he'll pull through. They put him back in a normal ward yesterday. The doctor says he's as tough as old boots.'

The relief made Harry grin. 'I wouldn't have thought you needed a medical expert to tell you that. But I must visit him later on today. If he's up to it.'

'He'd like that. Though he'd never admit as much. I went to see him this morning. For the first time, he'd started to complain. His pillow wasn't comfortable and the breakfast hadn't been up to much. He couldn't understand why he wasn't allowed a full-scale fry-up. I took that as a good sign.' Stephanie passed her tongue across her lips. 'But things will have to change. He'll have to take things easy for a while.'

'Better wear protective clothing when you break the news to him.'

For the first time, she smiled. 'Oh, if anyone can handle him, I can.'

'I bet you're right. The answering machine was quite a coup.'

'Hard work, believe me.' She leaned forward. 'But then, I'm not afraid of that. And now Jonah will be forced to trust me with assignments more demanding than serving writs and keeping tabs on errant husbands. Which brings me to Vera Blackhurst.'

'What's the latest? The trustees would be thrilled if you discovered she'd just finished a five-stretch in Holloway Prison.'

'I bet. At least I'm beginning to make progress through talking to people she met while she was working with Charles. There are one or two leads. She knows North Wales well, for example, and she once let slip that she lived in Colwyn Bay for a number of years. I'm planning to go over there on Saturday afternoon to find out precisely what she got up to there. I gather she may have grown up in Cheshire.'

'I realise Jonah's illness will slow the inquiry down.'

'Thanks, but I do want to be professional about this. The show must go on and all that. I'd hate to let any client down after I've only been in the business five minutes. Especially such a high-profile client as the Kavanaugh Trust.'

'Don't worry. Besides, the trustees probably feel they are too high-profile for their own good at the moment. You heard about Luke Dessaur?'

She nodded and a smile began to spread against her face, though he guessed she was trying to suppress it.

'What's up?'

'You want the honest answer?'

'Usually,' he said with a grin.

'It's just that when Jonah mentioned Dessaur's death to me, he said, "Ten to one, Harry will start poking his nose in where it isn't wanted".'

Her mimicry of her uncle's gruff tones was startlingly accurate and Harry laughed out loud. He was beginning to realise that it would be a mistake to underestimate this young woman.

'He was right, as usual.' He hesitated. 'And the fact is, the further I've poked my nose in, the more I've become convinced there is something to smell.'

'Such as?'

Almost without realising it, he found himself relating the whole story. By the time he was finished, Stephanie's eyes were rounder and larger than ever. 'So what do you intend to do?'

'What can I do? The body has been buried, there's no forensic evidence to prove that Luke was murdered. Nor will there ever be.'

She frowned. 'Surely you won't be content to let it go at that?'

'Well,' he admitted. 'I thought I might ask a few questions. Perhaps talk to the trustees away from the formality of the board meetings. See whether or not Ashley is barking up the wrong tree.'

'That's more like it.' She smiled. 'Jonah's told me about you. One thing he always says is this: you never give up. He once even described you as one of the stubbornest buggers he'd ever met. You should be flattered. It's the highest praise he can bestow.'

He laughed. 'Look, I must sort out a few things here before I go to visit him. And one other thing.'

'Yes?'

Forget Jim and his disapproval, he thought. 'If you wouldn't mind, I'd like to come over to Colwyn Bay with you at the weekend.'

She stared, unsure whether to be offended. 'Thanks, but I really don't need a chaperon.'

104

'I'm sure you don't,' he said hastily. 'That wasn't what I meant at all. But I've always been fascinated by detectives – and I'm dying to find out the truth about Vera Blackhurst's past. I'd never have had the courage to ask Jonah if I could accompany him.'

She took her glasses off and gave him a smile which transformed her earnest face. 'I can imagine what he would have said. Of course, I'd be glad of the company. And I can pick your brains about the law on the journey. For my exam.' She giggled at his bafflement. 'I'm taking a course in private investigation.'

'Jesus. What happened to the glamorous life of the gumshoe?'

She gave his scuffed Hush Puppies an appraising glance. 'Same as happened to the wealthy lifestyle of the Liverpudlian lawyer, I expect.'

Chapter 10

The Labour Club's wizened doorkeeper looked as if he'd been around since the days of the Tolpuddle Martyrs and found little to smile about in the intervening years. He sat on a wobbly plastic chair behind a Formica-topped table. Behind his head, a huge orange poster with black lettering announced that *The Great Timothy* was appearing tonight. Even in this stronghold of socialism, there was a place for private enterprise: a placard on the table offered the cheapest tinned tobacco on Merseyside. But the doorman's demeanour reminded Harry of a picket outside the dock gates, constantly on the look-out for scabs trying to scuttle past. When Harry and Kim registered in the book for non-members, he pored over their signatures with thinly veiled suspicion.

Kim watched him with barely suppressed amusement and, when they had finally escaped his clutches, she linked her arm with Harry's and whispered, 'He probably suspects you of being a spy from Conservative Central Office.'

He handed their coats to a girl on cloakroom duty. 'Being in the company of the honourable Matthew Cullinan must have rubbed off on me. By the way, I've been asked to a select dinner party with Matthew and his lady love. They suggested I bring a guest, but I thought you...'

'From what little you've told me of the honourable Matthew, I'd rather pass,' she said. 'It's years since the one and only time I made the mistake of attending a dinner party for toffs. I had a brief relationship with a solicitor who worked in-house for one of the big printing companies. He was invited to his boss's mansion over on the Wirral and took me along. Our very first date, would you believe? God, it was an experience I'll never forget. Five hours of small-talk about private school fees and goings-on in the local Tory Association.'

'End of a beautiful friendship?' he asked as the girl returned from her inner sanctum and handed him a receipt.

'Not all that beautiful,' Kim said. 'I'm afraid you'll be better off taking someone else.'

They entered the concert room. The stage was in darkness but the place was filling up and a crowd had already gathered at the bar. As Harry waited to be served, he glanced at the silent television in the corner. A handful of people were clustered around it, watching a boxing match on a satellite channel. He looked around. The walls were festooned with notices. *Do Not Walk On The Dance Floor When The Artiste Is Performing. Anyone Found Bringing Their Food Or Drink On To The Premises Will Be Ejected. No Swearing. No Dogs. Have You Paid Your Annual Subscription Yet?*

'Takes me back to my schooldays,' Kim said when the drinks had been bought. 'My father used to be the steward in a club exactly like this. I spent my formative years watching housewives playing bingo, throwing my pocket money away on the one-armed bandits, eavesdropping on the gossip about the latest scandal, the latest bit of in-fighting between committee members.'

Harry grinned. He'd found Jonah in characteristically crusty form that afternoon and it had lifted his spirits to see that the old curmudgeon was on the mend. 'These places are all the same. My old man used to be the coach at a non-league football club. When I was a boy, he used to give me coins to keep me occupied on the jukebox whilst he chewed the fat with his cronies.'

'So we have something in common, apart from the law?'

'More than maybe either of us realise.'

Quickly, too quickly for Harry's liking, she returned to her original theme. 'I remember that every now and then I would spot the Member of Parliament popping his head round the door once his constituency surgery was done for the week. He'd have a quick look to see if there was anyone he needed to be pleasant to. If not, he'd do a bunk faster than you could say "train to London paid for by the tax-payer". Leaving the local barons to rule the roost. See the four men huddled over there? Members of the committee, bound to be. Conspiring against someone, I expect.'

Harry laughed. 'I'd expect nothing less of political animals.'

'Believe me, the Tories won't be the target. In any group of people, the enemy within is always the real danger. The committee may have no time for the Matthew Cullinans of this world, but the people they really hate are the comrades who cross their paths on their own territory.'

'Why don't you tell me more?' Harry asked gently.

She took another sip from her drink. 'My father was a strong-minded man. He spoke his mind, didn't care who he upset if he believed he was right. It's not a recipe for popularity. One fine day, when I was still at school, his manager sacked him. It was a terrible disgrace. Nothing personal, mind. All the bar staff went. Money had gone missing and no-one could prove who had taken it. So the committee decided it was safest to dismiss the whole bunch of them.'

'Employers still do that.'

'And it's no fairer now than it was then,' Kim said fiercely. 'My father suffered from that act of cowardice for the rest of his life. Oh, he found other work. He was good at the job, no-one could deny that, and he didn't mind long hours. But his heart was never in it afterwards. He'd been accused of stealing and nothing could ever be the same again. Even the blow to his pride didn't hurt as much as the frustration of having done nothing wrong, yet being punished at least as much as the true culprit. Whoever that was.'

'Agatha Christie called it an ordeal by innocence.'

'A good way of putting it.' Kim gave a bleak smile. 'I never thought of your beloved Dame Agatha as a social commentator.'

'She never tried to be. That's the whole point. But I didn't mean to distract you. What happened to your father?'

'They broke him. He had a heart attack when I was sixteen. At least it was a quick end. But he was only fifty-three. Such a waste.'

'I'm sorry.'

She touched his hand. 'Ever since then, I've felt a kind of personal responsibility to make sure that things are put right.'

'You feel you owe it to your father?'

'Exactly – but it's an impossible task. For every miscarriage that can be rectified, a dozen others pass unnoticed. However hard MOJO tries. And that's something else I need to put in the balance: even if I take this job in London, what are the chances that I will manage to make any difference? Is it simple vanity that makes me think I can?'

They finished their drinks in silence, while the sound of Gene Pitney drifted across the room. He was singing 'True Love Never Runs Smooth'.

'Too right, Gene,' Harry muttered.

'Sorry. I didn't catch that.'

'Nothing.' Besides, was what he felt really love? Harry could not be sure; perhaps he should take that as proof that it was not. He cared for Kim, cared deeply. But it was not the same as the love he had felt for Liz. 'Let me buy you another drink and then we'll find a seat next door before the show begins.'

As they left, he couldn't help noticing the latest on the television screen. One of the boxers was sprawled across the canvas; his right eye was closed and blood was leaking from a cut on his temple. The referee had raised the victor's arm aloft. Someone had switched up the volume and the commentator was talking about another triumph for the champion.

By the time they were settled in the concert room, a compère had appeared on the stage and started cracking politically incorrect jokes that would have had the chic socialists of Hampstead and

Islington retching into their vodka and limes. A story about a bad-tempered barmaid and three Irishmen with a speech impediment had even Harry cringing. But the regulars loved it. Especially when the compère confessed that he came from Kirkby. A place so rough, he said, that the first prize in the local pub quiz was an alibi for two for a fortnight. But it was better than Wigan, a parochial town, where a kebab was no more than a meat pie on a stick.

The daughter of one of the committee members made a brief onslaught upon the greatest hits of Shirley Bassey before the Great Timothy was at last introduced. Tim Aldred strode out on to the stage kitted out in top hat and tails and brandishing his wand as if he were conducting at the Last Night of the Proms. The top hat was slightly askew, the jacket carelessly buttoned. Harry's heart sank: Tim might be able to get away with an act that had been out of date in the fifties when entertaining the Darby and Joans. A Labour Club, even on a charity night, was a different proposition. There was a ripple of applause, but plenty of people in the audience kept talking as Tim started his patter. When he asked for a volunteer, a youth in an ill-fitting suit who had evidently taken advantage of the all-day drinking laws put up his hand. After Tim chose a meek woman with acne to assist him, the drunk started shouting abuse until a heavy in a dicky bow put a menacing hand on his shoulder.

'Nice suit, young man,' Tim said. 'Got it in a car boot sale, did you?'

The youth bellowed something unintelligible. Tim shook his head sadly. 'Now I've heard everything – a dyslexic heckler.'

It began to dawn on Harry that the Great Timothy had little in common with the Tim Aldred he thought he knew. He had a nice line in self-mockery and an unexpectedly quick wit. And he was good, very good, at conjuring. In truth, there was nothing unexpected in the tricks that he performed. Bits of nonsense with playing cards, silk handkerchiefs and a ten-pound note were followed by a sequence in which he invited his helper to bind his wrists with rope and then tie him to a chair. The knots seemed elaborate and impenetrable, but with a shrug of the shoulders he freed himself and took a bow. He sent the woman back to her seat, and then called her back to recover the bracelet which he had discovered inside the crown of his top hat. For a finale, he lay on the stage and covered himself in a huge black cloak. A drum rolled and gradually it seemed that he was levitating above the ground.

By now, the audience's chatter had died away. Even the drunk was quiet. When the Great Timothy landed back on terra firma, shrugged off the cloak and took a bow, the applause was hearty and prolonged. As the curtain fell, Harry turned to look at Kim. To his surprise, her brow was furrowed.

'Penny for them.'

She started guiltily. 'Oh, it's nothing. Nothing.'

Disco lights began to flash and the thud of dance music echoed around the room. He said, 'Shall we escape next door?'

'Good idea.'

'So what did you think of the Great Timothy?' he asked after he had replenished their glasses.

'I recognise him from somewhere. It will bug me until I remember.'

'Let me know when it comes back to you. In the meantime, how do you rate his act?'

'Fun,' she said. 'Simple stuff compared to the illusions you see on the box, but he put it over well.'

Harry nodded. '"It's the way you tell 'em." I must admit I hadn't expected him to be such an accomplished performer. I couldn't help thinking back to when I was a kid. Magic fascinated me. I seem to remember that at the age of nine, it was my ambition to become a conjuror.'

'Seriously?'

'Seriously. My parents even bought me a magic set. As I recall, it contained a simple version of the rope trick Tim performed.

Trouble was, I kept forgetting to make sure that the cord went the right way around my wrists. Result: I was trussed up without a hope of making an escape. Houdini must have been spinning in his grave.'

She laughed. 'So you decided on mature reflection to concentrate your efforts on hocus-pocus in the Liverpool magistrates'?'

'The only spells they understand involve a couple of years inside. Ah, here's the Great Timothy in person! Good to see you. This is Kim Lawrence. Kim, meet the star of tonight's show.'

Tim Aldred smiled. 'Enjoy it?'

'Wonderful. You're wasted at children's parties.'

'You think so? I promise you, compared to a dozen eight-year-olds, performing in front of this lot is child's play. All the same, a pint of bitter will do no harm.'

'I haven't been to a magic show since I was a kid,' Kim said after Harry returned from the bar. 'And I loved it.'

Tim nodded. A dreamy look came into his eyes. 'I got the bug myself when I was nine or ten. A boy I knew had a birthday party with an old man pulling rabbits out of a hat. The whole class was invited. Most of the lads weren't impressed; television had spoiled them. But I was entranced and went straight to the local library so I could borrow every book they had on magic. I felt that if I kept people entertained, they would accept me. I learned to play the piano as well. Same reason. Sounds pathetic, I realise that, but I'd always been a bit of a loner, an odd one out. Still am, I suppose.'

'You've always worked in show business?' she asked.

'Heavens, that's too glamorous a name for it. And the answer is no. Perhaps I lacked the courage of my convictions. I let my mother persuade me that I needed a proper job. The only time in my life I didn't do as she said was when I married young. Of course, I should have listened to Mum. Soon I had not only a wife, but two little girls and a mortgage to cope with. I spent too long working for a firm of ship repairers before I saw the light.'

'You gave up your job?'

'It gave me up,' he said uneasily. 'Fewer vessels on the river; those that remained were better built, less in need of our services. I finished up on the dole. By then my wife had long since run off with someone she worked with, and taken our daughters down to Slough with her fancy man. And my mother had died.' He paused, as if casting his mind back to the past. 'Eventually, I realised that for the first time in my life, I was able to please myself. So I became a magician and occasional pub pianist. And I love it, believe me, I love it.'

Kim said, 'One thing has been bothering me all evening. Have you and I ever met before?'

Tim studied her face, as if seeing her for the first time. 'I'm sure I would have remembered,' he said. No question, Harry thought. His smile was anxious.

'It's only that... oh, never mind.'

'I'm a very ordinary-looking chap,' he said. 'I expect you've confused me with someone else. Anyway, I'm glad that the two of you were able to make it. Thanks for coming.'

Harry said, 'At least tonight we don't have to plough through a pile of minutes or discuss the latest appeals for funds.'

'Thank God. It can be wearisome.'

'And Luke worked so hard on behalf of the Trust, his suicide is bound to throw an additional burden on the remaining trustees.' Harry paused. 'I suppose it *was* suicide?'

Tim started. 'What do you mean? You think it was an accident?'

'Not necessarily. As you demonstrated on stage, appearances can be deceptive.'

'That was entirely different. Personally, I've always thought that Luke killed himself.'

'But why? He was a successful man. Well-respected, in good health as far as anyone knew, not short of money. His death is inexplicable.'

113

Tim shrugged. 'Inexplicable things happen all the time. As for the Trust, well, Luke's death is a serious blow. But thank God we have Frances Silverwood. She's as sound as Luke – and a marvellous person. We're lucky to have her.'

'I agree. And then there's Matthew Cullinan.'

'I'm sure he's very capable,' Tim said stiffly. 'But I must say – this is just between you and me – I find him rather patronising.'

'I don't expect Roy will allow him to get on his high horse too often. He has a flair for bringing people like that down to size.' When Tim grunted in response, Harry added quickly, 'Don't you agree?'

'I must be honest with you. As far as I'm concerned, Frances and Luke have been carrying the Trust for a long time. Frankly, Roy couldn't care less about managing the investments or checking out applications for funding. It takes up too much valuable drinking time. Besides, it's not his money, so he's not bothered. We'd be bankrupt tomorrow if it were left to him. In fact, as far as I can see, we are close to the precipice right now.' He leaned forward. 'I think it's time for a few hard questions to be put to our so-called treasurer. Gervase Kavanaugh endowed the Trust generously. Charles was always supportive. What I'd like to know is: where did all the money go?'

Harry said quietly, 'Where do you think it went?'

'How should I know? I'm no accountant.' Tim hesitated. 'But as you found out yourself the other day, I take a professional interest in the watches people wear. Look, Harry. I know you act for Roy Milburn and I don't expect you to comment on this. But you might like to ask yourself one thing. Your client spends half his time in an alcoholic haze and isn't exactly a high earner. So how did he afford the new Rolex he was wearing at Luke's funeral?'

Chapter 11

By noon the next day, Harry was starting to think that he too qualified for membership of the Magic Circle. Roy Milburn had been banned from driving, but his fine had been affordable and, even though this was his second over-the-limit offence, there had been no prison sentence. Inside the courtroom, Roy had been neat and respectable in his wool and polyester suit – nothing too flash – and had bowed his head in remorse as the prosecution recounted his misdeeds. No-one but himself had been hurt in the crash and he was the very model of a sadder and wiser man. Harry's plea in mitigation had gone like a dream. It was a great escape: the heroes of Colditz would have been envious.

Once they were outside the court building, Roy punched the air and let out a roar of delight. Davey Damnation paused in the middle of a diatribe about Jezebel seducing her servants to commit fornication and pointed a bony finger.

'And when the thousand years are expired, Satan shall be loosed out of his prison!'

'What about time off for bad behaviour?' Roy asked cheerily.

The brimstone and treacle man glared at him and moved forward, arms aloft, as if to strike a blow. But Roy simply whooped with laughter and tossed a twenty-pound note into Davey's upturned hat, threw an arm around Harry's shoulder and began to limp along the street.

'We must celebrate! Come on, I won't take no for an answer.'

Harry glanced back at Davey. He still had half a mind to try to talk to the man, to see if he could get any sense out of him and perhaps put his mind at rest by proving to himself that Davey could not be the Scissorman. But Roy was not to be denied. 'That's very kind.'

'Not a bit of it. Let's push the boat out. Slap-up meal, champagne, the whole works. It's the least you deserve. You had them eating out of your hand by the end. Another five minutes and you'd have been demanding compensation for false arrest. Where would you like to go? Believe me, money's no object. Take your pick.'

An idea occurred to him. 'I've heard the lunches are good at the Hawthorne Hotel. And it's handy for the office. Would that suit you?'

Roy paused. 'Odd choice. In view of – recent tragic events.'

'You're thinking of Luke's death? Of course, if you'd rather try somewhere different, I'll understand.'

He looked directly at his client, as if to emphasise that he'd thrown down a gauntlet. Roy squared his shoulders and picked it up. 'No, no. If that's what you prefer, then it's fine by me.'

They set off in the direction of the river and the Hawthorne. It had begun to drizzle and for a few minutes, neither of them spoke, but as they turned into James Street, Harry blinked the rain out of his eyes and said, 'It still seems hard to credit that Luke is dead – and in such circumstances.'

'I agree. When Frances phoned me with the news, I thought it was a leg-pull. But then she broke down in tears and I realised that she was telling me the truth. Luke really had committed suicide.'

'But *why?* It doesn't make sense.'

'You're a lawyer,' Roy said. 'You make a living out of things that don't make sense. Why did I jump into that car when I knew I'd had a skinful? I've asked myself the question a hundred times since that night. The chairman of the bench was right. I could have killed someone. I damn nearly killed myself and don't I know it? The pain from this bloody leg can be excruciating sometimes. But people aren't logical, Harry. That's the top and bottom of it.'

'In most cases, I'd agree with you. With Luke, though, it was different. He's the last person I would ever...'

'Isn't that so often the way?' Roy interrupted. 'Where others are concerned, we spend so much of our lives pretending to be something we aren't. Luke wore a mask like the rest of us. Deep down, he was obviously as mixed up as you and me. Ah, here we are. The scene of the crime.'

'Suicide hasn't been a crime for years,' Harry said mildly.

Roy flapped a hand dismissively. 'Figure of speech. God, you lawyers are so literal. You ought to relax more. A glass or two of bubbly is just what you need. And incidentally, do you know why sharks don't eat lawyers? Professional courtesy.'

The Hawthorne stood on the Strand, facing out towards the landing stage. A national chain had bought it eighteen months earlier and spent a good deal of money in transforming it into a Mecca for tourists who paid in dollars or by American Express. Harry and Roy passed through revolving doors into a vast and thickly carpeted foyer. In the centre was a pedestal bearing a bust of Nathaniel Hawthorne; a placard beneath it explained that the author of *The Scarlet Letter* had been American Consul in Liverpool in the 1850s and had occupied an office a stone's throw away. From discreetly hidden speakers came the strains of 'Rhapsody in Blue'. A couple of impossibly pretty girls behind the reception desk were urging guests checking out to have a nice day.

Harry gazed in wonder at the elaborate chandeliers suspended above them. 'Last time I came here, I was a trainee solicitor. In those days, it was a specialist conference centre and we were attending a course on accounts. Dullest day I spent in my entire life. I couldn't help remembering that in the eighteenth century the Goree Piazzas were around the corner.'

Roy furrowed his brow. 'Weren't they the old warehouses used for the colonial trade?'

'That's right. I've heard it said that slaves used to be bought and sold there. And when I was starting out in the law and signed up to articles of clerkship with Maher and Malcolm, I used to think I had a lot in common with those poor souls.'

Roy laughed. 'Well, now, what's it to be? I see that a bunch of sales reps have taken over the Eleanor Roosevelt Suite, but never mind. Would you like a drink first at the Herman Melville Bar or straight into Washington Irving Restaurant?'

'Let's eat.'

'Fine. Only one condition: no hamburgers.'

Half an hour later they were both washing down the best salmon steak Harry had tasted in years with another glass of champagne: his second, Roy's fourth. Their conversation had been light and jokey and Harry rounded it off with an account of Tim's magic show at the Labour Club.

'So you were impressed?' Roy gave a disbelieving guffaw. 'I'd always imagined he would be hopeless. Getting tied up with his own rope tricks, that sort of thing. I even sympathise with that prat Matthew Cullinan when he gets pissed off with poor old Tim.'

'Do I gather you're not a fan of Matthew?'

Roy pulled a face. 'Recruiting Matthew was the Dinosaur's attempt to turn the Trust into a slicker operation. He needn't have bothered. I've not seen any evidence yet of Matthew's marvellous financial acumen, have you?'

'Do you and he discuss investment policy together?'

'Our discussions about money mainly consist of Matthew telling me that the stuff we thought was blue-chip is really a load of crap.' Roy put down his knife and fork. 'You're asking a lot of questions about the Trust, Harry. I thought your partner was the man with the eye for detail. I can't believe you find us such fascinating clients.'

'If you knew my other clients, you wouldn't be so sure. I'm sorry to be nosey, but I am interested. Luke's death startled me. I've begun to realise that I hardly knew him.'

Roy shrugged. 'Let's face it. He may have had many admirable qualities, but being a warm lovable human being wasn't one of them. Frances Silverwood would disagree, of course. So would Ashley Whitaker. But even though I've known the Dinosaur since I was a student, I've always found him as difficult to read as a novel in Chinese.'

'I never realised the two of you go back a long way.'

'Oh yes, I first met him when Ashley and I were at university together. Must be well over ten years ago.'

'When I was a student, I never got to know the godparents of my pals.'

'You're forgetting that Luke and Mrs Whitaker used to be an item. They may have married other people, but they always kept in close touch. With Ashley's father and Luke's wife both dead, they saw even more of each other. So, if you were in touch with the Whitakers, you couldn't fail to meet the dear old Dinosaur. I met him when Ashley invited me back to his home during the summer break. I didn't much care for him, to be honest. Too starchy.'

'You and Ashley don't seem to have much in common. Yet you've remained friends.'

Roy gave a lazy smile. 'Sort of. You might say Fate brought us together – blood brothers, you might say. And he did finish up with my ex-girlfriend.'

'You were involved with Melissa?'

Roy winked. 'For a time, yes.'

'And there wasn't a rift between you when Ashley married her?'

'Far from it.' Roy grinned. 'Easy come, easy go.'

'Most men in your shoes wouldn't have been so philosophical.'

'It was no big deal. Mind you, Melissa had everything: good looks, money, charm. But I told you before, she was as neurotic as hell – and she always kept her legs tightly closed. She told me she was determined to keep her virginity until her wedding night, would you believe? So I didn't have much fun. In the end I started to get bored and look elsewhere. Whereas Ashley was crazy about her from the start. Besotted. Truly, I think he is to this very day.'

'Happy marriages are rare,' Harry said, with feeling.

'Depends on your idea of happiness, doesn't it? She liked to have him dangling on a string, but even so, his conscience troubled him because he thought of her as my girl. I told him not to be so bloody stupid, there were plenty more fish in the sea.'

Roy laughed. Harry knew that his client had once been briefly married, to a woman he'd met in a night club. Since then Roy had preferred to have no ties. The one-night stands which Harry found so unsatisfying were still meat and drink to him. 'Besides, her father was a tough cookie. He ordered Melissa to end our relationship – and she was quite prepared to obey him. A real daddy's girl. My attitude was – rather Ashley than me.'

'I don't think he's complaining.'

'Oh sure,' Roy said lazily. 'And don't be fooled by that vague manner of his. Take it from me, he was always at least as horny as yours truly – but he always tended to fantasise rather than do anything about it. Not like me at all in that respect. I suppose you could say he's much more patient. Married to Melissa, I bet he's had to be.'

'Tell me more about Luke. Did he ever live with Mrs Whitaker?'

Roy shook his head. 'Not likely. You knew the Dinosaur. Talk about Victorian values – but he was more strait-laced than most Victorians, if you ask me. He was just as bad as Melissa, he never subscribed to the permissive society. He would never have countenanced living in sin. Not even with Mrs Whitaker, much as he cared for her.'

'Why didn't they marry?'

'Your guess is as good as mine. My bet is that she wouldn't have been averse to tying the knot again. She'd been devoted to Ashley's father, but after a decent interval there was no reason why she shouldn't try to find happiness elsewhere. The Dinosaur was a handsome devil in those days. She was a shade on the plump side, maybe, but that's not the end of the world, is it?' He grinned. 'As a matter of fact, I quite fancied her myself. I was going through an older-woman phase at the time. Thank God it wore off, otherwise, I'd be necking with pensioners whilst I was still in my prime.'

The waiter took their orders for dessert and Harry found himself unable to resist a Rip Van Winkle mousse. In the conversational lull, an outlandish idea occurred to him.

'I must admit I'm intrigued by the tie-up between Luke and Ashley. Frankly, if either of my godfathers was sitting in this restaurant, I wouldn't recognise him. Yet Luke and Ashley saw a great deal of each other. I was wondering if the relationship might have been closer than anyone ever admitted. Is it possible' – he paused – 'is it possible that Luke was Ashley's father?'

Roy stared at him. 'Now you really are in the land of make-believe. Whatever gave you that idea?'

'Just a thought. Do I gather that you're not convinced? I realise there is no physical resemblance...'

'Whereas, to judge from one or two photographs I've seen over the years, Ashley is the spitting image of his dad.'

'Maybe I'm wrong, then.'

Roy grinned. 'Detective fever. You're trying to solve a puzzle that doesn't exist. Luke carried a torch for Ashley's mum. He became genuinely fond of his godson. Their friendship was strong enough to survive the death of Mrs Whitaker. My guess is that, if anything, it brought them together. The Dinosaur found it hard to get close to people. Maybe he leaned on Ashley more than any of us realised.'

'What makes you say that?'

'I don't suppose it's a coincidence that when Luke finally snapped, Ashley was in Canada.'

'You're suggesting that if Ashley had been here, the Dinosaur might have told him about whatever was on his mind?'

'As you hinted a moment ago, Ashley was his natural confidant. If Luke had been able to talk with him, maybe the outcome might have been different.' Roy smiled. 'But don't tell Ashley I said that. He's got enough on his mind as it is. No need to burden him with guilt for the death of his godfather.'

'I still don't understand why Luke should want to kill himself.'

'Neither does Ashley, so far as I can gather.' Roy yawned. 'If you two mystery buffs are baffled, what chance is there for the rest of us to fathom it?'

Harry said, 'Do you think it could have been trouble within the Kavanaugh Trust that drove Luke to suicide?'

Roy was scornful. 'For God's sake. Now you are letting your imagination run away with you. Okay, Luke cared more about the Trust than the rest of us. In my case, frankly, that wasn't difficult. And the Trust is on its uppers. The Charles Kavanaugh bequest would have been a godsend, but Vera has put her spanner in the works.'

Harry leaned forward. 'So as far as you are concerned, the Trust had no connection at all with his death?'

'Of course not. How could it have?'

'Then why do *you* think he killed himself?'

'Like I said, I don't have a neat and tidy answer. Life's messy; so is death. Very different from the books that you and Ashley devour.'

'I suppose – you are sure it *was* suicide?'

Roy gave him a shocked stare for a moment before rocking back in his chair and starting to roar with laughter. 'Now I'm certain you have been reading too many mysteries. What's bugging you, Harry? Do you think Tim bumped the Dinosaur off so that he could try his luck with Frances? How much champagne have you drunk?'

'Too much, I expect. Shall we order coffee?'

'I could do with some. But why don't you come round to my eyrie to drink it? I only live just around the corner. Have a look at my studio.'

'I suppose I really ought to be getting back to work...'

'Forget it. Come on, you'll be billing me an arm and a leg anyway. You can afford to take a little time off after such a famous victory.'

'About your bill,' Harry said. 'I've put in a good deal of time on this case.'

'No problem,' Roy said expansively. 'I'm quite flush at the moment. Forget what I said originally about giving me a discount. I'm happy to pay top dollar. You deserve it after today. Hang on a moment while I settle up, then we'll walk to the flat.'

Whilst he was waiting, Harry mooched around the reception area. Glancing through the door into the Herman Melville Bar, he noticed Don Ragovoy talking to a young man who was polishing glasses, the one who had accompanied him to Luke's funeral. Then out of the corner of his eye he spotted a small swarthy man in a porter's uniform carrying a couple of heavy suitcases. The badge on the man's lapel said *Julio*. Moving as swiftly, for once, as in his footballing days, Harry intercepted the porter on his way to the goods lift.

'Excuse me. I believe you spoke to a friend of mine, a Mr Whitaker, about the man who died here recently – Luke Dessaur.'

The man gave him a sullen look. 'Listen, mister, I don't want any more trouble. I had the police round asking questions after your friend came here.'

'There's not going to be any trouble. You gave my friend a lot of help. I simply wonder if you can remember anything else about the argument you overheard.'

The man shook his head vigorously. 'Not a thing, mister. Not a thing.'

'Was it a woman in Mr Dessaur's room or another man?'

'Listen, I tell your friend, I dunno.'

'What time was it?'

'I dunno. Just before eleven, maybe.'

123

'Not later?'

'It was plenty late enough. I was dog tired.'

'You weren't the porter who found the body, were you?'

'No, that was my pal. He was on the eleven to seven shift that night. Now look, mister, these bags are heavy.'

Harry flourished a couple of notes from his wallet in the hope of refreshing the man's memory. But it was no use. In his haste to be off, Julio even forgot to tell Harry to have a nice day.

Roy returned. 'You all right?'

Harry hesitated. He was trying to work out timings. The argument Julio had overheard had taken place before Luke tried to phone Ashley in Canada and about an hour and a half before his death. So what was its significance? 'Yes – yes, of course. Shall we go?'

A couple of minutes later Roy steered him round the corner from Water Street into India Court and pointed at a building on the left-hand side. 'There it is.'

He stared. Roy was indicating a boarded-up shop that had once sold discount office equipment. Crusoe and Devlin had once invested in a couple of their filing cabinets but within a fortnight the drawers had become stuck. Although the prospect of having his most intractable case files entombed forever had appealed to Harry, Jim had decreed that future purchases would be made from more reliable suppliers. Presumably other customers had taken similar decisions, resulting in the sad note on the bolted front door that any enquiries about the business should be addressed to its duly appointed receivers.

'I don't see any sign...'

Roy smiled and, producing a hefty bundle of keys, unlocked the padlock on a gate at the side of the disused store. They went down an alley to a back door and Roy opened up.

The place was dark, with a faint musty smell. They were surrounded by wobbly typists' chairs, battered knee-hole desks and other oddments of ergonomically incorrect office furniture.

'There's no place like home,' he said.

'So where is your studio?'

'Follow me.'

Roy directed him through into the back and towards a narrow staircase. 'I hope you're fit. There were lifts for goods and customers, but both of them have been condemned by the health and safety people. It's either this or the outside fire escape and that's a death trap after overnight rain.'

He led Harry up six flights. By the time they reached the top Harry was gasping for breath and Roy's features were creased with pain. 'Out of condition?' he gasped. 'The exercise will do you good. Imagine how it feels with a dodgy leg.'

Harry looked around. They were standing on a small landing. In front of him were three large and solid doors. A strange clicking and hissing emanated from behind the one in the middle. Roy nodded at each of them and said, 'The lift motor room. The tank room – hence the background music. And my front door. Come in.'

Harry followed Roy inside and along a long narrow passageway, at the end of which was a door which opened into a small sitting-room-cum-studio. The floor was covered with hessian matting and there was a stale whiff of Indian cooking in the air. The walls were festooned with the originals of cartoons that Roy had drawn. There was, Harry thought suddenly, a cruel streak in Roy that came out in his work. He had the skill to capture character with a few sharp strokes of the pen and the most acute images were always the most savage. A prominent councillor with two faces, an inarticulate soccer star with his boot in his mouth. There was a sketch book on the table and Harry began to leaf through it. The picture on the first page startled him. It showed a rabbit looking disgusted to have pulled a goggle-eyed Tim Aldred out of a hat.

He turned over. There was the honourable Matthew Cullinan naked except for a nappy and sucking a silver spoon. Next page: Frances Silverwood cuddling a shrunken head in her arms as if it were a new-born babe.

'Have you met Uncle Joe?' Roy asked. He'd come back into the room so quietly that Harry started and hurriedly put the book down on top of a little grey filing cabinet in the corner. 'Yes, I can tell from your expression that you have. Naughty of me, I suppose. Most women in search of a child-substitute choose a pet. Frances is the only one I know who mollycoddles a shrunken head. Weird, or what?'

'Sorry. Being nosey.'

'I suppose I shouldn't mind my brief knowing my secret vices.' He gave a wolfish grin. 'Though knowledge is power, isn't it? That's always been my motto. But I've got so many guilty secrets that if one or two of the little ones are found out, it doesn't matter much. There are plenty more in that cabinet. Only snag is, the bloody drawers are almost impossible to open.'

'Tell me about it,' Harry said, glad to relieve his embarrassment by changing the subject. 'The cowboy who used to work downstairs sold me a couple of them.'

Roy grinned. 'Good old Donal. Consistent only in his total lack of reliability. I wonder what he's up to now?'

'You knew him?' Donal was the young salesman who had seemed to be in charge here. A dark-haired fellow with the gift of the gab.

'An old pal of mine – and the reason I'm here. He was managing the shop for some rogue from Belfast. This is supposed to be a caretaker's flat, but Donal thought up a cunning plan. He lived out at Aigburth, but he would install me here and save on expenditure. I could save money too and the place was ideal as a studio. Ever since my bloody ex took our house, I've rented rather than bought, but the dump I was living in was costing an arm and a leg at a time when I was desperate for cash. When the shop went kaput, Donal pissed off back to Ireland, owing money to half of Liverpool. I did a deal with the receivers. They like saving money too. Rather than try and evict me, they agreed that I could stay here for the time being, provided I kept an eye on security. So I'm still here.'

'And doing well on it, judging by the cost of the lunch we've just had. You've come into money lately, then?'

Roy tapped the side of his nose. 'Ask no questions and you'll hear no lies. Now, how about taking a look outside?'

He opened the double windows and they went on to the roof of the building. The wind was roaring in from the river, much fiercer up here than at street level. He turned round slowly, absorbing the scene. A low railing ran around the perimeter of the rooftop, enclosing an area that combined terracotta pots containing hardy green and yellow plants with boiler flues, lengths of hose and black rolled steel joists for window cleaners' cradles. On the street side, a flagpole reached up into the sky. Roy saw him looking at it and laughed.

'I'm tempted to run up the skull and crossbones. One of these days, maybe.'

Harry could see the river through a gap in the buildings that edged the Strand. One of the rooftops must belong to the Hawthorne. Suppose Luke had discovered that Roy was embezzling from the Trust. Might he have booked in to the hotel because it was convenient to meet Roy there after the meeting at the Piquet Club? He walked over to the edge to look at the tiny figures on the ground. As he gazed down, he began to feel dizzy. He took a step back and wondered if it had been like this for Luke. What it would feel like, to look down upon the ground from the hotel window and know that within moments one's body would be lying on it? And there was still the old question: did he jump or was he pushed?

'You look miles away,' Roy said softly.

He turned back to face his client. 'Sorry, it's nothing. I just remembered I'm going to see *Vertigo* tomorrow night.'

Chapter 12

Matthew Cullinan and Inge Frontzeck shared a flat in a four-storey neo-Georgian block which looked out over the River Dee. The cars parked in the courtyard were Alfas and BMWs; blue, white and yellow winter pansies cascaded from vast hanging baskets beside the main door. A discreet sign next to the entry phone informed Harry that the occupants of the block did not welcome free newspapers or unsolicited callers and that they were active members of a neighbourhood watch security scheme.

The Jericho Lane Labour Club was only half an hour's drive away, but it belonged to a different world in which he was much more at home. He felt rather like a pub singer who has wandered by mistake on to the stage at Glyndebourne. As he rang the bell marked with the name of his hosts, he conquered with difficulty the urge to make a face at the closed circuit television cameras mounted on the courtyard walls.

Inge directed him to take the lift to the top floor and buzzed him in. When she opened their front door to him, he presented her with a bouquet of flowers.

'You're so kind,' she said.

As she touched his cheek with her lips, he felt her breasts press against him for a moment and for the first time found himself seized by envy of the Honourable Matthew Cullinan. He had no regrets about the lack of blue blood in his veins and the world of financial consultancy held as much appeal for him as a spell in Strangeways. But the warmth of Inge's body as, without a thought, she gave her social greeting reminded him that he had been celibate for too long.

She led him into an L-shaped living-room stuffed with more antiques than the Lady Lever Art Gallery. Vivaldi was playing on a Scandinavian sound system that reminded him of something out of *Star Trek*. A Persian rug was stretched across the floor and he guessed it must have cost a fortune.

Not a place to be sick on the carpet, he told himself.

On the mantelpiece were half a dozen framed photographs showing Inge at various stages of her life since childhood. She had been a shy little girl and a dumpy teenager. Only in the most recent picture was she smiling: it had been taken in front of a snow-laden ski lodge where she was gazing into Matthew's eyes.

Her boyfriend was standing next to a cocktail cabinet in the shape of a huge globe, checking the labels of a couple of bottles. Harry uttered a silent prayer that Matthew would not ask him which particular vintage he favoured. His host moved forward, hand outstretched. 'Grand to see you. Can I offer you a glass of champagne?'

'I ought to say no,' Harry said. 'I was on the Moët at lunch-time.'

'My God. It's a tough life being a Liverpool solicitor, eh?'

'Special occasion. I was with Roy Milburn.'

'Of course, I'd forgotten. Court case went well, did it? I rather gained the impression that if you kept him out of the nick, you'd be achieving a minor miracle.'

'Some you win, some you lose. But I've learned a lesson from him and come over here in a cab. So – pour away.'

As Matthew opened a bottle of Bollinger, he said, 'I don't want to talk shop, but I must be honest with you. Sometimes I worry about Roy.'

'Why's that?'

'Here, good health. Well, it's a question of reliability, I suppose. I do wonder whether Roy's the ideal man for the treasurer's job.'

A masterpiece of understatement, Harry thought. 'He only took the job on as a favour because the trustees couldn't find anyone else and he'd once trained as an accountant.'

'I gather he flunked his exams. Hardly reassuring. I'm not sure how close an eye he keeps on the Trust's finances. I don't pretend to have gone through them with a fine-tooth comb, but they seem in a pretty parlous state to me. Luke once said that when Roy was appointed, the Trust was not simply in the black but in a very healthy state indeed.' Matthew shook his head. 'I'm not convinced that the management of our investments has been sound, so I have tried to make a number of changes for the better. Of course, I'm the new boy on the board, but I can't stand idly by while the whole shooting match falls apart.'

Harry sipped his champagne. He was beginning to understand why he had been invited, although he still could not quite reconcile the way Matthew talked with his reputation as a low-profile do-gooder. 'Did you discuss your concerns with Luke?'

'I may have mentioned them in passing.'

I bet. 'And what was his response?'

Matthew paused and Harry sensed that his host was measuring his words with care. One thing was clear: this meant more to him than a bit of casual, bitchy gossip. 'He said very little. Just between you and me, I felt my remarks didn't come as a complete surprise. But now we will never know what was in his mind. Oh well, Roy is your client. I don't want to embroil you in a conflict of interests. I simply feel that I owe it to Luke to do what I can to protect the Trust's interests.'

'How did you feel when you heard of his death?'

Matthew spread his arms. 'Bolt from the blue, wasn't it? Couldn't believe it at first. He simply didn't seem the type for suicide.'

Harry was about to ask whether there really was such a type when the doorbell rang and Inge called out from the kitchen. 'Darling, will you get it?'

'Right-ho.' Matthew winked at Harry. 'Our other guest. You'll have to excuse me.'

'Yes, of course. Sorry, I didn't realise anyone else was expected.'

Matthew gave a mischievous grin and ambled out to the hall. Harry heard the door open and words of welcome exchanged before Matthew ushered the new arrival into the room.

'Harry! How lovely to see you again.'

Juliet May had exchanged her working clothes for a strapless evening gown which so emphasised her curves that it was difficult not to stare. The way she smiled at the sight of him made it clear that his presence here was not unexpected. That puzzled him, but he felt an irrational burst of pleasure at seeing her again that outweighed even the fear that she intended to spend the evening in urging on him the vital need for Crusoe and Devlin to smarten up their image. As Inge had done, she brushed his cheek with a kiss and he told himself that perhaps he had underestimated the virtues of middle-class customs.

'I never knew you were a friend of Matthew's,' he said.

'Oh, I love nothing better than hobnobbing with the aristocracy. But as a matter of fact, I met Matthew through Inge. The firm I used to work for had a contract with her father's company and when I set up on my own, she was kind enough to ask me to help her out with marketing her catering business.'

Inge came into the room and exchanged cheek-pecks with Juliet. All very different from the earthy familiarity of Jericho Lane. 'Darling, you look terrific. As always. You've already met Harry, I believe.'

'That's right. Didn't you tell him that I'd been asked along to make up the four? I saw the way his jaw dropped when I walked through the door. I thought he might try to make a run for it before I could persuade him to put on a seminar for his clients on cutting the cost of litigation.'

'Hang on a minute,' Harry said. 'We don't want to give them any ideas like that.'

'An honest solicitor,' Juliet told Inge. 'A rare creature.'

'Quite a challenge for you,' Matthew said. 'Glass of bubbly, Juliet? Let me top you up, Harry.'

'Thanks.' Juliet turned to Harry. 'Please don't get the wrong idea. This evening is for pleasure, not business. I'm really not going to spoil it by making a pitch for the Crusoe and Devlin contract.'

'You make it sound like a major exercise in competitive tendering,' he said. 'Truth is, we've never gone further than putting an advertisement for divorce work in all the local papers the first week in January. When families come together for the season of goodwill, we're guaranteed an increase in business.'

'I think our legs are being pulled,' Matthew said. 'Seriously, Harry, you could pick up a spot of useful free advice tonight. Lawyers need to promote themselves these days, same as soap powder salesmen. The people I use have a marketing budget equal to five per cent of turnover. They pay a good deal

of attention to areas in which Juliet has expertise. Like relationship marketing.'

Juliet giggled at Harry's evident bewilderment. 'Don't worry, I don't go round encouraging people to have affairs in order to increase demand for legal services. It's a question of targeting clients who have other solicitors, obtaining initial instructions from them, perhaps on a single project, and then seeking to earn their loyalty over a period of time, becoming their regular retained lawyers.'

'That's nothing new so far as criminal advocates are concerned. We've been touting recidivists for business since the Krays were first put on probation.'

She smiled. 'I suspect I might not be able to teach you as much as Matthew would have you believe. Even if your tongue was slightly in your cheek, the divorce idea is fine. Identifying the clients' needs, that's the idea. I must remember to give you a ring next New Year's Day, when Casper and I are coming to blows after I've had a week's exposure to his parents, his brother and sister and their appalling kids whilst he's spent most of the time on the fax to New York.'

'Oh yes, Jim Crusoe told me you were married to Casper May.'

She giggled again. 'It's a mixed blessing being married to someone so...'

'Notorious?' Matthew suggested drily.

'That's probably as good a description as any,' Juliet said with a rueful smile. 'I take it you've heard of my husband, Harry?'

Harry nodded: when in doubt, say nowt. In his twenties, Casper May had been one of the city's most feared loan sharks. His methods of persuading his debtors to pay him what he thought was due had attracted the attention of the police more than once. He had then diversified into the security business. Liverpool abounded with rumours that his technique for winning new business owed less to keen pricing than fear that to turn him down would result in unexplained break-ins or arson attacks within days rather than weeks. In recent years he had been keen to clean up his image and nowadays he was fêted by the local press for his highly visible work for charity. He was a highly effective fund-raiser. Even if the grievous bodily harm days were over, when Casper May asked you to make a donation to a good cause, you checked out your insurance before saying no.

'Where did you say he was at present?' Inge asked.

'In Florida with the general manager of one of his disability charities. Why is it I suspect she's blonde with long legs?' Her smile did not diminish the sting of her words. 'I happened to mention to Inge yesterday evening that I would be at a loose end tonight and she was kind enough to invite me over here.'

Harry caught an exchange of looks between Inge and Juliet, but found it impossible to interpret them. Inge said, 'I hope you don't mind, Harry, but when Juliet told me she had actually met you the other day, it seemed a perfect opportunity to have you both along.'

'I'm glad Fate has brought us together again.'

'Do you believe in Fate?' Juliet asked.

'Why do you ask?'

'Juliet reads the Tarot,' Matthew explained. 'I must admit it's not my cup of tea, but Inge swears by it.'

He gave his girlfriend a contented smile. His expression was no doubt meant to seem affectionate, but Harry thought he sensed something hidden beneath the surface. What did it remind him of? Perhaps the sly glance a hardened criminal might give to an inexperienced defence lawyer, whom he would string along simply because he needed his help. Very odd. Perhaps he was imagining it. Certainly, Inge seemed unaware that anything might be wrong. Her eyes were bright; Hal David might have been thinking about her when he wrote his lyric about the look of love.

'Are you interested in the Tarot, Harry?' Juliet asked.

Jerked out of his reverie, he said, 'I know nothing about it. But any help with my lottery numbers would be more than welcome.'

She leaned forward and rested her hand on his arm. 'Please don't think it's simply a load of nonsense. I'd be happy to give you a reading if you're interested. I've met a good many people who have had their lives changed as a result of a Tarot reading.'

'That's exactly what terrifies me.'

She removed the pressure of her hand. 'I promise you, the Tarot is much misunderstood. Even by intelligent people. I gave a reading to a friend only the other day and turned up the Death card. My friend was terribly upset and yet there was no need. The card can have different meanings.'

'All the same, perhaps I'll give it a miss tonight, if you don't mind.'

Inge said, 'You should change your mind, Harry. But now it's time to eat. Would you like to come into the dining-room?'

The food was predictably superb and as the alcohol continued to flow freely, Harry realised to his surprise that he was thoroughly enjoying himself. Inge was an accomplished hostess as well as cook and had an unexpectedly sly wit. Matthew was content to treat her to that amiable, superficial beam and keep refilling the glasses; Harry noticed that Juliet's needed replenishing at least as often as his, and he wasn't in the mood to be abstemious. There was no sign that the drink was having any noticeable effect on her, but she was funny and voluble, coming out with a string of entertaining stories about people who had embarked on elaborate public relations exercises only to get their comeuppance in embarrassing fashion. Harry listened idly to the anecdotes, but paid more attention to the look of her in the glow of the candle-light. Once she cast a quick glance in his direction and caught him studying her figure. He moved his eyes quickly in the direction of Inge, but not before he'd noticed the glimmer of a smile on Juliet's lips. A few minutes later, he felt the toes of a stockinged foot brush against his leg. He turned towards Juliet and this time returned her smile.

He had almost forgotten the reason why he had agreed to come here in the first instance when during a brief lull in the conversation Inge said to him, 'Well, Harry, what news about this Blackhurst woman?'

Briefly, he summarised the latest. Matthew Cullinan's eyes began to gleam even before he had finished. 'Excellent news. If she's a fraud, we must be able to put a good deal of pressure on this lawyer of hers. Sounds as though he's making a complete ass of himself.'

'It must be true that love is blind. I don't know what he sees in her.'

'Oh, I can think of a couple of things,' Matthew said and gave him a man-to-man wink. 'So what happens next?'

Harry described his plan to accompany Stephanie on her trip to North Wales and Juliet clapped her hands with enthusiasm. 'Wonderful! So you really are going to play the detective?'

'Juliet loves a mystery,' Inge said. 'I think if she had her time again she'd be a female private eye herself.'

136

'It would make a change from simply reading the books. You know, that wonderful shop called the Speckled Band? I haunt it. I feel as though I'm walking into an Aladdin's cave each time I step through the door.'

'Then it's strange we haven't bumped into each other before now,' Harry said. 'I've been buying books from Ashley ever since he opened. And there is a connection with the Kavanaugh Trust. He is the godson of the former chairman, who died a few days ago.'

Her eyes opened wide. 'I didn't know that.'

Harry gave her an edited account of the mystery surrounding Luke's death, watching Matthew's face as he described how, in the last few days of his life, Luke had given the impression of being afraid of something. His host remained impassive until Harry said that Luke had apparently argued with a visitor in his hotel room on the night of his death.

'Are you suggesting there was something – untoward about his death?'

Juliet said briskly, 'Come on, Matthew, let's call a spade a spade. It sounds as though Harry's suggesting this is really a murder case.'

'It's ridiculous,' Matthew snapped. 'Luke killed himself. Failing that, he had an accident. Murder is out of the question.'

'Don't get so heated, darling,' Inge said. 'It's not like you.'

'Sorry, my love,' he said, instantly contrite. 'It's just that I don't like to have his death treated as some sort of parlour game. It's a human tragedy. Let's leave it at that, shall we?'

'Of course,' Juliet said and her ironic inflection told Harry that, beneath the civilised chit-chat, she had little time for Matthew Cullinan. The more he saw of her, the more he warmed to her.

Putting on his most genial expression, Matthew said, 'Tell you what, Harry. Why don't you have a listen to this?'

He moved over to the sound system and selected a compact disc from the cabinet which he put into the player. The room was filled with discordant music and Harry had drunk enough to be unsure whether it was the booze or the din that was giving him a headache.

Juliet grimaced. 'What in God's name is this?'

'Real fist to the piano stuff, eh? Yet without it, Harry and I would never have met.'

Harry stared. 'How do you mean?'

'I take it you're not familiar with classical music of the thirties?'

'Not – not if you exclude Gershwin.' *Oh God, I'm beginning to slur my words.*

Matthew chuckled. 'This, my friend, is the most successful piece Gervase Kavanaugh ever wrote. A little number called "Suite for Lucifer".'

Harry listened for a little while to the screeching violins and crashing cymbals and said, 'Well, it proves one thing, doesn't it?'

'What's that?'

'It's just not true that the devil has all the best tunes.'

Chapter 13

The telephone woke him at ten the next morning. He picked up the bedside receiver and groaned his name.

Kim said, 'Good dinner party, was it?'

The thudding inside his head made Status Quo sound like the Swingle Singers. 'Whoever said the rich are different was right,' he mumbled. 'They have the constitution of an ox. I don't think I'm cut out for the high life.'

'You disappoint me. I always thought you could take your drink.'

'Beer's one thing, but I've never had much practice with champagne.' He was trying to remember. *Had* he been sick on the carpet after all?

'Call yourself a solicitor?' She was in breezy mood. A morning person, Kim, unlike himself. 'I take it you had a wonderful time?'

'Sort of.' An image began to form in his mind, fuzzy at first but becoming clearer. The face of Juliet May.

'You must tell me about it when the hangover clears.' She paused. 'I simply rang to beg your forgiveness.'

'What for?' He had an uneasy recollection of Juliet's leg pressing against his. Even now he thought he could smell her perfume.

'I'm going to have to cry off *Vertigo*. Quentin and his partners are having a meeting over dinner tonight. It's a regular event in their calendar, but they want to talk over their offer with me. I shall have to make up my mind soon whether or not to accept.'

He sensed that she was waiting for him to respond, but he could not think of anything worthwhile to say. 'I suppose so. Good luck.'

'Sorry about the film.'

'Doesn't matter. Let me know how you get on.'

'I will. And Harry – '

'Yes?'

'Oh, nothing.'

After she had rung off, he sat on top of his bed hugging his knees for a few minutes, telling himself that he should have handled the conversation better. But his mind was jumping around like the playback on a faulty video recorder. He could vaguely recall being helped into a taxi the previous evening by Matthew whilst Inge asked if he would be all right. He had protested that he felt fine, absolutely fine whilst Juliet said something – was it about seeing him again some time? The one thing he could be sure of now was that the queasiness in his stomach was not due solely to the alcohol he had consumed. It was senseless to deceive himself. He wanted badly to see the woman again. Never mind that she was married to Casper May. For the moment, he cared more about whether in his drunken state he had made a fool of himself in front of her than the outcome of Kim's meeting with the partners of Windaybanks.

A shower, a potful of black coffee and a couple of hours later, he was walking from his flat past the police headquarters and in the direction of the city centre. It was the coldest day of the year so far and flecks of snow were falling, but at least the raw wind coming in from the Mersey was helping to clear his head. He felt less fragile now that he had a sense of purpose. He had remembered Juliet mentioning that on Saturdays she often stopped off at Ashley Whitaker's shop in the middle of the day.

Yet there was no sign of her when he arrived at the Speckled Band Bookshop. Ashley was behind the counter, debating the merits of Dorothy L. Sayers with a gnarled customer in a huge camel overcoat. Melissa was sitting on one of the tables in the middle of the ground floor, kicking her long and elegant legs as she leafed through *Strangers in a Train*.

'I don't often see you here,' he said.

'I keep away. Ashley's the detective story fan. Personally, I prefer poetry. I think Sylvia Plath is marvellous.'

'Oh. Right.' Harry decided that Melissa wouldn't be an ideal choice as a fun companion on a desert island. Maybe Roy hadn't simply been jealous of Ashley when he'd described her as being as neurotic as hell. 'Can I interest you in an exchange of murders?' he asked, nodding at the Highsmith book.

She glanced in Ashley's direction and gave a high-pitched laugh. 'There are times when I might be tempted. He lives in a world of his own, frankly. Do you know, he spent the whole of yesterday evening on the phone to some crime nut in Milwaukee, having promised faithfully to take me out for a slap-up meal? He's obsessed. I don't think anyone could blame me if I agreed a murder-swop. But who would you wish to do away with?'

'The list is endless. It starts with the Lord Chancellor and goes all the way down to the computer salesman who told me that his system was idiot-proof.' He shook his head. 'By the way. I was talking to one of your customers last night. A woman called Juliet May.'

'Casper May's wife? That's right, she spends a lot of money here.' She grimaced. 'I'm glad someone does. Where did you meet her?'

'Matthew Cullinan invited me to dinner. It turned out that Juliet May is friendly with his girlfriend, Inge Frontzeck.'

'The German girl? She's the daughter of Uwe Frontzeck, isn't she?'

At last he remembered where he had heard the surname before. 'Isn't he...?'

'The businessman. He owns Frontzeck Clothes. They have a chain of shops. Very up-market.'

'The name did ring a distant bell. But I've never been at the cutting edge of fashion.'

She gave a faint smile. 'Perhaps you'll have seen him mentioned in the financial pages of the Press.'

'I don't read them,' Harry confessed.

'I sympathise. My father used to study the share index in the same way that Ashley pores over an Agatha Christie for clues.'

'Your father was in business as well, wasn't he?'

Melissa's tone softened. 'Yes, he ran a brewery. I used to complain that he loved the company more than me, but it wasn't true and deep down I always knew it. My mother died of a stroke when I was young and he did everything he could to make sure I was looked after. He was always wonderful to me. And then some bastard killed him in a hit-and-run accident and things were never the same again.'

Harry pushed aside a pile of paperbacks so that he could sit next to her. 'My parents died when I was still at school. A fire engine screaming through red lights hit them broadside. They never stood a chance. They were killed instantly, or so I was told. But I've always wondered whether, in the last few seconds, they realised what was about to happen, knew that they were helpless and that there was no escape. Silly of me. Morbid.'

'I'm sorry.'

'The fire engine was answering a hoax call,' he said. 'The one thing I've never been able to do is defend kids accused of raising false alarms. Again, it's stupid, unfair. I act for rapists, murderers, men of violence. Even drink-drivers. But hoax callers – no, I can't hack it.'

'And if I had my way,' she said, 'the kid, whoever he was, who killed my father would hang. I still wish I could meet him, to tell him what a wonderful life was destroyed that day. It's a human reaction, I suppose. But as everyone has always told me, life must go on.'

'Most people realise that,' Harry said. 'I suppose that's why Ashley and I find it so difficult to believe that Luke would have killed himself for no good reason.'

She gave him a searching look. 'So he's been sharing his pet theory with you?'

'I understand you're not convinced.'

She shook her head. 'Ashley's getting carried away. He does that. Every so often, he gets a wild idea into his head and nothing can shift it. Like marrying me, for instance.'

'He once told me it was the best thing he ever did in his life.'

'He's kinder than I deserve. No-one could accuse him of marrying me just for my money. The last ten years can't have been a picnic. I'm not easy to live with, Harry. I've spent more hours in therapy than you've had hot dinners, but still I have days when I find life is simply – too much. Perhaps I had that in common with Luke.'

'How close were you to Luke?'

'We knew each other for years, yet we never talked intimately. But I always sensed that somehow he was – dissatisfied with life. He was lonely. Which is why he liked to spend so much time with us. Ashley wasn't a blood relative, but he was the closest to family that Luke had.'

'So you're not surprised by the idea that Luke might have committed suicide?'

'I could understand it. He was in his fifties, a widower.' She sighed. 'When I told myself that life must go on, I was barely twenty-one, still with everything to look forward to. Very different. Besides, in a strange kind of way, perhaps something good did come out of my father's death. Daddy took the view that no young man would ever be good enough for his only daughter. Ashley is a dear, but he would never have been Daddy's cup of tea. He's never been a go-getter, never will be. But as soon as I phoned him with the news that Daddy had been killed, he rushed back from France. He'd been out there back-packing. We've been together ever since. Whenever I think I'm going to scream if I hear one more word about clues and red herrings, I remember that. He was a tower of strength when I needed one.' She mustered a smile. 'So perhaps we won't go ahead with the exchange of murders plan, after all.'

Harry looked across to Ashley. He was sealing up a parcel which contained an ancient and dust-jacketed copy of *The Unpleasantness at the Bellona Club*. Its cost to the purchaser was fifty times that of an immaculate modern reprint, but collectors prized scarcity over substance. Harry shook his head. Not all the mysteries of crime fiction were to be found between book covers.

When her husband had bidden farewell to the collector and ambled over to join them, Melissa said, 'Harry knows Juliet May.'

'I understand she is a regular here,' Harry said.

'One of my best customers. She loves mysteries, buys them by the carload. As a matter of fact, she often calls in around this time on a Saturday.'

'Matthew Cullinan introduced them,' Melissa said. 'Harry dined at Matthew's last night.'

Ashley's eyebrows rose. 'Rubbing shoulders with the aristocracy, eh?'

'After sampling Inge's cooking at the Piquet Club, I felt the invitation was an offer I simply couldn't refuse. Though I should have gone easier on the champagne. My head's still buzzing.'

Melissa slipped off the table. 'I must go. Keys please, darling.' As she held out her hand, she said to Harry, 'My car's in dock until Monday. I only popped in to borrow the Lexus. And see what happens? I end up kicking my heels for half an hour whilst he prattles on about Dorothy L. But I enjoyed our chat. See you.'

Ashley blew a kiss at her departing back. 'Can't be easy, being married to a crime book-seller. Did I tell you I'd picked up a collection of first editions by Freeman Wills Crofts? He's one of my all-time favourites. Not exactly Tolstoy, but it's still sad that his work is so neglected today. Anyway, tell me about your dinner. Did you happen to touch on – the matters we spoke about the other day?'

'Matthew and I did have a word about the Trust.' Harry paused. He was conscious that he acted for the Trust and for Roy Milburn as an individual, as well as for Ashley. His instinct was always to interpret freely the professional rules on conflicts of interests if it seemed right to do so. Nevertheless, he would have to tread carefully. 'Matthew did mention that he was concerned about the state of the Trust's finances. He'd even raised the matter with Luke.'

'What exactly was the problem?'

'Well...'

'Sorry, I'm being too inquisitive. But it's not just idle curiosity on my part. If there is anything connected with Luke's death that needs to be exposed, I hope you will be prepared to... Hello! Were your ears burning a few minutes ago?'

Ashley's last remark was addressed to Juliet May, who had appeared in the doorway laden with bags. But Saturday shopping did not seem to have ruffled her; evidently her head for champagne was better than Harry's.

'Hi, you two. Harry – we must stop meeting like this. And why should my ears have been burning, Ashley?'

'I gather you both dined with Matthew and Inge last night.'

'A thoroughly enjoyable evening.' She gave Harry a cheeky grin. 'Don't you agree?'

He felt himself blushing. 'It's good to see you again.'

'You too. Ashley, have you had any luck with the Fredric Brown?'

'It's in the back room. The shipment from the States arrived yesterday and I haven't finished unpacking it all yet. Hang on a couple of ticks and I'll dig the book out.'

As he disappeared from sight, Juliet said, 'Small world, don't you think?'

Harry cleared his throat. 'I have a confession to make.'

She raised her eyebrows. 'Sounds interesting.'

'I remembered you saying that you often called in here around the middle of Saturday. I've been killing time with Ashley and Melissa in the hope that you'd turn up.'

'I'm flattered.'

'You see – I've been meaning to watch a rerun of *Vertigo* at the Philharmonic Picture Palace tonight. You mentioned last night that, with your husband being away, you were at a loose end at present, so I wondered...'

She clapped her hands in delight. 'How kind!'

'Of course,' he said hastily, 'I realise you probably won't be interested at all. And I wouldn't want you to get the wrong idea. If you don't...'

'I promise,' she said in a solemn tone, 'I haven't got the wrong idea. And I am interested. I love that film. Thank you.'

Ashley returned, carrying a book in a protective plastic wrapper. 'Here you are,' he said to Juliet. 'A first edition of *The Screaming Mimi*. Shall I put it on your account?'

'Please.' She turned to Harry and said, 'Lovely to bump into you again.'

'And you.'

After she had gone, Ashley said, 'Lovely woman.'

'Yes.' Harry had an uncomfortable sense that his face and mind were too easy to read. In his haste to change the subject, he found himself offering to buy rather more books than he had space for in his flat or time to read. All the same, it had been a worthwhile visit.

***

Less than two hours later, he and Stephanie were together in his MG, taking the turn from the A55 that led to the centre of Colwyn Bay. It had begun to drizzle, reminding Harry of a wet holiday spent here with his parents when he was six or seven. He could remember sitting in his dad's old Austin 1100, parked on the promenade, waiting for the next train to emerge from the tunnel in the cliff at the edge of the bay, since the old man had promised him an ice cream then if he hadn't made a nuisance of himself in the meantime. The Costa del Sol it wasn't, but he cherished the memories, all the same.

On the way over here, he had been regaling Stephanie with tales of the unexpected from the life of a Liverpool lawyer. She was a good listener and his story about a matrimonial dispute over custody of the single set of false teeth possessed by a couple from Huyton had kept her entertained all the way from Connah's Quay. 'Back to business,' he said as they stopped at traffic lights. 'Where do we go from here?'

'Vera told Charles's next-door neighbour that she used to live in a mansion just up the road from the Welsh Mountain Zoo. Look, there's a sign to it.'

They climbed the hill that overlooked the resort and the bay and soon found a group of large houses which might, allowing for a little poetic licence, have fitted the account that Vera had given of her time here. Stephanie started knocking on doors, with Harry at her side, spinning a yarn about a long-lost aunt whom they were looking up on the off-chance. It had enough of a ring of truth to prevent the doors being slammed in their faces.

'You lie admirably,' he said after they had drawn a blank for the third or fourth time.

'I'll take that as a compliment,' she said. 'Put it down to a vacation job I had before I went to uni. I worked in telesales.'

'Ever considered employment in a legal aid office? Anyway, one thing is beginning to bother me. Suppose Vera lied too? She may simply have come here once on holiday.'

She shrugged her shoulders. 'That's the life of a private detective. Come on, let's try this place before we start down the mean streets of Mochdre.'

This time they struck lucky. Their call was answered by a sweet little grey-haired lady who proved to have both time on her hands and an axe to grind. Harry was impressed by the way in which

Stephanie sensed at once the need to demonise the missing aunt and adjust her story accordingly. Her talent for telling a tall story would have been envied by any of his criminal clients.

Within a few minutes they were ensconced in Amy Lewis's sitting-room, taking tea and listening to the story of how, almost five years earlier, her path had crossed with that of Vera Blackhurst.

'I used to play bridge with a man called Ieuwan Croft, see? He and his wife Blodwen had retired to that huge place you may have seen on the other side of the road. Tara, they called it.'

Stephanie and Harry nodded. It was a miniature Versailles with a spectacular outlook; they had seen a Bentley and a sports car parked outside. Ieuwan Croft, they were told, had run one of the largest haulage firms in Wales until a mild stroke had prompted his retirement. He and his wife had become friendly with Amy Lewis and her husband and when Mrs Croft had died, Ieuwan had needed to advertise for a housekeeper.

'And guess who answered?' Amy Lewis demanded.

'Not Auntie Vera?' Stephanie cried, clapping a hand to her mouth. 'My dear old mum always used to say that

she would come to a bad end! She'd never have guessed

that Auntie would have wound up keeping house for a millionaire.'

'And not just keeping house either, if you ask me,' Amy Lewis said darkly. Her own husband had died a matter of days before Mrs Croft, and Harry deduced that she had fancied herself as a suitable second wife for the wealthy Ieuwan. But Vera had been more than a match for her.

'A brassy tart, if you ask me,' Amy Lewis said. 'Sorry, dear, I know she's your auntie, but I have to speak as I find.'

'No, no,' Stephanie said. 'My mum used to say exactly the same. Those very words, even. She had no time for Auntie Vera, that's why I never tried to look her up whilst Mum was alive.' She gave their hostess a trusting smile. 'You know, it's funny, you remind me a lot of dear old mum. Something about the eyes.'

'That's sweet of you, dear. Another fairy cake? Well, where was I? Oh yes, within a matter of weeks Ieuwan had given up playing bridge and was spending all his time out on the seafront, sitting arm in arm with her ladyship. I knew her game, all right. But there was nothing I could do.'

Six months after Vera's arrival in his life, Ieuwan Croft suffered another stroke and died. Natural causes, nothing suspicious about it, Amy Lewis grudgingly admitted. 'And no prizes for guessing who he left most of his money to?'

'Surely not Auntie Vera?' Stephanie cried. She was living the part. Harry was in serious danger of collapsing into hysterics. 'No wonder she never got in touch again!'

'Was there no other family?' he asked, trying to suppress his amusement.

'No children, but plenty of cousins, nephews and nieces who had no liking for that Vera Blackhurst. Ieuwan had made the will only a couple of months before he died. They tried to challenge it, but their solicitors advised them their case wasn't strong enough to take to court.'

In the end, a deal had been done. Vera had not hung out for every last penny; indeed, she had offered a compromise which seemed so generous that the family had bitten her hand off. But she'd still walked away with a small fortune.

Amy Lewis's little blue eyes gleamed with bitterness. 'Not a bad investment for six months of her life, I'd say.'

Harry nodded. He was trying hard to contain his good humour. He could not wait until he got the chance to tell Geoffrey Willatt all about his lady love's profitable past.

Chapter 14

Vertigo was a film in which he found something new each time he saw it. It often troubled him that he was so fascinated by a film about infatuation with a dead woman: it was dangerous to see parallels between life and art. Liz, like Hitchcock's Madeleine, was dead and beyond recall. He would never forget his wife or the passion he had for her, but he knew that she belonged to the past. Melissa Whitaker was right: life must go on. And yet, he realised, as he parked near the Philharmonic Picture Palace, he had failed to find anyone who had begun to make him feel the way he had about Liz. There had been a brief affair with an older woman who lived at the Empire Dock, a local barrister and then the uncertainties of his relationship with Kim. He cared for Kim, cared for her a good deal, but it was not the same. Perhaps he'd needed to spend time with a woman quite different from his dead wife. But the truth, he was beginning to recognise, was that caring a good deal was not enough. He needed to experience again the hot desire he had only ever known with one woman. If it was possible to experience it again.

So why had he fixed up a date with a married woman? It didn't make sense. Adultery had wrecked his own marriage and he told himself that he had no intention of wrecking anyone else's. He had seen too many clients make that mistake. Besides, Casper May was not a man to cross. So he must behave himself and make the most of her company while he had it. Talk about murder mysteries past and present. And perhaps try to guess the answer to the trickiest riddle of all: what was a woman like Juliet doing married to Casper May?

He could see her waiting for him on the steps that led to the cinema. Her auburn hair was in a shaggy perm that spilled on to the shoulders of her black jacket. She was leaning back against the wall with her arms folded and smiling as if she owned the place. At once he cast all other thoughts aside and remembered his reason for inviting her out tonight. She made him feel good: it was as simple as that.

'Am I late?' he asked guiltily.

'No. I'm early. I've been looking forward to this, even though I've seen the film once before. How about you?'

'I must have watched it half a dozen times. It fascinates me.'

She looked at him intently. 'I have the impression you don't do things by halves.'

'Jim reckons that's one of my weaknesses.'

'He's wrong. If you care about something, you should give it all you've got. No holding back.'

With a grin, he took her arm and led her inside. The Picture Palace had been open only a couple of years, but the owner had faithfully recreated the ambience of an old-time cinema, with faded plush seats and even an organ that rose from beneath the floor to play a few tunes before giving way to the dark rhythms of Bernard Herrmann once the main show began. He always found the film engrossing, could not help becoming absorbed in James Stewart's obsession with the mysterious blonde. But tonight for once he found his attention wandering. When at last he succumbed to temptation and moved his leg experimentally against hers, he was rewarded by an answering pressure. Later, she leaned her head on his shoulder and when, an hour into the picture, he dared to stretch an arm around her shoulder, she did not try to edge away. He felt her permed curls brush lightly against his cheek and closed his eyes, inhaling her perfume, wondering what it would be like to take her home for the night.

It was over too soon and as they emerged into the chilly night air she smiled at him and said, 'Thank you. I enjoyed that.'

'Can I offer you a drink?'

She shook her head. 'Thanks, but I ought to be getting back.'

'Surely you have time for...'

'No, I'd love to. But it wouldn't be a good idea. I need to be up early tomorrow morning. I have to drive to Manchester Airport to meet my husband.'

The brush-off? He scanned her face, desperate to find a clue to her thoughts. 'Perhaps some other time?'

'I do hope so, Harry.' She bent towards him and kissed him chastely on the cheek. 'Thank you so much for asking me to come with you. I've had a lovely evening. And I do hope we'll see each other again before too long.'

'I'm bound to need your help with my first press release.'

'If you do, give me a call.' She thought for a moment. 'But even if you don't, perhaps you'll give me a call anyway?'

And then she was gone. He watched her thread through the crowd, raising an arm to hail a passing taxi. Not until the taxi had disappeared did he move. By then he knew that he needed to see her again. Like a junkie craves the needle, he already yearned for another fix of her company.

When Kim rang him the next morning, he could tell straight away that she had made her decision. The careful tone of her suggestion that he come round for a meal that evening told him that the news was bad.

'I thought – we could talk,' she said.

'Sure.'

'Would seven o'clock suit you?'

'I'll be there.'

He put the receiver down wishing that he could share the win-a-few-lose-a-few outlook of a man like Roy Milburn. At least he'd been given a little time to become accustomed to the idea of her departure for London. And at least he'd met Juliet May.

But Juliet's out of bounds, he told himself. *Stop thinking of her.*

The phone rang again. Stephanie, this time. She sounded exasperated. 'You'll never guess. Jonah discharged himself from hospital last night. He refused to stay there a moment longer, the cussed old thing. I said he ought to listen to the doctors, that it would serve him right if he dropped down dead the moment he got home, but he wouldn't be told. I'm over at his flat now. Of course, as soon as he arrived back here, he found out he was still very weak. He's spending his time watching telly and complaining about the programmes.'

'So you won't be free this afternoon?'

Driving back from North Wales, they had agreed to follow up another lead that Stephanie had picked up from Charles Kavanaugh's neighbours. Vera had mentioned that she came originally from Warrington and the plan was to try to check out her past and see how far it varied from the story she had been telling.

'Not a bit of it. Jonah's insisting we pursue the inquiry. I think he's afraid of me using his illness as an excuse for slacking off. Can you pick me up here in half an hour?'

On his way through a downpour to Jonah's flat, Harry reflected that perhaps he had more in common with the old battleaxe than he would like to think. Since the death of their wives, they had both tried to lose themselves in their work, in solving other people's puzzles. It wasn't simply a way of killing time: it made it easier to forget the past.

The last time Harry had visited the flat, it had been as chaotically disordered as his own, with dishes piled high on the draining board and a layer of dust on every surface. It was a single man's home, somewhere to doss down for a chap who contended that life was too short for housework. But things had changed. As Stephanie showed him in to the living-room, he almost had to shield his eyes from the shine on the brasses adorning the opposite wall. It was as if they were expecting to host a photo-shoot for *Ideal Home*.

Only Jonah made the place look untidy. He was hunched up in an armchair, wearing a mutinous scowl and a cardigan that looked as though it dated back to the days of clothes rationing. He looked up from the *Radio Times* and said, 'Load of bloody rubbish. That licence fee is daylight robbery.'

'Do I gather you're on the mend?'

Jonah grunted and jerked a thumb in his niece's direction. 'To hear some people talk, you'd think I was at death's bloody door.'

'If you don't keep your promise to the doctor about no more roll-your-own cigarettes, you'll be slamming the door behind you,' Stephanie said.

'The sooner I get back to normal, the better.' Jonah indicated their surroundings with a melancholic wave. 'She's even tried to do a bit of tidying. Didn't ask first, of course. I used to know where everything was. Now I can't find a bloody thing.'

Harry grinned. 'Better be careful. If you don't keep your eyes open, she'll be making you redundant.'

Jonah snorted. 'Oh aye, I've heard all about yesterday. The two of you got a lucky break, fair enough. But believe me, the case is only over when the money from the client is safely in the bank.'

Stephanie raised her eyebrows to the heavens and said, 'We'd better go, Harry, before the temptation to strangle him overwhelms me. Lucky break? Huh!'

'So what do we know about Vera's connection with Cheshire?' Harry asked as they drove along the M62.

'She actually mentioned growing up in a black-and-white manor house just outside the town. She became all nostalgic and complained about the government taking part of the family estate when a viaduct was being built for the motorway. I know the area quite well.' She coloured. 'As a matter of fact, I used to go out with a boy from Stockton Heath. I spent quite a bit of time there before he ditched me, the bastard. One thing I'm sure of. There's only one motorway viaduct, on the M6 at Thelwall. That should make life easier for us.'

The rain had stopped and the grey-blue sky had begun to brighten. As he glanced to his right, Harry saw the huge chimneys of the power station at Fiddler's Ferry glinting in the sunlight. He told himself that it didn't take long for things to take a turn for the better. There was nothing to be gained by agonising over Kim. Stephanie was no Juliet May; she was little more than a kid. But even if Colwyn Bay and Warrington were hardly Miami Beach, he was keen to make the most of his chance to play the detective. Besides, she was good company.

'So you always had your heart set on working with Jonah?' he asked.

'Why not? There are plenty of worse fates. A girl on my course at uni started working part-time as a stripper to pay off her student loan. Another took a job as a guide at some tea-towel museum down on the south coast.' She grinned. 'I remind myself of them whenever I get fed up with studying for my NVQ.'

Harry was puzzled. 'NVQ?'

'National Vocational Qualification.'

'Yeah, I know, but what in?'

She sighed at his ignorance. 'Private investigation, of course. It's a recognised subject. Gone legit, you might say. There are thousands of us now, you know. Even though we're not overseen by any statutory body.'

'Don't be in a hurry to invent one. You might end up with something like the Law Society.'

'There are too many cowboys in this job,' she said seriously. 'It damages the reputation of all of us. This is the consumer age. We need to offer proper client care.'

'Don't tell Jonah or he'll have a relapse,' Harry said.

She laughed. For all her earnestness, she didn't lack a sense of humour. It was one of the things he liked about her. The ex-boyfriend had been a fool as well as a bastard. 'So what's the appeal of detective work to you?'

'Put it down to insatiable curiosity. I've always liked puzzles and mystery stories. Trouble is, the mysteries keep spilling over into real life – and I can't resist getting involved.' He hesitated. 'I've even started wondering if I might have a clue about the identity of the Scissorman.'

Stephanie's eyes widened. 'Tell me more.'

He explained the theory that Davey might be the Scissorman which had remained obstinately at the back of his mind. 'For what it's worth, he did turn up in town just before the Scissorman killed a Liverpool girl for the first time.'

'It's not much to go on.'

'I realise. And of course, he might be entirely innocent.'

'So what are you going to do?' she demanded.

'I don't know,' he said helplessly. 'I just don't know.'

'That must be it,' he said after they had parked on the road which ran under the Thelwall Viaduct. Between their lay-by and the hump-backed bridge which carried the road over a canal was a gatepost marked *Massey Brook Manor*. A curving drive led up to a splendid black-and-white building of the type often found in Cheshire. At one time it must have been one of the finest homes in the area. The only problem was that now it commanded a spectacular view of eight lanes of motorway traffic. Harry wound down the car window, which was beginning to mist up, but the roar from the viaduct almost deafened him.

She pointed to a sign which informed them that the place was a residential home for the elderly. 'I suppose it's lovely if you're hard of hearing. You know what? It wouldn't surprise me if Vera did live here once. But I can't see it as her ancestral home. Maybe she was a live-in care assistant, something like that. Shall I tell them about my dear old uncle who thought the sun shone out of her? Yes, I think I'll invent an older brother for Jonah: someone as trusting as he is cynical.'

Her guess about Vera's past proved to have been inspired, but the voluble deputy matron who talked to them evidently found it hard to swallow a story which elevated Vera to near-sainthood. It turned out that she had left them in the lurch nearly ten years earlier and the deputy matron had yet to forgive her.

'Oh aye, she was local. Grew up in Statham, I gather, but she always liked to give herself airs and graces. She'd worked in several other homes before she landed up here. She certainly took in Mr Edghill, the chap who used to own the Manor. I always said that men were fools about Vera. They could never see through her, though any woman could.'

Harry nodded. He was thinking about Geoffrey Willatt. 'How did she get on with the residents?'

The deputy matron frowned. 'With the blokes, too well, if you want my honest opinion. She toadied to them. I didn't care for it at all. Of course, I was quite new here myself, I couldn't do anything about it. But she was constantly trying to wheedle things out of them. They never cottoned on, of course. They were just flattered. Heaven knows what they saw in someone so brassy.'

'Why did she leave?' Stephanie asked. 'Was there a row?'

'Oh no, Mr Edghill pleaded with her to stay. Quite ridiculous, we were well rid of her, if you ask me. But she found a comfier billet for herself, it was as simple as that. She'd worked out that there was more money to be made from looking after lonely old men on their own. One night she went out to a pub and met a retired farmer who didn't have any family to inherit his business.' The woman shook her head at the naïvety of the male sex. 'He didn't stand a chance. And less than twelve months later he was dead.'

'So Vera Blackhurst turns out to be a serial beneficiary,' Stephanie reported to Jonah when they were back in Liverpool.

'How did the farmer kick the bucket?' Jonah demanded. 'Another convenient stroke?'

'You're wasting your time if you want to pin a murder on her. I'm sure that isn't her style. No, this fellow went into hospital for a gall bladder operation and had a heart attack from which he never recovered. Vera made a good show of being mortified, but she had half his fortune to cheer her up. The other half went to charity. Same story: he'd changed his will shortly before his demise. This is one very persuasive lady.'

'Vera isn't the only one,' Harry told Jonah. 'Your niece is a born detective. The way she coaxed the story out of the woman had me lost in admiration.'

Stephanie blushed. 'We aim to please.'

'You never told me that before, Jonah,' Harry said with a grin.

The old man grunted. 'You realise she's put a lot of time into this job? It'll cost, y'know.'

As Stephanie showed him out half an hour later, Harry whispered, 'How is he, really?'

A cloud passed across her face. 'He still can't adjust to the fact that he's not a well man. That's what worries me. But I do think he's on the mend. He's starting to fuss about money again and that must be a good sign. Except for our clients.'

'Don't worry about the trustees. I'll make sure they cough up.'

'You're sure they can still afford my services, despite their financial problems?'

'You're not seriously worried about that, are you?'

'Jonah didn't want me to tell you this, but he did get me to make one or two discreet enquiries about the Trust to make sure they were good for the money. I know a chap who is involved with the Charity Commission and he suggested that the Trust's finances were causing his people a bit of concern.'

'I didn't know they had wind of any problem.'

'Don't underestimate them. They may not move like greased lightning, but they're no fools. They are starting to sniff around. Not so long ago, the Trust had money to burn. Now it's on its uppers. Where has the money gone?'

'They are a philanthropic organisation,' Harry said. 'They dole out money right, left and centre to people in the arts world who apply for it. That's the reason Gervase set the Trust up in the first place. A spot of carelessness here, one or two iffy investments there – and before you know where you are, you're strapped for cash.'

'Maybe. But from what I hear, I don't think it accounts for anything like the whole of the problem. And I guess you think much the same. Which makes me wonder – why did Luke Dessaur let things slide?'

'You're not suggesting he was on the take? I simply can't believe that.'

'He killed himself, or so most people think,' Stephanie pointed out. 'Guilty conscience?'

'Listen, I haven't met many men I'd describe as honest through and through. Most men have their price. But Luke was an exception.'

'Okay, okay. But maybe his control wasn't as tight as it should have been.'

'Could be. But if you want the truth, I don't think it's a coincidence that the perennially poverty-stricken treasurer has been blowing the dust off his wallet lately.'

She raised her eyebrows. 'Well, well.'

An angry voice from the sitting-room demanded, 'What the bloody hell are you two whispering about?'

'You'd better go,' she said, 'before he accuses me of chatting you up. He seems to think I've only got to meet an unattached man to want to have my wicked way with him.'

'Keep in touch,' Harry said. And on the way back to Empire Dock, he couldn't help thinking that, an unattached man, it would be lucky if Stephanie did have her wicked way with him.

'I suppose you've guessed what I have to tell you,' Kim said that evening.

They were in her sitting-room, having a drink before dinner. She was looking as lovely as he had ever seen her, in a cream silk shirt and black trousers. Once or twice in the past he'd risked her wrath by saying that the baggy sweaters and crumpled corduroys she favoured didn't make the most of her slim figure. As soon as she'd opened the door to him, his heart had sunk. If she was staying in Liverpool, she wouldn't have made such an effort to please him.

'It's the right decision,' he said. 'For you.'

'Yes, it is. Though that doesn't mean it was easy to take.'

'Thanks for thinking twice.'

'I owed you that, at least.'

'You don't owe me anything. If you hadn't accepted MOJO's offer, you'd always have regretted it. One thing I'm sure of is that they need you as much as you need them. You'll make a difference.'

'I hope so.' She sighed. 'I'm excited about the challenge, of course I am. But I'll miss you.'

'You'll let me know how you get on?'

'I wouldn't dare not to. We must keep in touch.'

'Yes, we must,' he said. But he felt they were like two holiday-makers who had enjoyed a brief romance with the aid of sun and sand and Sangria. Once check-out time came, they would go their separate ways. It would be better not to see each other again. Memories were always more comfortable if they were not disturbed by fleeting, ill-at-ease reunions.

He raised his glass. 'To the future.'

'To the future, Harry.'

During the meal she let out a small exclamation and clapped her hand to the side of her head. 'I almost forgot.'

'Mmmm?' For once she had forsaken her vegetarian cookbook and Harry was relishing the Châteaubriand.

'Your friend, the Great Timothy. I remembered where I'd come across him before. It was after he killed his mother.'

'*What?*'

She laughed. 'Do I have your full attention now? Yes, he strangled his dear old mum.'

'Tim Aldred? You're pulling my leg.'

'Gospel truth. Mind you, there were extenuating circumstances.'

'Like what? Did she throw his conjuring set in the dustbin?'

'It was a mercy killing. And joking apart, it was a sad case, one of the saddest I can recall. I was only on the fringe of it, though. It all happened while I was an articled clerk. My principal acted for Tim Aldred. I simply did some of the leg work.'

'What happened?'

'As far as I can remember, he lived at home with the old lady. By then his wife had already run off with the kids. His mother suffered very badly from arthritis. The pain was agonising and the doctors could do nothing for her. Even the maximum dosage of morphine couldn't touch it. To cut a long story short, she begged him to kill her. For a time, he resisted, but in the end he granted her wish. He tried to make it look as though she'd committed suicide, but he wasn't as good at covering his tracks as he should have been. Perhaps his skills as an illusionist weren't so well-developed in those days. The police began to ask questions and although at first he denied having helped the old girl out of her misery, eventually he started contradicting himself. Before long, his story fell apart. So they charged him with murder.'

Harry swore. 'Was there any financial gain?'

'She owned a house and she'd put a few pounds away in the building society. He was an only child and everything was due to come to him anyway. No motive for murder on any sensible view of the case. The two of them were very close. His marriage had failed and as soon as he was charged he lost his job.'

'So he wasn't made redundant, as he claimed?'

'No. I remember feeling sorry for him at the time. He was turfed out by the company before the case ever came to trial. They seized on it as an excuse to avoid a hefty pay-out, I suppose. That was Tim's trouble. He was one of life's losers. I only met him the once, that's why I didn't recognise him straight away, even though the case made a great impression on me. By the time it came up at court, I'd qualified and joined another firm. I read about it in the papers, though. He wasn't even lucky in his judge. We thought he'd get a suspended sentence at worst, but he came up across old Womble. The bastard jailed him.'

Harry whistled. 'So he's served time?'

'Yes, though on appeal the sentence was cut and he got out fairly soon. I can understand why, with that experience, he concentrated on magic. The real world had let him down badly.' She looked at him. 'Is any of this important?'

'It's very interesting. Important? I dunno. Could be. Depends on whether Luke Dessaur found out about it – and, if so, on whether it bothered him at all.'

'You're not suggesting that the threat of removal from a board of trustees is a sufficient motive for murder?'

'Unlikely, I agree.' Harry paused. 'On the other hand, from what you say, Tim does have a track record. He's killed once before and tried to pass it off as suicide.'

'That was different,' Kim snapped. 'You and your bloody detective theories. You didn't see him all those years ago. I did – and I can tell you that I've seldom seen a man so penitent. There was only one reason why he strangled his mother. He did it out of love. It was a unique case. You can't imagine he would turn into some sort of serial killer. I must say, I'm starting to wish I'd never opened my mouth.'

For a moment neither of them spoke, then Harry said softly, 'Sorry. I was only thinking aloud. It's a bad habit. We shouldn't quarrel, not tonight of all nights. I'm sure you're right. Let's forget about it, shall we?'

She gave him a sheepish smile and nodded. Yet the mood of the evening had changed and he was almost glad when the telephone rang. Perhaps after she'd dealt with the interruption they could rescue something from the wreckage. Kiss and make up. She went out into the kitchen to take the call and whilst she was away he dipped into her music collection and put on something by Roberta Flack. If that didn't soften the atmosphere, nothing would.

But when she came back, he realised it was all in vain. She'd already put on her outside jacket and her face was ashen.

'Look, Harry, I'm really sorry about this, but something's come up. I have to go to the Bridewell. To see a real murderer, this time. The Scissorman has tried to kill another working girl. But they've arrested him.'

He bit his lip. 'It isn't by any chance Davey Damnation...'

She stared at him. 'How on earth do you know about Davey?'

'I started wondering the other day. I've always thought he was harmless, but he kept on about harlots and retribution. Maybe he's one of those who thinks he hears the voice of God, telling him to slay them.'

'You're not serious? You don't think Davey's the *Scissorman*?'

'Well, didn't you just say so?'

'No, I didn't. He's in hospital at the moment, recovering from the attack.'

'I don't understand.'

'Davey's been walking the streets of the red light district at night, haranguing pimps and prostitutes whenever he sees them.

163

He saw some vagrant with a pair of scissors in his hand approaching a working girl. Davey let out a yell and tried to pull the fellow off her. He was stabbed in the chest for his pains, but the girl got away and raised the alarm. A passing panda car picked the man up and he's in custody now.'

'And Davey?'

'In hospital. They reckon he'll make it, thank God.'

'And he'll be a bloody hero,' Harry said, feeling dazed. Perhaps he ought to leave the detecting to Jonah and Stephanie after all.

Chapter 15

If Harry needed any reminder that breaking up was hard to do, he received it back in the office the next morning. His first client of the day was a middle-aged, middle-income middle-manager whose solution to a mid-life crisis had been to embark on a torrid affair with his secretary. A dab hand at photography, he had taken dozens of snapshots of his girlfriend in a variety of unambiguous positions. When his wife had discovered them, she had determined to divorce him and take him for every penny that he had not squandered on flowers, perfume and chocolates for her younger rival.

'You know the mistake I made?' the man demanded.

Harry was tempted to say that he was spoiled for choice, but contented himself with a wary shake of the head.

'I left the pictures in the glovebox of my car. The one place my old lady was likely to look. If only I'd tucked them up inside the owner's manual. She'd never have opened that.'

It was true, Harry reflected, as he wrote down the depressing details. One of the things that divided the sexes was their respective attitudes towards motor vehicles. When he asked a woman client about the make of car her husband used, she tended to say it was a blue one or, if pressed, 'I think it may be a Ford.' Kim said that when she put the same question to a man, he would bore her to death with the detail and be able to recite the chassis number. Though he would often forget how many bank accounts he possessed.

When the meeting was over, he called Frances to tell her about his trips with Stephanie to uncover Vera Blackhurst's past history as a befriender of wealthy old men.

'My God! Should we report this to the police?'

'What is there to report? As far as I can see, she's committed no criminal offence whatsoever.'

'It sounds to me as if having Vera Blackhurst as your housekeeper can seriously damage your health.'

'There's no evidence that she played a part in the death of any of the old men who left money to her. She simply has a track record of going to work for widowers who were on their last legs. But there's nothing in the report from Jonah's niece to suggest that the wills were improperly executed. As with Charles Kavanaugh, she simply wormed her way into the affections of the men she worked for, then waited for nature to take its course.'

'It stinks.'

'Sure, but Vera's not the first person to behave that way, far from it. What's different is that she's made a career out of inheriting money. Some people might say good luck to her. For all we know, she makes the twilight months of her benefactors happier than they would otherwise have been. They were all lonely as well as rich.'

Frances sighed. 'So what do we do?'

'Stick to our original plan. We wanted to strike a deal. This information gives us the chance to do just that. Vera may be as innocent of crime as a new-born child, but I doubt whether she'd welcome notoriety. Besides, when Geoffrey Willatt finds out what's been going on, I guess he'll stop being starry-eyed about her. He'll advise her to settle out of court as soon as possible and then drop her like a hot brick.'

'And you think she'll take that advice?'

'It won't be the first time she's opted for taking a fast buck.'

'Fine. Will you go ahead and talk to Willatt, please? In the meantime, I'll tell the other trustees. Anyone I can't reach by phone I should see this evening. It's the first night of that musical the Trust has backed, *Promises, Promises*.'

'Any good?'

'I certainly hope so, given the amount of money we've pumped into it. Look, why don't you come along? I have a couple of spare complimentary tickets. Bring a friend.'

As soon as he put the phone down, Suzanne buzzed to say that Roy Milburn had rung and asked for a return call. Harry tried his number but found himself talking to an answering machine. He left a message and then phoned Kim. She sounded hoarse, weary and depressed after a night in the company of the police and the mentally disabled tramp who had been identified as the Scissorman.

'Sorry, I've not slept. And at four o'clock this morning, my client sacked me.'

'What happened?'

'He wouldn't take my advice. As far as I can tell, he has a good chance of pleading diminished responsibility, but right now he needs a psychiatrist as much as a lawyer.' She sighed. 'As least he's not my problem any more. Not that I would have been around to act for him even if he hadn't decided to conduct his own defence. I suppose in my heart I'm glad. He may be ill, but the murders were savage. My flesh crept as I sat next to him. It made me think I've made the right decision. I'm better suited to working in MOJO's head office than trying to defend people who scare the shit out of me.'

Harry couldn't help saying, 'You're a better lawyer than you'll ever be a bureaucrat.'

A short laugh. 'I suppose I ought to take that as a compliment.'

'It was meant that way.'

'One thing's for sure, at least this time there won't be a miscarriage of justice. He's as guilty as that creep Norman Morris was innocent.'

'To say nothing of Davey Damnation.'

'Yes, what on earth was all that about last night? Good job you kept your thoughts to yourself.'

Apart from telling Stephanie. God, she'll laugh when she hears the news. I'd better give her a wide berth for a while. 'How is he?'

'The last I heard, the tabloid press were forming a disorderly queue outside his hospital room, hoping to sign up the story of how he nailed the Scissorman. I can see the headlines already. "Dedicated evangelist risks life to trap crazed killer."' She yawned. 'Anyway, I just popped in to the office for half an hour to clear a few things. After I've finished, I think I'll go home to catch up on my sleep.'

'Will you be up in time to come to the theatre with me?'

He told her about the invitation to see the musical and to his surprise she said yes.

'I feel awful about leaving you like that last night.'

'We both know it comes with the job.'

'Even so. I'd love nothing better than a relaxing evening with not a religious fanatic in sight.' She paused. 'Besides, it may be our last chance for some time together for a while.'

'London's only at the end of the railway line from Lime Street,' he said. But he knew it might as well be on the other side of the world.

After he rang off Suzanne buzzed him to say that Roy Milburn had called back. 'He said not to worry, he'd decided he didn't need to speak to you after all. And another thing, he'd heard from Ms Silverwood about someone called Vera Blackhurst. He asked me to write down a message for you.'

'Which is?'

'"I'd love to be a fly on the wall when you speak to Vera's fancy man."'

Harry grinned and asked her to call Geoffrey Willatt. He was going to enjoy this conversation.

The Pool Theatre occupied a redbrick Victorian building down a narrow lane off Chapel Street. Once it had been a swimming baths; the conversion had saved it from the bulldozers which ploughed mercilessly through Liverpool in the sixties, reducing much of the city's history to rubble. Nowadays a number of local amateur dramatic groups put on productions here. The Waterfront Players were, according to the programme which Harry bought from a girl at the main door, a small group formed a couple of years ago. Tonight's show would be their biggest so far.

A narrow flight of steps led down from the entrance to the passageway with a tiny box office at the end. As Harry picked up the tickets, Kim joined him.

His lips brushed against her cheek. 'How are you?'

'Okay, thanks. I've spent most of the day trying to put the Scissorman out of my mind.' She shivered, but then moved her shoulders up and down in a visible effort to shake off the memory of her night's work. 'Thanks again for inviting me. I need something to take my mind off the evil that men do.'

'Let me lighten your day, then.'

He recounted his conversation with Geoffrey Willatt. It had been a joy. As with a play by Harold Pinter, the pauses had counted for as much as the words. He had particularly appreciated the long silence which followed his quoting the deputy matron's opinion that, for all her tartiness, Vera preyed on rich old men because she was greedy for money and not in the least interested in sex.

'So what did he say?'

'That he would take instructions. By that stage, his voice sounded as if there was a garrotte around his neck. And the rustle of the white flag being hauled up was almost audible.'

She laughed and took a look at their surroundings. Up above, a gallery with iron railings ran around the building at street level, a relic from the old swimming bath. 'I've never been here before, even though it's only a stone's throw from the flat. Always meant to come, but somehow or other I never quite made it.'

'Me too. The things we don't get round to doing.'

In one corner of the smoke-filled bar, Frances was deep in conversation with Tim Aldred. She was talking nineteen to the dozen; his expression was rapt. Harry wondered if, with Luke gone, the two of them might get together. Frances looked up and caught sight of him. As if reading his mind, she blushed before waving them to come over.

'I spy the Great Timothy,' Kim said.

'Magician and mercy killer. Shall we have a word?'

Frances greeted them warmly and insisted on buying drinks. 'To celebrate the news about Vera Blackhurst. Your detective has done a good job, Harry.' She lifted her glass. 'Here's to a prosperous future.'

'Cheers. I've spoken to Geoffrey. Somehow I don't expect Vera's asking price for a deal will be too high.

'It's marvellous. And we need that money so badly.'

'I gather you've talked to Roy. He left a message at my office this morning but we missed each other after that.'

'Yes, I called him as soon as I put the phone down after speaking to you. His last words were, "See you tonight", but he hasn't turned up yet.'

Tim grunted. 'He's hopeless.'

Frances smiled. 'You would do a much better job as treasurer, I'm sure of that. Now, if you'll excuse me for a few minutes, there are one or two people I ought to say hello to in my capacity as acting chair of the Trust, before the curtain rises. Talk to you later.'

As she moved away, Kim turned to Tim and said, 'I've remembered where we met before.'

He flushed. 'I didn't recognise you at Jericho Lane to begin with, but it began to dawn on me that your face was familiar. You were Manny Greenberg's articled clerk, weren't you?'

'It feels like a long time ago.'

'To me too. But you haven't changed all that much.'

'Thank you.'

An awkward silence hung over them like a shroud. Finally Harry said, 'Kim told me about your mother.'

Tim swallowed. 'Whatever you may think, whatever the court may have decided, I still believe I did the right thing. She wanted to die. She was in agony. She begged me to put her out of her misery.'

'I know,' Kim said and touched his hand. 'I couldn't believe the sentence.'

'I was treated like a common criminal. It was so unjust. The one mistake I made was trying to dress her death up as suicide. I should have come clean from the outset. Lack of guts on my part, I suppose.'

'I don't think you lacked guts,' she said.

'I feel ashamed of myself. I don't think it's logical. As I said, I have no regrets about helping her to do something she was incapable of doing herself. But prison leaves a mark.'

She nodded. 'It puts you on the outside, however much you regard yourself as a victim of injustice.'

'That's right. And it's why I never talk about it. I'm stigmatised. I dread the idea that people may discuss me behind my back, point a finger, say I murdered my mother, imply that I did it for personal gain.'

'Did Luke know?' Harry asked gently.

'Of course not,' Tim said. 'You know what a stickler he was. He would never have understood.'

'I'm not so sure.'

'I am. I had enormous respect for him, but he expected everyone else to live by the same standards as he did. If he'd known I'd done time, he would have wanted me off the board.'

'You shouldn't assume... Evening, Matthew. Hello, Inge.'

Matthew Cullinan and his girlfriend were arm in arm. He beamed at Harry. 'Grand to see you again. Frances rang to let me know about Vera Blackhust. Tremendous. I always knew that bloody woman was on the make. I expect now she'll make herself scarce.'

'She hasn't committed any crime,' Harry pointed out.

Matthew grunted. 'No smoke without fire, if you ask me.'

Inge Frontzeck patted his shoulder. 'Perhaps now you can relax, darling.' She gave them a rueful smile. 'You'll never believe how worried he has been about the Trust's financial difficulties.'

Matthew coloured. 'I must admit I've been bothered about the money side. Hopefully that's all now in the past. We should be able to negotiate a reasonable share from the Kavanaugh estate.'

'So now you can enjoy this evening without fretting about how much it has cost the Trust,' Inge said.

Frances smiled. 'I've only just noticed your ring, Inge. So you two have named the day at last?'

A huge diamond was sparkling on the third finger of Inge's left hand. She beamed and allowed everyone to inspect it. Matthew squeezed her hand and confessed that he had proposed that very afternoon.

'To my surprise and delight, she said yes.'

'He even got down on bended knee to pop the question,' Inge told them. 'After that, I didn't have the heart to refuse.'

'I'm a great believer in the old traditions,' her fiancé said.

'How marvellous!' Frances said. 'So we have a double cause for celebration.'

'We must have a toast,' Harry said. 'What would you all like to drink?'

Tim said, 'Don't you think we ought to take our seats? The show's due to start any minute.'

'You're quite right,' Matthew said. 'Everyone's moving through. We'll save the toast for later. Champagne on me, if the theatre bar runs to it.'

As they took up their seats at the far end of the second row, Kim whispered, 'Call me a bigoted old socialist, but that man Cullinan gives me the creeps.'

'You're a bigoted old socialist,' Harry said. 'Now be quiet and watch the show.'

He enjoyed the performance much more than he had expected. He'd never been a fan of musicals and occasional viewing of the works of Rodgers and Hammerstein or Andrew Lloyd Webber on the small screen had convinced him that the choice was usually between sentimentality or lush melodrama. A sixties sex comedy with a chorus line of seedy middle-aged businessmen clicking their fingers as they bemoaned the complexities of playing away from home was more to his taste.

'Like it?' Tim asked as they queued at the bar during the interval.

'Mmmm. "Where Can You Take a Girl?" was fun.'

'At least you and I aren't married men. We don't have to feel guilty if – we get involved with someone.'

'I don't know about you,' Harry said, trying to keep Juliet May out of his mind, 'but sometimes I wish I had cause for a troubled conscience where women are concerned.'

Tim gave a sceptical laugh and then said quietly, 'Can I speak to you – without prejudice, as you lawyers might say?'

'Go ahead.'

Tim fiddled with his tie and it dawned on Harry that the other man had made a special effort to look smart this evening. It helped that, for the first time in their acquaintance, he was wearing a suit that seemed the right size.

'You may have guessed this already...' Tim bit his lip. 'You see, the fact is, I've become very fond of Frances. I don't think she realises. Of course, while Luke was alive, she only had eyes for him. I'm not naïve, I knew that she'd never bother with me.'

He paused while Harry gave the barman his order. 'But what I wanted to say is – do you feel you have to tell her about my past?'

Harry stared. 'You mean, the business over your mother's death? Look, it's history. And the way Kim tells it, you were desperately unlucky. But whatever makes you believe Frances wouldn't take exactly the same view? She's a sensible woman, I'm sure if you tell her the full story, she'll understand. Talk to her. I don't think you'll regret it.'

If I had my time again perhaps I should come back as an agony columnist, he thought as he rejoined Kim. Soon he was absorbed again in Neil Simon's take on the battle of the sexes. The second half of the show entertained him as much as the first. The three-piece band was playing a score written for a thirty-five-strong orchestra, but they made up for lack of numbers with such verve that they managed to drown a couple of the songs. Towards the end, after the latest betrayal of her two-timing boss the heroine sang 'Whoever You Are, I Love You' before taking an overdose. As the lyric washed over him, Harry mused about the impulses that can lead a person to end it all. For the hundredth time, he wondered if it was possible that he and Ashley were mistaken and that Luke Dessaur had indeed killed himself. But what could be the reason, what motive was strong enough?

Just before, in time-honoured fashion, Fran and Chuck finally got it together, they performed the duet that everyone in the audience had grown up with. The one in which they agree that what you get when you fall in love is lies and pain and sorrow. So – for at least until tomorrow – they'd never fall in love again. *The story of my life*, Harry thought as the curtain fell for the last time to continuing applause.

'Great fun, wasn't it?' Frances asked as they made their way out of the auditorium. 'You two don't have to rush off home, do you? Come and meet the cast and the backroom team.'

'They did well,' Harry said. 'Tell you the truth, I didn't expect to enjoy it so much.'

'I'm glad,' she said. 'It's such a relief when you think of the money we've invested in it. Far more than I thought wise, frankly.'

Tim nodded. 'If only Luke had been here today, he could have seen that his faith was vindicated. I must admit that I had my doubts. Musicals are so expensive, even when they are produced on a shoestring and the run is only from Tuesday to Saturday. They must be one of the highest-risk investments of all.'

'Why was he so keen?'

'Oh, he insisted that it was precisely the sort of imaginative venture that Gervase Kavanaugh established the Trust to support all those years ago.'

'That's right,' Frances said. 'The producer persuaded him that the show broke the mould of Broadway musicals, but once its run came to an end it disappeared from sight. The Waterfront Players were strapped for cash and he was keen to back their enterprise. Even though his taste in music was more Bach and Verdi than Bacharach and David.' Suddenly she caught sight of someone and raised her voice. 'Bruce! I've been looking round for you. Congratulations! A terrific production.'

Bruce was a tall, slender man in a leather jacket and denim jeans who had just been smooching with the leading lady. His face was flushed with champagne and excitement. Harry recognised him from somewhere, and not just because of a passing resemblance to the young John Travolta, but for the moment could not place him.

'I must admit I'm ecstatic,' Bruce drawled, extricating himself from the clutches of the girl who had played Fran Kubelik and coming over to join them. 'Thanks from the bottom of my heart. If it wasn't for the Kavanaugh Trust, we'd never have been able to make it this far.'

'Oh, I'm sure you would have managed somehow.'

'Believe me, it's true. In terms of conventional box office appeal, *Promises, Promises* isn't exactly *My Fair Lady* or *The Phantom of the Opera*.'

'I thought it was more fun than both of them put together.'

'Me too. Maybe it's because I come from New York City and I just adore Neil Simon's one-liners. But whichever way you look at it, we owe the Trust a lot.'

'It was Luke's baby. He drove it through, he was the one to thank.'

A shadow passed across Bruce's face. 'Yes – yes, of course.'

'By the way, you know Tim, of course, but have you met Harry Devlin? He's the Trust's solicitor and this is his friend Kim Lawrence. Meet Bruce Carpenter – he's the man who made the whole thing happen. The producer of the show.'

They said hello and then Harry asked casually, 'I thought I recognised you and now I've remembered. Didn't I see you at Luke's funeral?'

'Yeah, I was there.' Bruce's smile faded. 'Well, it was the very least I could do – in the circumstances. Anyway, it's been great to meet you. And now – I really must circulate.'

As he disappeared, Frances said, 'A very charming young man. Rather too young and handsome for an old maid like me, but a good talker, that's for sure. He could get most people eating out of his hand, I suspect.'

'Is he a full-time producer?'

'Heavens, no. The Waterfront Players are amateurs. They all need a day job to survive. At the dress rehearsal Bruce told me that he works as a barman. He'd love a career in showbiz, but he needs to keep body and soul together whilst he hopes for a break. Maybe tonight is just what he needs. Everyone seems to have loved the production.'

She sighed and surveyed the crowded room. A champagne cork exploded and Matthew beckoned them over.

'Come and have a drink with us to celebrate!'

He broke off to kiss his bride-to-be and people cheered. The place was thick with smoke and everyone seemed to be talking at the same time. A press photographer approached the happy couple, but Matthew feigned shielding his face and pointed at Bruce Carpenter, who had rejoined a group of cast members.

'Please, those are the people you should be taking pictures of. They've worked very hard to make tonight such a success.'

Bruce shook his head graciously and said, 'Like I just said to Frances, we owe it all to you and your friends from the Trust.'

A flashbulb popped anyway, to Matthew's evident embarrassment. Frances turned to Harry and said, 'Just one thing bothers me.'

'What's that?'

'Why isn't Roy here?'

Harry spread his arms. There were other things that were bothering him. For example, he had just remembered that he had seen Bruce Carpenter on another occasion after Luke's funeral, polishing glasses behind the bar at the Hawthorne Hotel.

Chapter 16

Dale Street didn't seem the same without Davey Damnation's wild eyes and pointing finger. As Harry left the magistrates' court at half eleven the morning after the show, he turned his collar up against the rain and thought about the pavement prophet. The newspapers were full of his story. Davey was the hero who had single-handedly ended a reign of terror that had defeated the police forces of four counties. It was only a question of time before he became a card-carrying darling of the media, a lovable eccentric, perhaps a rent-a-quote pundit on ecclesiastical affairs. And what was wrong with that? At least he'd helped to make sure that the Scissorman would not strike again. Whereas Luke Dessaur's murderer – if there was one – was still at large. It was time to have another word with Ashley Whitaker. Harry was convinced Ashley knew more than he had yet been prepared to admit and thought he might now be able to guess what it might be.

The Speckled Band was quiet, as usual. Ashley was sitting behind his desk at the back, leafing through an old Inspector French mystery. He waved as Harry walked in.

'Skiving off work? Don't worry, my lips are sealed.'

'I've just come from court. My client is an amateur footballer, a very good player. He scored a hat-trick in a vital match and now he's in trouble with the law because of it.'

Ashley tutted. 'What went wrong?'

'He was videotaped scoring the winner. The film was taken by inquiry agents acting for a local authority. Twelve months ago, he sued for crippling injuries he said he'd suffered after stumbling into an uncovered manhole. Claimed he was in constant pain and would never be able to play sport again. He was awarded two years' salary. A good result, I was delighted with it. Of course, he didn't tell me he was turning out for this pub team twice a week. Now he's been sent down for obtaining by deception.'

Ashley chortled. 'Never mind, the coffee's on and there are a few old pulp magazines on the shelf behind you, if you're interested. Good stuff by Joel Townsley Rogers and Jonathan Latimer. Have a browse and a shot of caffeine while you lick your wounds.'

'Thanks, but I really came to see you rather than the merchandise.'

'Sounds intriguing.'

'Specifically, I wanted a word about Luke's death and the Kavanaugh trustees.'

'Any more news? I saw a review in the morning paper of the musical Luke was so keen to back. Though there was probably more ink spilled over Matthew Cullinan's engagement than there was about the show.'

'He reckons he likes to hide his light under a bushel, but he's news, isn't he? Liverpudlian society isn't exactly swimming with blue blood. As for the other trustees, there's now a minor mystery about Roy Milburn.'

Ashley's face became inscrutable, but his tone remained light. 'Not got himself into another scrape, surely?'

'Dunno. It seems he's disappeared.'

'Hiding from his creditors, I expect. It wouldn't be the first time.'

Harry perched on a stool. 'He and I missed each other on the phone yesterday, but Frances Silverwood spoke to him. She wanted to let him know we've found out Vera Blackhurst's past. She has a track record of cashing in on the wills of wealthy old men. The odds are that we'll be able to strike a deal with her over the Kavanaugh money.'

'Luke would have been glad about that.'

'Yes, but it's by the by. Roy was supposed to be at the Pool Theatre last night, but he failed to turn up. And though I tried to ring him again this morning before I went to court, there was no answer.'

'I've known Roy for a long time,' Ashley said. 'He's a great character, but I wouldn't ever claim that reliability is one of his virtues. Ten to one, he's picked up a woman in a pub somewhere and persuaded her to take him home for the night. Going AWOL is nothing new for him. I wouldn't worry too much if I were you.'

'I'm not exactly worried. Curious, yes. The Kavanaugh Trust is surrounded by more than its fair share of mysteries.'

'Shall we have that coffee while we chat?' Ashley went to the front of the shop and put up the *Closed For Lunch* sign. 'Rather early, but I don't think I'm missing out on too many customers. Keep talking.'

'For example,' Harry said as Ashley fiddled with a filter machine in the back room. 'Why was Luke so keen to put a large chunk of the Trust's money into a little-known American musical at a time when funds were short?'

Ashley frowned. 'He did mention it to me. He had a good deal of faith in the Waterfront Players.'

'Did he ever mention the name of Bruce Carpenter to you?'

'I can't recall it. Why?'

'Carpenter is the producer of *Promises, Promises*. He accompanied Don Ragovoy to Luke's funeral. And he works at the Hawthorne Hotel.'

Ashley shrugged. 'I'm not surprised he attended the funeral. As for the Hawthorne – I don't see the connection.'

'Neither do I – yet. But perhaps there is one. I'd started thinking that Luke stayed at the Hawthorne because it was convenient for Roy's place just around the corner. But if he wanted to see Roy, why not have a quiet word with him after the meeting at the Piquet Club? If Luke wanted to see Carpenter, that might explain why he turned up at the hotel.'

Ashley blinked. 'To discuss what?'

'Maybe Roy misled Luke about the Trust's finances. If he put more money into the show than was wise, he may have wanted to pull the plug. He and Carpenter may have been the pair Julio overheard quarrelling – and Carpenter would have had a motive for murder. The man is crazy about the theatre. He might have flipped.'

'Ingenious,' Ashley admitted. 'But I'm not convinced. As I understand it, Carpenter owed – and still owes – an enormous debt of gratitude to Luke. I can't imagine them having a serious argument. Besides, if you're right, why would Luke book an overnight stay? Sorry, but it doesn't stack up. Anyway, the coffee's ready.'

After Ashley had poured, Harry said, 'All right, then, what's your theory? Let's assume Luke was murdered. Whodunit?'

Ashley started. 'I don't know.'

'Come on. You're a murder buff, you're as bad as me if not worse. You can't read a report in the papers about a mysterious crime without playing your own guessing game. You regard people who peek at the last page of a detective story long before they've finished reading as little better than savages. Your godfather is dead, you believe murdered. You must have ideas about a possible culprit.'

Ashley pursed his lips. 'I've never pointed the finger at anyone.'

'Would you agree that if Luke was murdered, the truth is likely to have some connection with the Kavanaugh Trust?'

'It seems an almost inevitable deduction,' Ashley said. 'He was retired and lived alone – not the sort of lifestyle where you make enemies. The Trust was his main interest in life.'

'If we leave aside Bruce Carpenter, then Luke's fellow trustees are the obvious suspects, given that one of them was deceiving him.'

'I can't disagree with what you say,' Ashley said hesitantly.

181

Harry finished his drink and put the cup down on the desk. 'Don't take this the wrong way, Ashley, but I've felt from the outset that there was something you were keeping from me.'

Ashley's features had become expressionless. 'What makes you say that?'

'I'm used to being lied to,' Harry said. 'I've had years of practice. It comes with the job. And it's occurred to me that Luke may have been more forthcoming about his worries with you than with me. He claimed that he hadn't and my original instinct was to believe him. But you were close, he trusted you. To you, he might just have been prepared to name the person he had in mind, perhaps even spell out what had happened. Talking to a solicitor, his instinct would have been to remain discreet, especially if he had little hard evidence. He wouldn't want to defame anyone. It wouldn't fit his sense of propriety.'

Ashley bit his lip. 'I suppose I owe you an apology. You've always been frank with me. Perhaps I should have been more careful to return the compliment.'

'So Luke did spill the beans?'

'You're no fool, Harry. He did use me – well, as a sounding board, I suppose. I did think about telling you, but it didn't seem fair to the person concerned. Several reasons for that. First, I might have been wrong about Luke having been murdered. I didn't think so, but I couldn't be sure. Next,

the things Luke mentioned to me might have had no link whatsoever with his death. I might have pointed you in entirely the wrong direction. And finally, just as Luke was unhappy about blackening someone's name without being able to prove a thing, so was I. It didn't seem right.'

'Might there have been a fourth reason?'

'Such as?'

'Perhaps a sense of loyalty to the person in question.'

Ashley flinched. 'What makes you say that?'

'Am I on the right track?'

'Maybe. But explain your reasoning.'

'The way I see it is this. As far as I know, you only know one of the trustees well. You and Roy Milburn go back years. I'd assume that if you were trying to protect anyone, it would be him.'

A long sigh. 'Of course, you're right. But it proves nothing, Harry, let me emphasise that. Just because Luke was unhappy about Roy, it doesn't necessarily follow that Roy killed him.'

'Why don't you tell me the story?'

Ashley shrugged. 'Now the cat's out of the bag, I might as well. Luke was bothered about a shortfall in the Trust's funds. A large sum of money had gone missing. Too much to be explained away as a downturn in investment income. He hadn't realised how serious things were when he promised to underwrite the musical. When he looked at the detailed figures, he was shocked. Theft was the only possible explanation. Roy fobbed him off with some lame excuse. Luke

knew Roy had been spending quite heavily and it didn't take much to put two and two together. When he spoke to me, he was thinking of asking a firm of outside accountants to undertake a special audit and find out how much money was involved. He wondered if he should give Roy a chance to make amends and repay whatever he'd taken before matters went any further.'

'And what was your view?'

'I thought it was a good idea. Roy is an old friend. I don't defend him – his behaviour can be appalling. But he's always been a survivor, managed to avoid really serious trouble. A fraud charge would be something different altogether. Call it foolish if you like, but I hated the idea that he might go to prison.'

'What did Luke say?'

'He said he would need to think it over. But yes, I thought he would at least speak to Roy. He didn't lack a heart. And Roy can charm the birds off the trees when he's in the mood. I hoped they could work something out between themselves. As long as Roy made amends promptly and resigned as treasurer, Luke might have been willing to leave it at that. He wouldn't have wanted the Trust to become involved in unseemly publicity if it could be avoided. At the same time, I'm sure he would have insisted on full restitution with the absolute minimum of delay.'

Harry said softly, 'And what did you think when you heard about Luke's death?'

Ashley's face darkened. 'Does it matter? I think I've answered the important question. You were right. Luke had cottoned on to Roy's defalcations.'

'I just wondered if you'd discussed with Roy your theory that Luke was murdered.'

Ashley fiddled with his cuff-links. 'You must understand, this is very difficult for me.'

'Because you suspect your old friend of having killed your godfather?'

The bookshop was silent as Ashley stared like a blind man at the packed shelves. Presently he cleared his throat and said, 'I'm sorry, Harry. I suppose I should have said something to you earlier.'

'Have you confronted Roy?'

A mute nod.

'And he confessed to you?'

'No!' Ashley said fiercely. 'He did not. He laughed at me, told me I'd always had a vivid imagination. Read too many detective stories for my own good. And then he brushed the whole thing aside and started talking about something else as if what I'd suggested was so absurd as not to deserve more than a moment's conversation.'

'But did he convince you he was innocent?'

'No,' Ashley said, bowing his head. 'Not at all.'

Harry scarcely noticed the rain as he walked back through town. Although the sky was dark, in his mind everything was becoming clear at last. The key to the puzzle must be the Kavanaugh Trust's financial plight. For all his eccentricities, Charles had been as generous a benefactor as his father and had covenanted a monthly lump sum right up until his death. Matthew Cullinan was an experienced investment adviser, whose acumen should have helped to shore up the finances. The cost of subsidising a stage musical might have been heavy, but it should not in itself have bankrupted the Trust. However strong his wish to support the Waterfront Players, Luke would not consciously have authorised a grant that was more than he believed was affordable. As treasurer, Roy was in the best position to milk funds for his own benefits. He was notoriously short of money, but Harry recalled the Rolex and his extravagant mood that lunch-time at the Hawthorne.

Luke had presumably asked Roy to meet him at the Hawthorne and decided to stay there so as to kill two birds with one stone. He could talk to Bruce Carpenter about the musical and then ask Roy how he intended to repay the money he had stolen from the Trust.

But Roy would not have been willing or able to make good the deficit. Easy to imagine his blustering denial of guilt followed by panic when Luke made his disbelief clear. Luke would have been insistent. If Roy could not put matters right, there would be no alternative but to call in the police. For Roy, though, there had been one alternative. The death of Luke, in circumstances that could be passed off as accident or suicide.

As he walked down Fenwick Street, Harry glanced up and caught sight of the old furniture store. For a moment he toyed with the idea of calling there to see if Roy was there. On second thoughts, better not – at least until he had decided how to handle any confrontation. Perhaps it was lucky he had not cottoned on to the truth at the time of his visit to the studio. The railing that ran around the roof of the building was alarmingly low. Roy might have started to make a habit of pushing people to their death.

As he hurried through the main door of the office, still deep in thought, he was stopped in his tracks by the sight of Frances Silverwood in reception. She looked haggard and ill; her eyes were red and she was blowing her nose. A copy of the local morning paper was spread across her knees.

'What on earth brings you here?'

She looked up and half-rose from her chair. 'Thank God you're here. I called you half an hour ago, but I was told you and Jim were both out. Your girl said she didn't know when either of you would be back. Because it was so important, I decided I'd turn up on the off-chance.'

'What's this all about? Is it something to do with Roy Milburn?'

Frances raised her eyebrows. 'No, nothing at all. Hasn't he turned up yet?'

'Not as far as I know,' Harry said grimly. 'What, then?'

She lifted the newspaper and Harry saw that it was open at the page with the report of the opening night of *Promises, Promises*. There was a small picture of Bruce Carpenter together with his leading lady, a much bigger one of Matthew Cullinan toasting his bride-to-be. 'I take it you haven't heard?'

'Heard what?'

Frances swallowed. 'It's about Matthew.'

Harry stared. 'What's happened to him?'

'My information is that at this very moment, the honourable Matthew Cullinan is in India. He's been seconded there for the last twelve months by a cancer charity that he works for, to help with a project to develop a specialist cancer hospital in Madras.'

'Don't be silly. We were with him at the Pool Theatre only last night.'

She shook her head. 'I'm afraid we weren't. The person we have been dealing with is someone else altogether. He's an impostor. And now he has disappeared.'

Chapter 17

'How did you find out?' Harry asked five minutes later. They had settled in his room and Frances had spread over the desk a copy of the newspaper report which had led to the exposure of the false Matthew Cullinan.

'I had a call this morning,' Frances said. 'From a local journalist, a young man called Des Reeve. He'd read the piece in his own paper about Matthew and Inge announcing their engagement. He was contacting me as acting chair of the Kavanaugh Trust. He said he'd called Matthew – or rather, the person we thought of as Matthew – but as soon as he started to probe, the phone was slammed down. When he tried again, the receiver had been taken off the hook.'

'What did Reeve tell you?' Harry asked.

'Apparently he started his career with one of the tabloid papers in London. When he was working as sidekick for a gossip columnist, he came across Matthew Cullinan. He knew that Matthew had been abroad for a long time and also that the man in the photograph taken last night bore no resemblance to him. Needless to say, he sniffed an exclusive. He sounds young, enthusiastic. I suppose he regards it as his big break. He tracked down Inge's number and dropped lucky. He spoke to Matthew – sorry, I keep calling him that – and tested him out with a couple of questions. With instant success so far as he was concerned. Matthew panicked. When Reeve couldn't get through a second time, he decided to get in touch with me.'

'What did you say?'

'At first I didn't believe him. I insisted on ringing off and calling him back at his office to check that it wasn't some kind of hoax. Whilst I was off the line, he took a message from someone else who had read the press report and reckoned the man in the photograph, far from being the honourable Matthew Cullinan, was someone

188

he'd been to comprehensive school with in Chester. His name's *Gary* Cullinan, apparently, and he has about as much blue blood in his veins as you or I.'

'So you're convinced?'

'Oh yes. I've never liked journalists. I don't trust them and this young fellow has an ingratiating manner that didn't cut any ice with me. But I decided he simply couldn't have made it up. Although it seemed incredible, once I began to get used to the idea, a good many things that had puzzled me started to make sense.'

'Such as?'

She puffed out her cheeks for a moment. 'As you know, he wasn't above boasting about his family and their money. Yet whenever I asked him about his father, simply to pass the time of day, he would change the subject. It struck an odd note. Looking back now, I realise that he was afraid of making a gaffe that would lead to his being found out.'

'He certainly fooled me,' Harry said ruefully. 'Made me think that I needed to watch my manners whenever I was in his presence. When I went to dinner with Matthew and Inge Frontzeck, I was a nervous wreck beforehand, worrying that I might forget myself and start eating peas off my knife.'

'Reeve has been busy,' Frances said. 'He's even managed to speak to Lord Gralam himself. The real Matthew hasn't set foot in England for the past year, but he was on the phone to his father from India only last night. The idea that he might be working in Liverpool seemed to cause his Lordship particular consternation. He'd much rather think that his second son was helping the needy in Madras than sinking in the squalor of Merseyside.' Frances sighed. 'It's sickening to realise how naïve we have all been. Let's face it, none of us really knew anything about Matthew Cullinan.'

'What about Inge?'

'Poor woman. I'm sure she hasn't the faintest idea about the truth.'

'Have you tried to call her?'

'Of course. Reeve was right – her number is unobtainable. Maybe when Matthew took the phone off the hook, she simply didn't notice it.'

'We need to talk to her,' Harry said. 'Any idea where she might be?'

Frances rubbed her chin. 'We could try the Cathedral. She has one of the catering concessions there. I remember she once told me she often looks in to make sure everything is under control.'

'I'll drive you there. But first we speak to Reeve together, yes? Better make sure of our facts before we start slandering one of the richest families in Britain.'

Des Reeve responded immediately to a call from Frances proposing a discussion about Matthew Cullinan. He suggested they meet in the gardens between Water Street and the parish church and within ten minutes he was greeting them there. He was in his early twenties and had masses of red hair, bright inquisitive eyes and an agreeable manner. Harry thought he resembled a squirrel and it would have been no surprise to see him chewing a conker as he ambled down the path towards them. His handshake was warm and he seemed eager to please. Harry had to remind himself that a squirrel is just a rat with a flair for public relations.

'You'll understand that I have to check any allegation that one of our trustees may have acted improperly with the utmost care,' Frances said. 'That's why I've asked our solicitor to come along.'

'Fair enough,' Reeve said amiably. 'I'm not surprised you find it hard to credit. You could have knocked me over with a feather this morning when I saw the picture in the paper

and realised someone was passing himself off as Matthew Cullinan.'

'You're quite certain about this?' Harry asked, in his best innocent-until-proved-guilty tone.

'We're supposed never to let the facts get in the way of a good story,' Reeve said with a disarming smile. 'But the bottom line is that I've interviewed Matthew. It was when I was down in London. He's a decent fellow and he was born with a silver spoon in his mouth – but even if he was richer than Croesus, he'd not be able to afford the plastic surgery to make him look like your chap. He's a small dark-haired fellow with a cast in his eye. See for yourself.'

He put a hand inside his Oxfam-issue jacket and pulled out a sheet, holding it with exaggerated care lest a gust snatch it away and carry it over the road and into the river beyond. Harry and Frances craned their necks to study it. It was a copy of a fax containing a press paragraph about the charitable deeds of Lord Gralam's son. The snippet was accompanied by a small head and shoulders photograph.

Harry let out a breath. 'Even I would have to admit it's fairly compelling evidence.'

Frances' eyes widened as she read the clipping and for the first time in their acquaintance Harry heard her swear. 'Shit. He's fooled us all.'

Reeve could scarcely conceal his pleasure at their reaction, but he attempted an off-hand tone as he stuffed the clipping away. 'The real Matthew Cullinan may be no Robert Redford, but as far as I can tell, he's genuinely caring. Let's face it, you'd have to be, to spend a year of your life in India raising money for people dying of cancer. He's been well-known for his charitable activities ever since he left Oxford. Depend upon it, he's still in Madras.' A pause. 'What I'm wondering is – where is Gary Cullinan?'

With caution worthy of any lawyer, Frances said, 'You realise I can't disclose the private address of a fellow trustee to a journalist?'

'Oh, no problem to any reporter worth his salt,' Reeve grinned. 'I soon found where our Gary lives. He's shacked up with Inge

Frontzeck, isn't he? I nipped over to Caldy a little while ago, but no joy. There wasn't a sign of either of them. My guess is, he's done a runner. As for her – who knows? Maybe she's gone with him. Any idea where they might be headed for?'

'None whatsoever,' Frances said sharply. The wind was blowing her hair into her eyes and she pushed it angrily away. 'What you suggest is quite impossible. I'm absolutely sure this will come as a bolt from the blue to Inge. She's been betrayed – like the rest of us.'

The wind was sharpening and Harry turned up his coat collar. 'So what do you know about Gary Cullinan?'

'Not much yet. I'm due to see the chap who gave us his name later today. Then I may be able to start piecing the story together. The way it looks at the moment, our Gary reinvented himself in order to do a spot of fortune-hunting. He chose well, didn't he? Uwe Frontzeck's daughter must be one of the wealthiest young women in the North-West.'

'She'll be heartbroken,' Frances muttered.

'She might find it helps to talk about it all,' Reeve said in a pious tone. 'Here's a card with my number. If she contacts you, would you ask her to give me a ring straight away? I'm sure she has a story to tell that our readers would love to hear.'

Half an hour later, Harry was walking through a tunnel lined with tombstones. He was completing a circuit of the Anglican Cathedral while Frances comforted Inge Frontzeck. The pathway that led down from the visitors' entrance passed underground for a short distance before sweeping out and round into a former graveyard which was now an area of parkland. He emerged into the open air and spotted the two women ahead of him, sitting on a bench, Inge's head on Frances's shoulder.

This place had once been a quarry; in Liverpool's pomp, much of the stone for its finest buildings had come from here. Later it had become St James's Cemetery, last resting place for many of the city's great and good. For the most part, their memorials remained: crosses, obelisks, small monuments. But Harry knew that there were catacombs here too, in which countless ordinary men and women had been interred and then forgotten.

He glanced up to his left and saw a pastiche Doric temple. The Oratory: a grand name for the old mortuary chapel, but Liverpudlians never did things by halves. Over his shoulder on the right loomed a place that always made him shiver. With its huge sandstone towers, the Cathedral was a house of God that inspired awe like no other.

Ahead of him, Frances looked up and caught his eye. She gave an imperceptible nod. On the way here, they had agreed that she would talk to Inge on her own before Harry started putting any questions. They could not be sure how Inge would react to the news that her lover was a fraud.

Inge's head was bowed, but as he approached, he saw that her cheeks were glistening with tears. He exchanged a glance with Frances. She put a finger to her lips.

Presently Inge said in a small voice, 'Sorry. It's childish to cry. I suppose I should have known it was all too good to be true.'

Frances put her hand on the younger woman's. 'He deceived all of us.'

'I love him, you know. Even now – I can't find it in me to stop loving him.'

Frances bit her lip. 'Men are like that,' she said fiercely. 'The more plausible they are, the more they hurt you.'

Spoken with feeling, Harry thought. Aloud, he said, 'Are you able to talk about – what happened this morning?'

'I was in the shower when I heard the phone ring,' Inge said. He could tell she was striving to compose herself, but there was no disguising the tremor in her voice. Her life was being put through a shredder. 'Matthew – sorry, but what else can I call him?

– answered it. I couldn't hear what was said. When I was dressed, I came downstairs and he was getting ready to go out. I asked who had called and he fobbed me off, said it was a business associate. Of course I never dreamed it had been someone from the Press. He told me he would have to go out to organise a business deal. It had cropped up unexpectedly and he had to deal with it at once. I was surprised, but of course I didn't question him closely. I – I've always trusted him implicitly.'

Her face crumpled. There were lines round her eyes and mouth that Harry had never seen before. 'My God, what an idiot I have been. I will be a laughing stock.'

Frances put an arm round her and Harry said, 'I realise this is difficult for you. If you'd rather not discuss...'

'No,' Inge said. 'I need to talk. I have to make some sense of it all. He – he said he would need to stay overnight and he'd be back tomorrow. I offered to help him pack, but he said it wasn't necessary. Ten minutes later, he was on his way. He said he was driving to the station.'

'I expect he was telling the truth,' Frances said. 'My guess is that he will want to put as much space between himself and Liverpool as possible now that he's been found out.'

'Did you really have no idea that he had been lying to you?' Harry asked.

Inge closed her eyes. 'I suppose that subconsciously, I already had a great many doubts about him. There were so many things that didn't add up. I'd been uneasy for a long time, but I'd been afraid to admit to myself the reason why.'

'Presumably he kept you well away from any members of his family?'

'Yes, you are right. I could never understand it. I've always been close to my parents and it was strange that whenever I suggested going down to see Lord Gralam or his elder brother, he made an excuse. I assumed it was just the way upper-class English families behave. They keep themselves to themselves. And I was amused by the way he never seemed to have any money.'

Frances stroked her jaw thoughtfully. 'Looking back, I see it now. We all assumed he was wealthy, but there was precious little hard evidence. I seldom saw him putting his hand in his pocket, even though he always dressed well and seemed to have an expensive lifestyle.'

'Who do you think paid for that lifestyle?' Inge asked wearily.

'He lived with you, of course.'

'And off me. The flat is mine. He never even contributed towards the upkeep. He always had an explanation for being short of ready cash. Something to do with the strict terms of the trust funds his father had set up. I never understood the details. He told me that even when he needed money, he was too proud to plead with his own flesh and blood. He would rather be on the bread-line. There was a story about a rift between them, something to do with Matthew yearning to do charity work whilst his father wanted him to be something in the City. I felt sorry for him, being deprived simply because he wasn't prepared to kow-tow to the old man. So I was always willing to help him out. My own father did express his concern once or twice, but I brushed it aside. Love is blind. Stupid, too.'

She let out a long sigh before adding, 'There was more. Occasionally I would catch him out in a little lie. Usually it was about something trivial. An old college friend he claimed to have been talking to or a business deal that he was trying to pull off. He always liked to impress me – but sometimes he overdid it. Believe it or not, I was rather touched. I thought it was sweet that, with his impeccable background, he would want to show off to me. It's stupid, but he made me feel good.'

'That's the art of the confidence trickster,' Frances said. 'He tried to convince us all that he was bestowing an honour merely by talking to us.'

'No wonder he claimed to be publicity-shy,' Harry said.

'That always appealed to me,' Inge said. 'He used to say he wasn't seeking public approval for his charity work. I admired his unselfishness, his modesty.'

Harry thought that Matthew had never seemed too modest when not threatened by the risk of public exposure. It was a contradiction that had always troubled him, and yet he'd never guessed the explanation. 'But he got carried away by the engagement and the excitement of yesterday evening. No wonder he cringed when the photographer insisted on snapping him. He must have been half-afraid that his luck would finally run out.'

Inge said softly, 'Shall I tell you what hurts me most?'

'What's that?' Frances asked.

'I don't know anything about him. Nothing at all. Last night I thought I was going to marry him and now he's gone. I may know his real name. But this – Gary Cullinan – is a complete stranger to me.'

For a time none of them spoke. The skies were darkening and lights gleamed from the Cathedral windows high above the hollowed-out park. Spots of rain were beginning to fall, but the wind had died and the only sound was the hum of the cars of kerb-crawlers cruising Gambier Terrace, looking for business.

Harry cleared his throat and said, 'The question is: what do we do now? Try to find him? Call the police?'

Frances winced. 'Heaven knows what harm this episode will do to the Trust. As if we haven't had enough to contend with lately.'

Inge said, 'The last thing I want right now is to see him again. I need time to think things over. And to talk with my family.'

'Of course you do,' Harry said. 'But remember, the journalist has his teeth into the story. He won't let go. You'll have to decide before long whether you're willing to speak to him.'

Inge coloured. 'Kiss and tell?'

'Not at all. But odious as it may seem, sometimes it's better to be frank with the Press rather than giving them the chance to make up the news. You know how they define a good story? Something that someone somewhere doesn't want them to know.'

Inge hauled herself to her feet and pulled her coat tightly around her. 'Very well. I'll consider it. But please, don't call the police. Not yet, anyway. There's probably no need. After all, as far as I know, I'm Gary Cullinan's only real victim.'

Harry said nothing. But he couldn't help wondering if she was right.

Chapter 18

After Inge had left them, Harry and Frances walked in silence along the path that curved under the shadow of the Cathedral. They were only a stone's throw from the red light area where Davey Damnation had confronted the Scissorman. In his mind he could hear Davey's echoing voice.

'I am he that liveth and was dead; and, behold, I am alive for evermore, Amen; and have the keys of hell and of death!'

Hadn't Shakespeare said that the devil can cite scripture for his purpose? Harry moved his shoulders up and down, as if it might help him to concentrate on the problem that had brought him here.

'Wasn't it Luke's idea to invite Matthew Cullinan to become a trustee?' he asked.

'Yes, he took the fellow at face value. It was quite a coup to have an investment expert offering his services free of charge. And naturally, it did the Trust no harm to have an aristocrat on the board.' She paused and said grimly, 'I suppose that if he's a rogue, that may explain what happened to the Trust's money.'

'But Roy is the treasurer,' Harry objected. His conversation with Ashley was still fresh in his mind, although he did not want to muddy the waters by revealing the suspicions which Luke had confided in his godson. 'He would have had to approve any expenditure.'

'Come on,' Frances said scornfully. 'Let's face it, Roy's an alcoholic. He couldn't look after a child's piggy-bank properly. Matthew – Gary – whatever his name is – will have been able to do exactly as he pleased. I'll call in the auditors to check over our books as a matter of urgency. We'll have to talk to the Charity Commission too. I suppose I ought to speak to Roy, though frankly I doubt if he'll have anything worthwhile to contribute.'

'Assuming that you find him.'

She halted in mid-stride and turned to face him. 'What do you mean?'

'He missed the show last night, didn't he? And I've tried to contact him by phone today with no joy. Ashley Whitaker reckons that he's gone off with some floozie, but I'm not so sure.'

'He'll turn up,' she said with a shrug. 'The proverbial bad penny.'

She started walking again in the direction of the car park. Harry hesitated before following her. He looked up at the forbidding bulk of the Cathedral. Again he felt a chill of unease, again he heard in his brain the voice of Davey Damnation.

'And I saw the dead, small and great, stand before God; and the books were opened!'

He sucked in a breath of the cold afternoon air and told himself that he must stop expecting the worst. He must dismiss the dread that lurked at the back of his mind, the cold fear that the killing was not yet at an end.

'So we weren't rubbing shoulders with the nobility after all,' Jim Crusoe said as they had a coffee together back in the office. 'I should have realised.'

'Why do you say that?'

'Last time I attended a trustees' meeting, I mentioned to him that Heather and I were thinking of taking a weekend break in Oxford. I knew he'd been to university there, so I asked his advice on hotels and the best places to visit. He was amazingly vague and I remember thinking to myself that it had been a waste of time plucking up the courage to ask the question. I'd picked up more from watching *Inspector Morse*. But of course I didn't draw the right conclusion. I thought he was simply too grand to take much notice of the sort of places that would fascinate an ordinary tourist. What's the betting he's never been near Oxford in his life?' Jim sighed. 'So the man who was supposed to be the saviour of the Kavanaugh Trust was the one who bankrupted it.'

'Why do you think that?'

'Obvious, isn't it? He's ripped off Inge Frontzeck over the last few months. He had the know-how and opportunity to do the same to the Kavanaugh Trust.'

'Luke thought that Roy Milburn was on the take from the Trust,' Harry said.

He recounted the story Ashley Whitaker had told him. Jim listened closely, his craggy face giving no clue to his thoughts.

'So Luke was mistaken. Nobody's perfect.'

'But he was a careful man,' Harry said. 'It wouldn't be like him to accuse someone unless he was sure.'

'He was circumspect when he talked to you,' Jim pointed out. 'He was obviously confident that he could rely on Ashley's discretion. As well as the fact that Roy was an old friend of Ashley's.'

'I suppose so. It troubles me, though. Who killed Luke? And why has Roy disappeared?'

'Luke is six feet under. There's no forensic evidence to suggest he was killed. As for Roy, my guess is that he's gone off on a bender somewhere. Or maybe he's seen sense and checked in to a drying-out clinic.'

'Now who's letting his imagination roam?' Harry hesitated. 'You know, even if Matthew was the one robbing the Trust, that doesn't necessarily exonerate Roy. He could have been at it as well. Luke may have asked him round to the Hawthorne, challenged him – and been pushed out of the window for his cheek.'

'You know yourself it's impossible to prove that, one way or another.'

The coffee had a bitter taste but Harry swallowed the last of it anyway. A kind of penance for not seeing the obvious sooner. 'I suppose you're right. But I'm sure I've missed something. Luke could have tumbled to the truth about Matthew himself, after he spoke to Ashley. He must have found that he had two problems to contend with. Not just a treasurer on the take, but a bogus financial adviser.'

'You're surely not suggesting that would have driven him to suicide?'

'No. But maybe Roy wasn't the only one with a motive to murder Luke. I never considered that the honourable Matthew was a serious suspect. But Gary Cullinan may have been.'

Jim raised his bushy eyebrows. 'Any idea where he's got to?'

'Des Reeve was going to speak to the man who gave him Cullinan's name after meeting Frances and me. Let's give him a ring to see if he's learned anything more.'

But the message from the newspaper office was that Reeve had not come back in that afternoon and was not expected at his desk again until the next morning. Harry tried Roy Milburn's number again but it kept ringing out. He gnawed at his fingernails in frustration. The need to do something was as insistent as a hunger pain.

'I'll go round and have a look at Roy's flat. See if there's any clue as to where he might be.'

'Wasting your time, aren't you? He won't have left a note on the door telling the milkman not to deliver and by the way, he's nipped off to Blackpool to spend the money he's stolen from the Trust.'

Harry gave his partner a wan smile. 'Maybe not, but anything's worth a try.'

Jim's eyes narrowed. 'What's eating you?'

'You'll think I'm being melodramatic.'

'I *always* think that.'

'Roy has been flush with money recently, right? Perhaps it's not because of his ill-gotten gains from the Kavanaugh Trust.'

Jim considered. 'You reckon he may have been blackmailing Matthew? Or Gary or whatever we are supposed to call him?'

'Why not? He likes to poke his nose into other people's business. If he thought Gary Cullinan had killed Luke rather than face exposure, he would have been more likely to try to cash in on his deduction than run off to the police. When I last talked to him, he actually said, "Knowledge is power."'

'So you think he may have pushed his luck too far?'

'Possible, isn't it? If Gary had killed once to preserve his secret, he probably wouldn't scruple at a second crime.'

Jim groaned. 'You said it yourself. You're eternally melo-dramatic. You're going on a wild goose chase.'

'I expect you're right,' Harry said, but he did not really believe it.

The old furniture shop was still deserted. Harry walked down the passageway at the side of the building, but found the back door locked. On balance, he decided, this was reassuringly consistent with the theory that Roy had disappeared on a frolic of his own and had not fallen victim to a desperate attempt by Gary Cullinan to conceal his imposture.

And yet – instinct told him that this was a story which would not have a happy ending. He leaned on the padlocked gate at the bottom of the alley and wondered what to do. Rain was falling steadily now and one by one the lights in neighbouring blocks were going out as people working in the city set off for home. Some of them walked past the top of the passageway, but none glanced down it.

The easy course would be to walk back to the street and head back to Empire Dock. But he knew that if he did that, he would not be able to settle until he could be sure that nothing untoward had happened to Roy Milburn. At least not here. He stood on tiptoe and peered over the top of the gate. It gave on to a tiny yard containing a bunker, a couple of dustbins and an ironwork fire escape. Harry recalled from his last visit that the stairway led to the roof. Why not climb it and just check that there were no signs of disturbance in Roy's studio?

Fortunately there was no barbed wire on top of the gate. If the receivers of the furniture business were relying on Roy for security, they were making a false economy. A few old bricks were lying around in the passageway and he used them as a platform to haul himself up and over the gate. He dropped down heavily on the other side: the aching of his knee joints as he hit the ground reminded him that he was neither as young nor as fit as he used to be.

The steps of the fire escape were sleek with rain and he took care to grip the cold railing as he began his ascent, remembering that Roy had described it as a death trap. He had no wish to emulate Luke by plunging to his doom from a great height. It occurred to him that it would be a good idea not to look down.

Slow as a septuagenarian, he made his way up towards the roof. When he reached the top he was out of breath, as much because of the tension he could not help feeling as the steepness of the steps. He squatted on his haunches at the foot of the flagpole, trying to recover his breath.

The last time he had come on to the rooftop had been in daylight. In the dark, it seemed different, shadowy and sinister. The wind was much stronger than before and Harry remembered that the guardrail around the roof had been low. A fierce gust coming in from the river might pick up even a grown man and toss him to the street below. And what was the noise coming from the direction of the fire escape? Was it possible that someone had followed him here?

He shivered and told himself not to allow imagination to conquer common sense. Jim was bound to be right. Roy had skipped and this was a waste of time. It would be absurd to peer down the fire escape and try to detect a non-existent pursuer. He clambered to his feet and squared his shoulders before walking across the roof to the window of Roy's studio.

The room was in darkness. The curtains had been drawn, but there was a crack between them. Harry peered through it. He could not see much, but it was possible to make out that there was someone sprawled across the sofa. A man who might perhaps be asleep – but Harry did not think so.

'Oh God,' he said.

Even as the words left his lips, he heard something behind him. Fear paralysed him. No doubt about it this time. Someone really had followed him up the fire escape. For a moment he thought he was about to throw up. He bit his bottom lip hard as he fought to master his terror. He could taste his own blood. It was no time to surrender to a man who had killed before.

It's him or me, he thought.

Then he turned, lowered his head and charged towards the dark figure who stood at the top of the iron stairway. But the other man saw him coming all the way and raised a gloved fist as he swerved to avoid a collision. Harry hit the guardrail and lost his footing. He felt himself falling and the last thing that passed through his mind before he lost consciousness was that now he would never know whether Gary Cullinan had killed Roy – or the other way around.

Part Three

Chapter 19

'It's a miracle that you're still alive,' Juliet May said over lunch a week later.

'After I came round,' Harry said, 'the paramedic said exactly the same thing. I rather had the impression that he thought I didn't deserve my good fortune. Not that I felt lucky for the next forty-eight hours. I ached all over. My head has never hurt so much in all my life. Not even when I was doing the Law Society exams.'

'You actually fell down the fire escape, then?'

'Seven or eight steps of it, to the first half-landing from the top. When I charged at the security man, I missed him but hit the rail, slipped and took a tumble.'

'You could easily have tumbled over the edge rather than down the steps.'

'Tell you the truth,' he said, giving the shoulder that still hurt him a rub, 'I've imagined it a thousand times since. Jim reckons that there's a lot of competition in the list of the ten stupidest things I've ever done in my life, but panicking on a dark rooftop probably tops the lot.'

He gave her a sheepish grin. They were sitting at the back of the posh wine bar which had recently opened on Drury Lane. She had called him the previous morning, his first back in the office since his calamitous expedition to the studio flat, to ask how he was. When he'd asked if she could make lunch on Saturday, she had said yes right away.

'At least you're a man of action,' she said with a teasing smile.

'That's not what the police said when they interviewed me at the hospital,' Harry confessed.

'Did the security man call them?'

Harry nodded. 'He spotted me sneaking up the fire escape while he was doing his rounds in the building next door. He's an ex-army bloke in his sixties and more of an action man than I'll ever be. He called the police on his mobile but couldn't resist nipping out and coming up himself to see what I was up to. He was sure I was up to no good, but I didn't look as though I could handle a rough-house.'

Juliet shook her head. 'How many burglars go about their business in a pinstripe suit?'

'Mine isn't a very smart suit,' Harry said humbly. 'And the coat I was wearing had seen better days. Besides, how many solicitors spend their time shinning up fire escapes in the rain? I could understand why the policemen took a bit of convincing that I wasn't a rather incompetent villain. Or, even worse, a murderer. Thank God I didn't have time to break into Roy's flat. I'd have had even more explaining to do if they'd found me standing over the body of one of my own clients.'

'You've never been tempted to kill a client, then?' she asked lightly.

'Tempted, yes. Many times. But I've always persuaded myself that it's a mistake to bite the hand that feeds. Even if what it feeds is sometimes pretty unpalatable.'

Returning his smile, she refilled his glass and hers. He'd noticed that she liked a drink before, when they had dined with Inge Frontzeck and the make-believe Matthew Cullinan. Well, what was the harm? He liked a drink himself. But he was bothered by her appearance today. Not even her expertise with make-up could disguise the bruise on her left cheekbone. He was still looking the worse for wear himself, but she didn't have the same excuse. He'd acted for too many battered wives not to be anxious about what the blemish might signify. But he hadn't plucked up the courage to ask her about it. He'd need more than a couple of glasses of wine to start treading on such dangerous ground.

'So Roy Milburn is dead,' she said. 'I heard a little about him from Inge. He sounded – quite a character.'

'To say the least.'

'Did you like him?'

Harry considered. 'I suppose if you'd asked me a week ago, I'd have said I did. It would have been an automatic response. He could make me laugh. And yet I always realised he had his darker side. Roy was a mischief-maker, forever stirring trouble. He had no self-control. He never knew when to stop.'

She raised her eyebrows and said, 'Which of us does?'

He found himself rubbing his leg against hers under the table. She giggled. *Things are getting better*, he told himself. Almost as an afterthought, he said, 'Whatever he's done, I'm sorry he's dead.'

'You said on the phone that he may have murdered Luke Dessaur.'

'I know a few people in the police and one or two of them now believe it's possible. But he can't be brought to trial. So it looks as though the whole business may be buried quietly. Like Roy himself.'

'And what do you believe?'

'Big question.'

'Come on! I'm not asking you to prove that God exists. You're a mystery addict, just like me. You know the score. Did Roy kill Luke?'

'I'm not trying to be evasive. I'm just finding it difficult to make sense of everything at present. Roy as a murderer, I can imagine. Roy the suicide I find more difficult to buy.'

'It isn't certain that it was suicide, though, is it?'

'No. Same story as with Luke's death. There's more than one possibility, but suicide is the favourite. He'd been drinking heavily and then he took an overdose. They found the pills in his kitchen. Pain-killers. Maybe it wasn't remorse, but just a spur of the moment thing. Perhaps his bad leg was playing him up. It gave him a lot of trouble – but it wasn't exactly life-threatening.'

'Paracetamol with codeine, wasn't it?'

Harry nodded. 'He'd taken enough to kill two or three men. A bit over the top if it was a cry for help. Besides, there was no-one for him to cry to. Maybe that was his real tragedy. He'd had hundreds of casual girlfriends over the years, by all accounts, but never anything really serious. I suppose I never regarded him as a serious character. Perhaps he had to kill himself to be taken seriously.'

The main course arrived: *nouvelle cuisine*, extortionately expensive and far from satisfying. Harry would have preferred steak with chips any day, but this place had been Juliet's suggestion and a little financial and culinary hardship was a price worth paying for the pleasure of her company. He toyed with his food for a while before adding, 'One way of looking at it is this. Luke's death was murder dressed up to look like suicide. And then his murderer *does* commit suicide. Very neat.'

She laughed. 'Why is it that I get the impression you're not convinced?'

He mimicked the sombre tone of a detective in an old black-and-white film: 'It's *too* damned neat.'

'Okay. Let's take it in stages. He didn't leave a suicide note?'

'No, but the police did find something in his flat which may come close to it. A cartoon of himself hanging from a gallows. Why else would he draw such a picture if he hadn't killed Luke?'

She wrinkled her nose. 'So the idea is that it had begun to prey on his mind that he'd ended someone else's life?'

He nodded. 'And there are parallels between the two deaths. Both men had been drinking before they died. In Luke's case, he may have invited Roy over to the Hawthorne. Perhaps he had a drink with Roy before coming out with his suspicions. Knowing Luke, he would have wanted to do the decent thing. He might have suggested that if Roy paid back everything that had been stolen, it wouldn't be necessary to call in the police. If Roy lost his temper, he might have started a brawl which finished up with him pushing Luke out of the window. The only snag is that Julio, the hotel porter, reckons the argument he heard took place an hour and a half before Luke died.'

The desserts were served and for a few minutes they concentrated on eating. 'How's the sorbet?' Juliet asked.

'I still prefer Death by Chocolate.'

'One-track mind,' she said. 'Didn't you say there were no signs of a struggle in Luke's hotel room?'

'Well,' Harry said, 'the idea that Roy killed him is only a theory. We'll never know the full story.'

'What about Roy's own death? Might someone else have been involved?'

'There's no sign of it.'

'The lynx-eyed security man saw no-one, then?'

Harry laughed. 'I gather he goes off duty at seven o'clock. The indications are that Roy may have died later than that. It was the evening he'd been meant to attend the first night of the show at the Pool Theatre. Possibly he had a change of heart and opted to stay at home and wallow in alcohol and remorse.'

'He doesn't sound to me like the sort of man who would be prey to conscience,' Juliet objected. 'Besides, he'd got away with it, hadn't he? He would never have been locked up for killing Luke. Why not just do a flit?'

'Perhaps he couldn't think of anywhere worth flitting to. The police can't be certain, but they think he was alone in the flat that evening and that I was the first person to turn up the day after. The fact that I found the door and gate locked suggests that.'

Juliet's eyes began to gleam. 'Don't tell me we're confronted by a locked studio flat mystery? A mystery buff's dream!'

'I hate to disappoint you, but round here the bad guys don't bother with icicles kept in vacuum flasks or blowpipes containing a poison unknown to Western science. When they want to settle a little difference of opinion about drugs or women, they rely on a

Stanley knife in the ribs or a few rounds from a submachine-gun. Subtlety isn't their strong point.'

'This could be the exception that proves the rule,' she insisted. 'You've told me yourself that half your clients are out of work and claiming benefit. But every once in a while you act for someone different like the Kavanaugh trustees.'

'Yeah, and look what's been happening to them.'

She sighed. 'Inge is heartbroken about Matthew.'

'You said on the phone that she stayed with you for a couple of nights after Gary Cullinan was exposed.'

'Yes. It seemed sensible for her to keep out of the way of the Press until she'd had a chance to gather her thoughts. Then we heard the news that the police had picked up Gary Cullinan.'

'In fact, I've been told he gave himself up. Apparently in his initial panic after learning that his cover had been blown, he decided to do a bunk. But then he changed his mind and contacted Reeve, the journalist, with a view to selling his story.'

'He's a shit,' Juliet hissed. Her eyes were wide and he was almost tempted to say *My God, you're beautiful when you're angry.* 'Poor Inge. In the end, she realised she couldn't keep hiding. After all, she wasn't the one who had done anything wrong. So she went back to her flat yesterday. I told her we would put her up for as long as she liked. There's plenty of room in our house, one advantage of having no kids. But I'm sure she did the right thing. By all accounts, Gary Cullinan has committed a string of crimes, but in my book the worst is the way he's betrayed Inge. He deserves to go inside.'

'Don't hold your breath for that. He's instructed Ruby Fingall to act for him, so he'll probably finish up with a public apology from the court for the trouble the legal system has put him to.'

'Surely the case against him is watertight?'

Harry shrugged. 'In the law, things are never so simple. Especially when two men who would be the key prosecution witnesses are dead.'

'Luke and Roy?'

'Yes. Gary's scam sounds neat. He complained that the investments held by the Trust had gone down in value and should be sold, with the proceeds reinvested. He produced low, bogus valuations of the old shares on fake stockbrokers' letterhead to back up his story and then creamed off the profit on the sales for himself. He put the money in a bank account he'd set up under his real name. All Roy saw was that money was leaking away. He was too lazy to check what he was being told. The *Financial Times* was never his preferred reading and he simply didn't realise that the original shares purchased by the Trust were still blue-chip performers. Talk about private finance initiative.'

'He's not a Robin Hood, you know. He's only ever been out for himself.'

'Sure, but he's back on the scene already. Frances Silverwood told me he phoned her yesterday and sounded full of the joys of spring. He was simply ringing to tender his resignation as a trustee.'

'So you think he may get away with it? I don't believe his nerve.'

'Frances says she chewed him out. But I doubt if it will have made any impression. Anyway, there are only two trustees left now. Shades of *And Then There Were None*.'

Juliet pushed a hand through her hair. It was a habitual gesture which Harry found appealing. 'And what about Frances Silverwood herself? Didn't she have a thing about Luke Dessaur? Suppose she discovered that Roy had... Good God, Harry, what's the matter?'

His eyes had become fixed on the entrance to the wine bar. Outside, Kim and a middle-aged man he did not recognise were peering at the menu in the window. He felt his cheeks burning. *Why should you feel embarrassed?* he asked himself. *You have nothing to hide.* Yet he suddenly had an idea of how Geoffrey Willatt must have felt on being discovered with Vera that night at the Ensenada. He found himself uttering a silent prayer that Kim and her companion would decide not to give the place a try.

As usual, his wishes were confounded. Kim turned to the man; he gave an authoritative nod and then ushered her inside. Harry noticed that as she paused on the threshold, the man put his hand on her shoulder. A casual gesture, no doubt. It would be a mistake to read anything into it. Yet Harry's stomach was tying itself in knots.

He started as Juliet repeated her question. 'Sorry. I've just recognised someone, that's all.'

'A sworn enemy, to judge by the look on your face.'

'Far from it,' he mumbled. *Oh shit, she's seen me.*

At the sight of him, Kim turned crimson. He watched as she hesitated and tried to guess what might be passing through her mind. Then she touched her companion on the arm and steered him over in the direction of their corner table. She moved clumsily between the other diners rather than with her usual lithe grace, as if she were struggling to compose herself before speaking to him.

She gave him a nervous smile of greeting. 'I didn't know this was one of your haunts, Harry.'

'I thought I'd try something different.'

She gave Juliet an appraising glance. At the sight of the bruise, her eyebrows rose. 'So I see. Well, how are you?'

'Much better than when you last saw me.'

She smiled. 'True, though it might not be saying much. You weren't a pretty sight after you took your tumble.'

She'd visited him first at the hospital and then at his flat after he'd been discharged. For a few wild moments her concern about his accident had made him think that she might change her mind about leaving for London. But of course it had been a fantasy: he'd soon realised that.

'Thanks again for coming to see me.'

'The least I could do,' she said. 'The very least. So now you're back at work? I meant to give you a call yesterday but – you know how it is.'

'Yes.' He nodded at her companion. The man was in his early forties, at a guess. Dark hair turning grey, smart casual clothes, expression so self-assured that it bordered on arrogance. 'Sorry. I should have introduced myself. I'm Harry Devlin. This is Juliet May. Juliet, meet Kim Lawrence and...?'

The man stretched out his hand. He was exquisitely manicured. 'Jethro Wood. I'm on the governing council of MOJO.'

'Ah.' Harry thought for a moment. 'Based in London, I presume?'

'That's right. I'm just up here for twenty-four hours to talk over a bit of business with Kim. You know we've managed to persuade her to become our Chief Executive?'

Harry nodded. 'You're lucky. She'll be a roaring success.'

'I'm convinced of it.' Wood patted Kim on the hand. It was the sort of gesture which would normally have made her flesh creep, but she gave no sign that she objected. 'Liverpool's loss is our gain. I've always admired her work up here. And at head office, she'll have the chance to make a much greater impact than any honorary regional representative. I'm at the Bar myself, a civil liberties set, but I find I spend a good deal of time on MOJO business. I'm looking forward to working with her very much. I think we'll make a good team. Which is important, because there isn't anything more important to a lawyer than fighting miscarriage cases.'

Especially if it looks good in the newspapers, Harry could not help thinking. Of course it was unfair to suspect Jethro Wood's motives. But come to think of it, the man's name did ring a bell. In his mind, he associated it with the sort of high-profile campaigning in which the campaigner seemed to count for more than the campaign.

'I've mentioned Harry to you, Jethro. He's a fellow solicitor.'

'That's right, I remember. I gather you're on the side of the angels, Harry.'

'I'm not sure many of my clients fit that description.'

'Come on now, you know what I mean. You're not on the side of the big battalions. Just like me. You act for the weak, the ignorant. People who really need us.'

Kim coloured again and Harry could tell she was wondering if the conversation was such a good idea. She said quickly, 'So are you a client of Harry's, Juliet?'

Juliet smiled and shook her head. 'I'm not sure if I can truthfully claim always to be on the side of the angels, but I'm in public relations, so I suppose I ought to.'

Kim pursed her lips. 'That's interesting. Don't tell me you act for Crusoe and Devlin?'

'Well, Harry and his partner are reviewing their firm's image and perhaps its position in the marketplace.'

Wood guffawed. 'Did I speak too soon? Hope you're not going to start pitching for business from the multinationals.'

'No danger of that,' Harry said.

'We all need to move on,' Kim said quietly. 'Speaking of which, I suppose we'd better grab a table. Those people over there look as if they are about to leave. Nice to meet you, Juliet. Harry, I meant to call you to say I've arranged an early handover with Windaybanks. I report to MOJO headquarters next Monday morning at nine.'

'So quick?'

'I'll be coming back here a couple of days a week to start with, so that I can help out with any of the problem files that Quentin Pike is taking over. But the plan is that I'll be full-time in my new job very soon.'

'We can't wait for her to start,' Jethro Wood confirmed.

'Good luck, then. I hope you'll keep in touch.'

'I promised, didn't I?' She glanced at Juliet. 'But I guess I'll be pretty busy for a while.'

He nodded. 'Of course you will.'

She turned to go, then looked back over her shoulder. 'By the way, I gather that it's all still happening at the Kavanaugh Trust.'

Harry managed a grin. 'The number of angels in that quarter is diminishing rapidly. Even the toffee-nosed benefactor turned out to be a conman.'

'And the word on the grapevine at court is that the treasurer who took an overdose may have killed the chairman.'

'It's a theory that suits everyone. It closes all the files.'

'You sound doubtful.'

Juliet smiled. 'I don't think Harry likes easy explanations.'

'When the police settle for an easy explanation, the end result is often a miscarriage of justice,' he said.

'If you're casting round for alternative suspects,' Kim said, 'take a tip from me. Tim Aldred didn't kill Luke Dessaur.'

'You must admit, he has the track record.'

She shook her head. 'You're the last person to fall for another easy explanation, Harry. Tim is a good man, I've always been convinced of it.'

Jethro Wood had begun to shift from one foot to another. As the waiter arrived with the coffee, he said, 'That table's free now. We'd better stake our claim.'

Kim turned to Juliet and said, 'Harry simply can't resist a mystery. Once he's hooked, he never lets go. You'll need to keep your eye on him.'

'Oh, don't worry,' Juliet said with a sweet and, Harry sensed, deliberately provocative smile. 'I'll do that.'

When they were alone again, she asked, 'Am I right in guessing that Kim is an old flame?'

He finished his wine. 'Sort of.'

'Nice-looking. You have good taste.'

'You say that after seeing the colour scheme in my office?'

She laughed. 'Sorry, I realise I shouldn't pry into your private life. You see, we share at least one vice in common. Insatiable curiosity. I simply can't help it.'

Now it was his turn to pour. After taking another drink, he said softly, 'So you won't mind if I indulge in a spot of vice too?'

'Be my guest.'

'How did you manage to come by that bruise on your cheek?'

She bit her lip. 'An accident.'

'I see a lot of women who have similar accidents.'

'Oh, I don't deny that Casper likes to give me a beating,' she said, with a sudden flash of bravado. 'The accident was that I let him make contact. Over the past few years, I've developed a better body swerve than half the footballers in the Premier League.'

He stared at her defiant expression and realised how little he knew about her. 'What happened?'

'He was careless. I found a letter from his latest lady friend in his jacket pocket. He decided attack was the best form of defence and accused me of being a snoop.'

'You don't have to put up with violence. Not in this day and age.' *And not*, he almost added, *with your kind of money*. There was no way Juliet May would finish up in a refuge or hostel.

'Oh believe me, Harry, I know that. I stay through an act of free will.'

'Are you afraid of him?'

She considered. 'Not often. And you mustn't get the wrong idea. This sort of thing' – she gestured to her cheek – 'doesn't happen often. Usually he turns his anger on other people. I'm only the last resort.'

'I don't understand.'

'I don't expect you to. I'm not sure I do myself. But none of us are rational all the time, Harry. We don't do the sensible thing. Wouldn't life be simpler if we did? But wouldn't it also be infinitely more boring.'

'You like that sort of thing?' he asked incredulously.

'No, I'm not a masochist. At least I don't think I am. The truth's more complicated than that. For all his faults, Casper is the most exciting man I've ever met. He's wild and dangerous, but he can be witty and charming.' She smiled. 'And when the black clouds lift, he swears it will never happen again. Of course logic tells me it will, but somehow I keep hoping things will change. I'm sorry to sound like something out of a women's magazine, but it's the way things are between us. He turns me on. Your friend Kim is lovely but she strikes me as a battle-hardened feminist. She would tell me that I should be ashamed of myself, that I'm a traitor to the cause of women. But I can't help it.'

'Sorry,' he said. 'It's none of my business.'

'But I can tell from your face you think I'm crazy to stay with him.'

'If you want a blunt answer, then yes, I do.'

She emptied her glass. 'And if you want me to be honest with you, then all I can say is that each time Casper and I have reconciliation sex, it's the best I've ever known.'

Horrified, he stared at her. Her expression was defiant rather than teasing. For a few seconds neither of them spoke. The bleeping of a telephone broke the deadlock. Juliet blushed and pulled a mobile from her bag.

'Inge? Well, it's not perfect timing, but of course I'm glad to hear from you...' Her face darkened. 'You're not serious? After everything that's happened? Have you taken leave of your senses? Only yesterday you were saying...'

Harry could tell from her face that the phone had been put down at the other end. She swore vividly and banged the mobile down on the table.

'What's happened?'

Juliet gazed at the heavens. 'Perhaps I should be the last one to criticise. You're going to think that every woman prefers pain to pleasure.'

'What did she say?'

'Only that she and Gary Cullinan have got it together again.'

Chapter 20

'I'd like to think that something good will come out of all of this,' Gary Cullinan said.

His tone was sober and he was holding Inge Frontzeck's hand as tenderly as if it were a fragile piece of china. The couple were sitting together on the sofa in the Caldy flat. Every now and then they gazed into each other's eyes. The air was heavy with the scent from a huge bunch of roses in a vase on the table. For Harry, there was an even greater risk of throwing up over the carpet than when he'd had a skinful on his last visit here.

'I'm sure it will, darling,' Inge said. Her head was on his shoulder. 'Our love has been tested. And we've found that it's stronger than ever.'

'I don't deserve you,' Gary said. 'And what's more, I'm quite certain Harry agrees with me.'

Harry writhed in his chair and thought: *For once in your life, you're telling no more than the truth.*

Inge turned to him and said, 'You saw how distressed I was when you and Frances told me about your discussion with the journalist. Of course, it was a great shock. But I wouldn't want anyone to think that I only cared for Gary because of his pedigree. Nothing could be further from the truth. It was the man I loved, not the family name. What upset me was the thought that I might have lost him. When Gary called me and begged me at least to give him the chance to explain, how could I say no?'

Gary stretched his legs out in front of him. The creases in his trousers were as sharp as ever; his shoes still shone as though a valet had spent half the night polishing them. 'I told her that I didn't expect her to take me back. How could I? I'd been living a lie. The truth is, that's what I've been doing for most of my life. Inge's a wealthy young woman, I thought she was bound to believe that my love for her was about as phoney as my identity as a well-born financial consultant.'

'But your doubts were overcome?' Harry asked.

'It only took a few minutes,' Inge said. 'I needed to hear everything from his own lips. Once I'd done that, all I had to do was decide whether I trusted my own judgment in Gary's character.' A pause, accompanied by a soft smile. 'It wasn't the most difficult decision I've ever had to take in my life, Harry, hard as you may find that to understand.'

'I find plenty of things hard to understand,' Harry said. *Like lust for reconciliation sex with a man who has beaten you up.* He'd parted from Juliet an hour earlier, still mystified by her willingness to tolerate brutality. He knew that if he had any sense he would make an excuse and not see her again. But where women were concerned, he never had any sense. 'Mind you, I have to admit it's a good story. I hope Reeve is paying you well.'

'Money isn't the main consideration,' Gary Cullinan said. It was rather, Harry thought, like a politician saying there was more to life than votes. 'We have to be realistic. The cat is out of the bag so far as my impersonation of poor Matthew Cullinan is concerned. This fellow Reeve is obviously determined to spill as much ink as he can over the story. He's even dug up some lad who went to the same school as me, someone I can barely remember. We may as well take the opportunity to put our side of the story. Stop misinformation being put about by the Press.'

He spoke as if committed to providing a public service. Perhaps one day a career in Parliament would beckon: he had the requisite chutzpah. It made Harry's flesh prickle and in any other circumstances he would have left by now, unable to bear any more of it. But there was still the chance that Gary Cullinan might help him to make sense of the puzzle surrounding the deaths of Luke and Roy.

'So you've given them your life story?' Harry reflected that Davey Damnation might be knocked off the front page any moment now.

'It sounds very grand when you put it like that,' Gary said in a self-deprecating tone. 'Really, I'd be the first to admit that there's plenty in my life to be ashamed of. Right from the start. I'm illegitimate, as it happens. Cullinan was my mother's maiden name. I never knew my father.'

'Who can tell?' Inge said with a smile. 'For all any of us knows, your father might have been a peer of the realm. Someone with a guilty secret who didn't dare to acknowledge your birth.'

Gary smirked. 'That would be a nice twist, wouldn't it? One thing's for sure, though, my dad never provided for either my mother or me. We lived in Birkenhead, near the old shipyard. Money was always short and Mum fell foul of the law. There was a business about some forged cheques – she had to go away. I was brought up by an elderly aunt, thinking that my mother was some glamorous gangster on the run. The truth was rather more prosaic. She was doing time.'

Inge squeezed his hand. 'It must have been dreadful for you.'

'I won't pretend life was easy. Of course, I dreamed that when I grew up, I'd make a fortune and look after my mother. She died before I had a chance to make the fantasy come true. I was only nine years old. I suppose after that, one thing led to another. I mixed with bad company.'

Over the years Harry had acted for many clients whose misfortune had been to fall in with a bad crowd. One of these days, perhaps he would meet someone who admitted to being the bad crowd's moving spirit, rather than one of its luckless victims. He said, 'So you got into trouble with the police?'

'Nothing too serious,' Gary said with a grin. 'I soon learned how to talk my way out of a tight corner. But eventually I decided that it was time for me to leave Merseyside. Seek my fortune elsewhere, so to speak. I wanted to make it big. Learn how to talk nicely, behave like the rich people I saw on the telly. I must have been all of fifteen.'

'Didn't you say you sold cars for a living?' Inge asked. It was clear that she admired his enterprise, his determination to better himself.

Gary gave a careless wave of the hand. 'Cars, office equipment, property. You name it. I went to Spain for a while and bought a share in a bar with an expat. For a time we did very well out of it. When things went sour, I came back to this country. I still hadn't found my niche, but I met a chap who had a financial services business. He needed a salesman and we joined forces. Some of the clients were high net worth folk. One was a blue-rinsed lady who was especially well-connected. She leapt to the conclusion that I was one of *the* Cullinans and I'm afraid I did nothing to disabuse her.'

'You are a terrible man,' Inge said fondly.

'I must admit I found it enormously entertaining that she thought that I was one of Lord Gralam's sons. So much so that I decided to check out the family. When I realised quite how rich they were, I started to think: wouldn't it be nice if I really were one of *the* Cullinans. It wasn't such a big leap to turn the idea into reality. I discovered that Matthew had departed for Madras. I fancied working for myself rather than making pots of money for someone else. So I decided to return to my home ground – not as Gary the likely lad, but as Matthew, the wealthy and respectable financial services guru. And you know what?'

'Go on,' Harry said.

'I could never call myself a wizard on investment business. I find it hard enough to pick a winner in a one-horse race. But people didn't seem to care. As long as they believed they were dealing with the son of Lord Gralam, they were happy to accept anything I said as gospel.'

'As Luke Dessaur did.'

'Exactly. It was amazing.'

'Perhaps,' Harry said slowly, 'Luke was more naïve than any of us realised.'

'I think so. When he invited me on to the board, I felt I could hardly say no. That's been my problem over the years, I guess. Like mother, like son. Neither of us were ever able to resist temptation.'

He stretched out an arm and began to stroke Inge's hair. 'And then a funny thing happened, Harry. I met Inge at a cocktail party – and I fell in love. But by then I was trapped. I was introduced to her as the honourable Matthew Cullinan. What could I do?'

'He thought I would drop him like a hot potato if I knew the truth,' Inge said. She gave Gary a gentle punch in the stomach. 'You should have had more faith in me, darling. It was you I was interested in, not your family background.'

'But I was afraid you would assume I was on the make, simply after your money. Let's face it, your father still does think precisely that.'

'He'll come round,' she said. 'He only wants the best for me. Once he sees that you give me everything I need, he'll share our happiness.'

Gary beamed. 'I must say, Harry, it's really a tremendous relief that the truth has come out. Even though I took fright when I first took the call from Desmond Reeve. And your fellow solicitor, Reuben Fingall, is a damned fine lawyer. I could tell the police were nervous of him. And when

I explained you acted for the Trust, he said how glad he was.'

Harry frowned. Such a compliment from Ruby was akin to a cannibal's expression of goodwill towards a missionary. 'What about the missing money?'

'Reuben said he was confident you would advise Frances Silverwood to take a reasonable view,' Gary said smoothly. 'Let's face it, the publicity would do no-one any good. Besides, the money will be repaid within the next forty-eight hours.'

'And where is it coming from, may I ask?'

'Harry, please,' Inge said. 'Don't look stern. It doesn't suit you. Can't you forget you're a solicitor and remember you're a human being.'

'The two aren't *always* mutually exclusive.'

'If it matters,' she said, 'the money will be coming from me. Together with the appropriate amount of interest. I will let Ms Silverwood have my cheque. In addition, I plan to make a personal donation. I had it in mind when we were at the Pool Theatre. The Trust obviously does a great deal for the arts in Liverpool. I'm keen to give it every possible support.'

'I don't want you to think I'm simply content to let Inge buy me out of trouble,' Gary said. 'We've argued about this for hours.'

'But I insisted,' she said. 'He needs to make a fresh start. We plan to start our married life with a clean sheet.'

'So the engagement is on?' Harry asked heavily.

'We plan to get married as soon as possible. This business – strangely enough, it has brought us even closer together.'

Gary said, 'What doesn't destroy you, makes you stronger.' Harry reflected that the journalists would love his mastery of the confession-story cliché.

'So I hope that the Trust won't press charges,' Inge said.

'It's not up to them,' Harry said. 'It's a decision for the prosecution service.'

'But you will urge Frances Silverwood not to be vindictive? I gather that she and Gary have never hit it off.'

'I've always regarded her as a fair-minded woman.'

'Spoken like a lawyer, if I may say so. Very careful. The important thing, surely, is that the Trust will not be out of pocket. On the contrary. And I gather there is a prospect of funds from the Kavanaugh estate.'

In the background, Debussy was playing on the hi-fi. At least things could have been worse: Gary might have chosen something else by Gervase Kavanaugh. Harry said, 'Vera Blackhurst's solicitor has confirmed that she's willing to agree a reasonable deal.'

Geoffrey Willatt had spoken to Jim whilst Harry was out of action. Apparently their old boss was a sadder and wiser man. And Vera was off on holiday to the Canaries. She was not expected to return to Liverpool.

'You can imagine how I felt when she produced that bloody will,' Gary said in comfortable reminiscence. 'I'd been relying on that money to tide the Trust over. Besides, I could tell from the start she was a con merchant.' He paused. 'Ah, Harry, I can read you mind. You're thinking: "It takes one to know one."'

'Something of the sort,' Harry admitted. How was it that a cheat and a bullshitter could put him on the defensive, make him feel that he was in the wrong? 'I can't make any promises. But I will speak to Frances and Tim.'

'It's Frances who concerns me, not dear old Tim,' Gary said. 'She can be very ruthless, I suspect, but he wouldn't hurt a fly.'

Although he killed his own mother, Harry thought. *And perhaps even a mercy killing demands a certain ruthlessness.*

Inge said, 'Frances has had enough heartache, she ought not to want to cause heartache to others. She knows what it is like, to lose the man she loved.'

Gary said, 'She lost him a long time ago.'

'What do you mean?' Harry asked.

'Only that Luke confided in me a little while back that she was keen to marry him. We'd had an evening together and a few drinks. He talked more freely than he usually did, said he was going to tell her it was impossible.'

'Did he say why?'

Gary looked puzzled. He was not, Harry sensed, someone who ever spent much time wondering what made other people tick.

'He told me he'd been very happily married. His wife had died tragically and I suppose he didn't think anyone else would ever live up to his expectations. Frankly, he gave me the impression that he was embarrassed by Frances's attentions. I think she was bothered by the passage of time. She must be – what? – getting on for forty. Remember that song in the musical at the Pool Theatre? "Tick Tock Goes The Clock"? I thought of Frances when the girls were singing that.'

'I wonder if Luke ever had that conversation with her?'

'Not sure.'

'Perhaps she guessed what was in his mind,' Inge suggested.

'Who can tell what a woman thinks?' Gary smiled and gave her knee a pat. 'Anyway, thanks for coming to see us. It's good to talk. And let's hope that this is one story with a happy ending.'

'But not for Roy Milburn.'

'Well, yes. Extraordinary, isn't it? To think that Roy is dead. I've heard a rumour that it may have been suicide.'

'It might have made more sense if he'd killed himself before Luke died,' Harry said carefully. 'After all, Luke suspected him rather than yourself of taking the money from the Trust.'

Gary shook his head. 'If only. Luke was old-fashioned and something of an innocent. But he did finally cotton on to me before he died.'

Harry raised his eyebrows. 'What makes you think that?'

'He told me so. A few days before his death, he asked me to have a chat. When we talked, he caught me off guard. I'd expected another cosy conversation over a drink, with Luke opening his heart about Frances again. But he was a good deal cooler this time round. Of course, he didn't know that I was not Matthew Cullinan, so he was very cautious. He said he thought I could cast light on the whereabouts of the missing money. I pretended to be baffled, but he persisted. I asked him if he'd spoken to Roy as treasurer and he gave me short shrift. Told me that Roy was useless. He'd checked the share valuations I'd provided and found out they were phoney.'

'As a matter of interest,' Harry said, 'what did you do with the money?'

'He was saving it to spend on our wedding,' Inge said. 'I'm as much to blame as Gary.'

Gary smiled and said, 'I played for time. Admitted nothing, but hinted that I'd simply – in effect – borrowed the money and that if the worst came to the worst, I could touch Lord Gralam for a loan. Meanwhile, I hoped something would turn up. Shades of Mr Micawber. I hadn't given up on Charles Kavanaugh's money – especially if you could turn the screw on the Blackhurst woman's lawyers. As a last resort, I'm ashamed to say I hadn't ruled out the possibility of borrowing from Inge. But then Luke died.'

'A lucky break.'

'Don't sound so disapproving, Harry. It doesn't suit you. I can't deny that when I heard the news, I breathed a sigh of relief. Who wouldn't? I'm only flesh and blood. I thought I'd escaped scot free – and so I had until I got careless and allowed that photographer to snap me at the Pool Theatre.'

'The euphoria of the occasion,' Inge said with a giggle.

'Exactly, darling. I was so excited – I got carried away. Do you know, for a time I almost thought I *was* the honourable Matthew Cullinan.'

'Darling, shall I tell you something? I'm glad you're not.'

They gazed lovingly at each other and Harry stood up. 'I have to be going.'

'You will – speak to Frances?' Gary asked.

'Yes, I hope to see her this evening.'

'Fine. Thanks. I'm sure she'll understand when you explain the position to her.' He beamed. 'So all's well that ends well, eh?'

'Oh yes,' Harry said. 'Except for Roy and Luke Dessaur.'

Chapter 21

Frances was singing an old Etta James number, 'Waiting for Charlie to Come Home'. She invested it with infinite yearning and as Harry watched, her eyes met those of the piano player and the couple smiled at each other like lovers reunited after years apart.

They were in the lounge of the Hawthorne Hotel and sitting at the piano was Tim Aldred. Harry had arrived ten minutes earlier, in the middle of a Cole Porter medley and Frances had acknowledged him with a fractional nod of the head during 'Love For Sale'. He had spoken to her on the phone earlier in the afternoon and arranged to meet her here. She had told him that she was performing, but had not mentioned the identity of her accompanist. Watching from the back of the room, Harry was struck by the delicacy of the big man's touch, the care which he took to ensure that the accompaniment did not distract attention from the vocalist. He had begun to realise that there was more to Tim than met the eye and, to judge by the look on her face, the same thing had dawned on Frances.

The song came to an end to a ripple of applause from the people in the lounge. The audience was composed almost exclusively of elderly Americans sipping coffee or wine after dinner in the restaurant. Frances and Tim bowed to them and said that they would be taking a break for half an hour. She walked briskly towards Harry. Tim lumbered along behind her, knocking a table as he passed it and spilling an old lady's drink.

'Congratulations,' Harry said.

She smiled. 'You liked what you heard?'

'Very much.' He turned to Tim, who had finished stammering his apologies to the old lady. 'You're a man of many talents. I knew you played, but I'm afraid I assumed you were a member of the honky-tonk school rather than Liverpool's answer to Vladimir Ashkenazy.'

'Isn't he the goalkeeper for Moscow Dynamos?' Tim asked with a blush that betrayed his pleasure at the compliment.

'You're quite right, Harry,' Frances said. 'Tim's always too modest. I had a terrible job persuading him to help me out tonight. Thank goodness I persisted. You were wonderful, Tim.'

She pecked him on the cheek and he reddened again. 'A bit rusty, really.'

'Nonsense. You were absolutely marvellous. Quite frankly, you ought to reconsider your priorities. I know you love conjuring, but you could do even better as a pianist. Especially if you worked with a true professional, rather than an amateur like me.'

He patted her arm. 'Frances, there is no-one I'd rather work with than you.'

For the second time in a matter of hours, Harry had the feeling that two was company, three a crowd. He said, 'So you've only just started working together?'

'Tonight is the very first time.' Frances said.

'I'd never have realised.'

'It's quite true. The man who regularly works with me had to cry off. His wife has been taken seriously ill and he needed to be with her. I thought I'd have to cancel our date here. I'd been in two minds about it since – since Luke died. I didn't know how I would cope with performing here. On the other hand, I hate to break an engagement. But I was on the verge of ringing in and making my excuses when Tim rang and I found myself asking him if he would be willing to help me out.'

'I was afraid I'd let you down,' Tim said.

'When you can play like that? Believe me...'

'Let me buy you a drink,' Harry said hastily. 'You both deserve it.'

When they were settled at a table in the bar, he told them about his conversation with Gary Cullinan and Inge Frontzeck. The glow faded from Frances's face as she listened and, when Harry told her that Inge was prepared to pay back to the Trust every penny that Gary had stolen and more, she snorted with contempt.

'I've a good mind to tell her what to do with her cheque. She ought to have more sense.'

Harry shrugged. 'She's fallen for his story hook, line and sinker. She seems to regard every lie that he's told as proof of his devotion to her.'

'Some women,' Frances said bitterly, 'never learn.'

'We mustn't be vindictive,' Tim said. 'I know you wouldn't want that, Frances. Perhaps he's learned his lesson.'

'That'll be the day.'

'Maybe. But I think we should accept the compensation and draw a line under the whole sorry business. Involving the police never does any good.'

'What about justice?' Frances demanded. 'The man's committed a crime.'

'Sometimes blind justice does no-one any good. Let's give him another chance. If he muffs it, that's his business.'

'And Inge's.'

'And Inge's. But she's a grown woman. If she makes a mistake, at least it will have been her choice. Let's not make a martyr out of him.' He turned his earnest face to Harry. 'What do you say?'

Harry remembered that Tim knew what it was like to face blind justice. 'I agree with you,' he said quietly. 'The Trust won't be any worse off. Besides, the prisons are full enough already. Mostly with my clients, I sometimes think.'

'Very well,' Frances said, unexpectedly meek. 'Tim, I've never known you be so eloquent.'

'I'm inspired by your company,' he said and then threw Harry a glance. 'Besides, there's something I'd like to talk to you about. Later on.'

So he was going to tell her about the killing of his mother. Harry was glad. But before he left them, he needed to find out if there was any substance to the theory that was taking shape in his mind. When Tim headed for the bar, he seized the moment.

'Frances. About Luke. I hardly know how to put this in a tactful way, but did he tell you recently that there was no chance that the two of you would get together permanently?'

Her eyes grew narrow. 'What makes you think that?'

'Gary Cullinan told me that Luke confided in him.'

She bowed her head. 'God, I loathe that man. But he was telling the truth for once. I've known Luke a long time. We were firm friends, we had a great deal in common. I suppose I started to think that it would be nice if we... well, you know...'

'Did he encourage you?'

'Oh no, quite the reverse. He was an entirely honourable man. But I persisted. Silly of me, I suppose. I should have realised that no-one could replace Gwendoline in his affections. In the end, I plucked up the courage to talk to him, ask if I was really wasting my time. And though in my heart of hearts, I didn't expect it, he told me I was. Kindly, of course, but he was absolutely clear. He didn't want to get married again. Once was enough.'

'It must have been hard for you,' Harry said.

'I was shattered. I suppose you could call me a private person. My work has always mattered a great deal to me. I've never had much time for personal relationships. Those I've had have been brief and disastrous. I'd given up hope of finding a decent man until I met Luke. I hoped he would read the signs – and respond. But he didn't.'

'You must have felt bitter towards him.'

She sighed. 'Perhaps, for a short time. But I soon realised I was being selfish. It would have been dreadful if I'd spoiled our relationship. When he suggested taking me to the dress rehearsal of *Promises, Promises* I was glad to accept. Even though just then it seemed I'd spend the rest of my life with Uncle Joe as my closest companion.'

'And now – you have Tim,' Harry said.

'Yes.' Her expression lightened. 'It rather looks as though I do. And do you know something, I was thinking only today that perhaps it's time for Uncle Joe to be interred with the rest of his mates in Everton Cemetery?'

'Good idea,' Harry said. 'You deserve better than him.

And here comes Tim with the drinks.'

She smiled. 'What's the betting he'll drop them?'

But Tim Aldred negotiated his way back through the crowd at the bar with unaccustomed skill. 'Cheers,' he said. 'Shall we drink to the Trust? With Cullinan out of the way and Vera Blackhurst sorted, it should go from strength to strength from now on.'

'We'll have to start looking for new recruits,' Frances said. 'Who would have thought that in such a short time we would lose Luke, Roy and Matthew?'

'It's an amazing coincidence,' Tim said.

'Is it?' Harry asked as he sipped from his glass.

'What do you mean?' Frances's voice was sharp.

'I'm not sure I believe in coincidences like that, Frances.'

'What else can it be? Presumably Roy got himself drunk as usual and then swallowed more pain-killers than he should have done.'

'There's an alternative theory.' He told her about the cartoon of Roy on the gallows and the theory that he had murdered Luke.

'But why?' she demanded. 'Roy didn't care much for Luke and the feeling was mutual – but murder...'

Harry finished his drink. 'What if Luke suspected Roy of being the one who was on the take from the Trust?'

'But surely now that Matthew has confessed...'

'Yes, well. For what it's worth, I don't believe Roy killed Luke.' He let out a breath. 'And I don't believe he committed suicide either.'

Both Frances and Tim were staring at him now. 'What do you think happened?' Tim asked hoarsely.

Harry said gently, 'I'll tell you when I *know* what happened. Meanwhile, I'd like to have a word with Bruce Carpenter while I'm here.'

'We saw him earlier on,' Tim said. 'We exchanged a few words.'

Frances gave a crisp nod. She had begun to recover her composure. 'I scarcely recognised him at first.'

Harry leaned forward. 'Why's that?'

'An Elvis Presley convention is being held upstairs and now that the show's run is over, he's been press-ganged into tending bar. And getting himself up as an Elvis look-alike.' She winced. 'Quite a racket up there. Not really my taste in music at all.'

'Pity I forgot my blue suede shoes,' Harry said. 'Elvis I can cope with. Just as long as I don't have to listen to anything else by Gervase Kavanaugh.'

Nathaniel Hawthorne must have been turning in his grave. The mezzanine floor was seething with Elvis wannabees from twenty-five to sixty-five. The place was a Brylcreem salesman's dream. Many of the men were wiggling their hips in a grotesque parody of the King whose voice was issuing from the huge speakers in the corner of the room. He was singing an old number one: 'The Devil in Disguise'.

'Harry Devlin, isn't it?' an American voice said in his ear. 'Forgive me, but you seem a little out of place here. Can I help you?'

The fleeting thought passed through Harry's mind that he seemed a little out of place almost everywhere, but he dismissed it impatiently. 'As a matter of fact, you can. I was looking for you.'

Bruce Carpenter raised his eyebrows. 'Perhaps I should be flattered.'

He had a tray of drinks in his hand and was wearing a white, gold and silver suit, the sort the singer had worn during his Las

Vegas period, together with dark glasses and cowboy boots. His hair was done in a quiff and at first glance it was possible to believe that the tabloid headlines had come true and the rock-'n'-roll saviour had come back to life. He noticed Harry looking at the boots and said with a smile, 'Would you believe it? Hand-stretched python skin.'

'Haven't I seen them on sale in the market at Toxteth?'

'As a matter of fact, I had to have them specially imported from the States. I only wear them for special occasions like this. They cost a small fortune and I'd hate to get them scuffed.'

Abandoning irony, Harry said, 'I didn't realise you were a fan.'

'Just because I love Stephen Sondheim, that doesn't mean I can't *adore* rock 'n' roll,' Bruce said teasingly. 'Remember what your local lad, John Lennon, said? "Before Elvis, there was nothing." I've been besotted with the King since I was a boy.' He paused, then said, 'But you didn't come here to talk about music, did you?'

'No. I wanted to have another word with you about Luke Dessaur.'

Bruce ran a hand through his quiff. 'Look, it was tragic about Luke. Tragic. But I don't know why you have to drag up the past. What's the point?'

'I want to know why Luke died.'

Bruce studied Harry for a moment. 'Don't you know already?'

'I think I may have guessed.'

'Well, then.'

'You're the one person who can confirm the truth.'

'What makes you say that?'

'You had a hold over him. An emotional hold, is my guess. Were you lovers?'

Bruce Carpenter rubbed his chin. Harry suddenly thought how young the man was. Not more than twenty-five, twenty-six. Half the age of the eternally respectable Luke Dessaur. For a while neither of them spoke. In the background Elvis was starting to ask: 'Are You Lonesome Tonight?'

'So you weren't fooled when I kept kissing and cuddling my leading lady?' Bruce said at last. 'Well, why should you be? I've been out for a long while. Not like poor old Luke. And yes, we were lovers, we had a brief encounter.'

'That's why Luke killed himself, isn't it?' Harry asked. 'Because for you it was just a passing affair. But he had fallen in love for the first time and couldn't face life without you.'

Chapter 22

'How did it begin?' Harry asked three quarters of an hour later. He'd had to wait until Bruce's stint of overtime had come to an end before he could start asking questions. They were in Bruce's own room on the top floor of the hotel. The walls were covered with framed posters advertising musical shows, shots of Elvis on stage and a couple of pictures of he-men with hairy chests that had been cut out of magazines. Harry was occupying the solitary chair, Bruce lying on his back across the bed with his feet resting on an anglepoise lamp.

'I approached Luke as chair of the Kavanaugh Trust while we were working on the show. Our main backer had pulled out and we were running over-budget too. We'd cut every corner with the music but we still needed money badly. Without it, I knew we'd never even make the first night. Luke was sympathetic. Of course, he was shy. He'd never dreamed of coming out. But I picked up the signals.' Bruce laughed. 'Lots of experience at that. The message was coming over loud and clear. He was prepared to help, cash-wise. And he fancied me.'

'He offered you a deal? Money in return for a relationship?'

'Oh God, nothing as crude as that. It was never expressed. Luke would have been horrified at the faintest whiff of bribery and corruption.' Bruce winked. 'But we all know what makes the world go round, don't we? No-one does something for nothing. You scratch my back and I'll scratch yours.'

Harry sighed inwardly. The hateful thing was that Bruce was probably right. 'So what happened?'

'He offered us all the dough we wanted, no strings. I was thrilled, of course. I told him how grateful I was and I suggested he come along to the dress rehearsal. Even then he brought a lady friend with him. Frances, his sidekick from the Trust. He liked to have a woman on his arm – but not in his bed. He told me later that she'd had the hots for him. He'd found it tough to deal with. She was a good friend and he didn't want to hurt her. Or give himself away. I said, "Why didn't you simply tell her the truth?" He nearly had a seizure.'

'He kept his secret well. I'd known Luke for a long time, but I never realised he was gay. It wasn't until I started to wonder why he'd been so keen to back your show that a possible explanation occurred to me.'

'Oh, he told me he'd always preferred boys to girls. But he came from the generation – and, more importantly, the background – when it wasn't what he called "the done thing". Lovely phrase, I think.'

'He'd been married.'

'So what? He told me all about that. More than I wanted to hear, truth to tell. God, he loved to talk, did Luke. He'd kept quiet for so long, that was the trouble. He poured his heart out to me – all the time. It was more than I'd ever bargained for.'

'The marriage was a sham?'

Bruce considered. 'Kind of. He'd had a repressed childhood, he said. Classic stuff for the shrinks. He went out with girls as a teenager, but they didn't give him a buzz the way some of the boys he knew did. He was afraid of himself. Bear in mind, this goes back to the dark ages, the days when gay love was illegal. He was fond of Gwen and then she was diagnosed as leukaemic. He married her as much out of pity as anything, I think – and then she went into remission.'

'He'd expected her to die when they married?'

'Yeah. He said they were happy enough, but it was never about sex for either of them. When he did lose her, he didn't need to get married again.'

'He was the sort of man a lot of women find attractive.'

'He *was* attractive – for his age. Believe me, Harry, I'm many things but I'm not a hooker. If he hadn't turned me on, I wouldn't have gone to bed with him that night of the dress rehearsal, money or no money.' Bruce paused and then a slow, mischievous grin crept across his face. 'At least, I wouldn't have gone to bed with him more than once.'

'What went wrong?'

'For Luke, having a relationship with another man was like busting a dam. He'd been celibate for so long, he'd actually *fought* against his instincts for over thirty years. Can you imagine? He went wild, never even gave safe sex a thought. Amazing. The whole thing was a big, big deal as far as he was concerned. Right from that first night together, I could tell he'd be the clingy type. Part of him was afraid of what might happen now that he'd succumbed to temptation. Part of him was desperate to make up for lost time.' Bruce shook his head. 'For me, it was scary. I'm not into commitment at this point in my life. I told him the honest truth, but he couldn't handle it. He wanted us to stay together. So naïve. He expected far too much.'

'He always had high standards,' Harry said slowly. He was trying to imagine the agonies of self-knowledge that Luke had been forced to confront in the days leading up to his death.

'Sure. And that's fine, so long as you don't impose your own standards on other people. That's where Luke went wrong. Within twenty-four hours, we were fighting. He wanted us to be together long term, go away somewhere he wasn't known. He had no family; apart from his godson he had no ties. I told him it was a crazy idea.'

'How did he react?'

'He threatened to kill himself. It was late one night. I'd had a bad day behind the bar and the latest rehearsal hadn't gone well. I was tired and pissed off and there was this old man bleating away in the background. I told him I'd had two lovers die on me through AIDS. Both of them I nursed right through to the bitter end. I wasn't going to lose any sleep if a guy I scarcely knew took an overdose.'

'What did he say to that?'

'Oh, he had a little weep and then he pissed off. Which was all I'd wanted. I thought maybe that was it between us. But then he turned up here again, white as a sheet. He said he'd been thinking about our conversation. I soon figured he was wondering whether I was HIV.'

'And you told him you were?'

'Right. It's not true, as it happens. I've been lucky. But it seemed a good way of making the break with Luke once and for all. Of course, I hadn't thought it through. He began to panic. He was convinced I'd infected him. For a nasty moment I thought he was going to attack me. Instead he broke down and cried. I had a change of heart then and told him I'd made the whole thing up. But he didn't believe me.'

'Frances told me he'd seemed afraid during the last few days before he died.'

'Now you know why. Silly, really. I told him, all he had to do was take a test and he'd prove to himself that he was in the clear. But he couldn't face it. He was much weaker than he seemed. One little lie and he lost it.'

It had been a cruel lie, but Harry let it pass. 'Tell me what happened on the day he died.'

'He checked in here after lunch. I couldn't believe it. God knows what was going on in his head. The last thing I wanted was a scene at my place of work. I kept my distance during the afternoon but he called me from his room and invited me to have dinner with him. I told him I had to go to the rehearsal and besides, it was against company rules for the staff to fraternise with the guests. He didn't like that, asked me what I thought we'd been doing together over the last few days. I said I didn't think 'fraternising' was the description I'd choose. We were behaving like a couple of bitchy drama queens, I guess. He was pretty persistent and in the end, I said I'd come to his room when I got back from the theatre.'

'So you went out that evening while he dined alone and then started knocking back the whisky in his room?'

'You've got it. I kept my promise and turned up to see him. I thought we might as well sort things out once and for all. Part as friends. You know.'

'Yes,' Harry said, thinking for a moment of Kim. 'How was he?'

Bruce began to nibble at his fingernails; it was as if, for the first time, he was experiencing a moment of self-doubt. 'I tried to explain there was no future together for the two of us. He'd put away a fair amount of scotch and he wasn't used to drinking. He became maudlin and frankly rather pathetic. I recall he pleaded with me to stay, but I wouldn't. We argued. It got heated.'

'The porter Julio heard raised voices.'

'Thank Christ he didn't recognise my voice or I would have had some embarrassing questions to answer. As it was, I told Luke he might as well check out first thing the next morning. He and I were finished. And I walked out on him.'

'And the next thing you knew he'd been found dead in the courtyard?'

'Uh-huh.' Bruce puffed out his cheeks. 'You can imagine how I felt.'

Yes, you selfish bastard. I bet you thought: 'Well, that's one problem solved.' 'You kept quiet about why Luke threw himself out of the window.'

'Who's to say it was deliberate? He was pissed, confused. Don Ragovoy will kill me for saying this, but it's just possible it might have been an accident.'

Harry shook his head. 'No, you're wrong. I'm sure he committed suicide.'

'How can you be sure? He didn't leave any sort of note.'

'Do you know something?' Harry said, 'I'm beginning to wonder if perhaps he did.'

Harry pushed his way through the Hawthorne's revolving door out into the street. By instinct, he turned in the direction of the waterfront; then he paused. It was pouring with rain and bitterly cold: not a night to stay out of doors, but he was not ready to return to his flat. His shoulders were tense and he felt restless; even if he did go back there was no chance of sleep. His mind was buzzing: he had a theory to test. Even as he gazed down into the pools of water on the pavement, glistening under the yellow streetlights, much that had puzzled him was becoming clearer. The gnawing in his stomach was a hunger to establish the truth. If there was even the faintest chance of satisfying his curiosity tonight, he was desperate to seize it.

He pulled up the collar of his coat and crossed the road, this time heading back towards the city centre. The rain was gathering in intensity, driven on by the wind from the river. At the Paradise Street bus station, a drunk was singing 'Lovely Rita, Meter Maid' and a few homeless people were huddling on cardboard in shop doorways. But the pubs and clubs had yet to close and for the most part, Liverpool was quiet. The Scissorman would not be on the prowl tonight.

He turned the last corner and came to a halt. Opposite him stood the Speckled Band. He knew that Ashley often stayed there late at night, sorting through stock and now and then succumbing to the temptation to pick up an old book and start reading it. Coming here at this hour in the hope of a chance to talk had been a long shot, though, and the place was in darkness. Shutters were down over the door and windows. But when Harry glanced up, he saw smoke curling from the chimney above the shop.

He caught his breath. Perhaps it had not been a wasted journey after all. He walked round the corner to the back of the building. There was a small yard which contained a rubbish bin; the gate which led into it was ajar. Harry went through, startling a cat which had been prowling along the wall round the yard into a squawk of indignation.

The door was heavy and painted black. Harry pushed and found it gave to his touch. He crossed the threshold and found himself standing in a narrow passageway. The walls were stained with damp. A door to his right was ajar; he could see steps leading underground. There was a smell of burning. He could hear the crackling of the fire in the shop, taste the smoky air on his lips.

He took a deep breath and called out, 'Ashley?'

For a few seconds, nothing. Then a door at the end of the corridor, the door to the shop, swung slowly open and Melissa Whitaker stepped out from the shadows.

'Harry.'

Her cheeks seemed hollowed-out, her eyes dim with despair. For the first time in their acquaintance she was wearing a tatty T-shirt and an old pair of denim jeans. He realised, too, that he had never seen her before without make-up. She never spared any expense in looking her best, but her skin seemed bare and coarse.

'Hello, Melissa. I didn't expect to see you here at this time of night.'

'I – I've been down in the cellar.' Her voice was oddly croaky. 'What do you want?'

'Where's Ashley?'

She cleared her throat. 'Why do you ask?'

'I need to talk to him.'

'Can't – can't it wait?'

'No.' He swallowed. She seemed as tense as he was. It was worth taking a chance. 'You know it can't wait.'

'Maybe you're right. But you can't talk to him. He – he's left me.'

'I don't believe you. He'd never do that. He's crazy about you.'

She closed her eyes. 'Too much so.'

'Can you and I talk, then?'

'There's no point.'

'There's every point.'

She sighed and waved him into the shop. As he moved forward, he could not suppress a shiver. Suppose this all went wrong?

Don't be a fool, he told himself. *This is a bookshop, for God's sake. Nothing can go wrong.*

The fire was blazing wildly, stoked by countless sheets of printed paper. Next to it teetered a stack of old detective stories. What was going on? If he were to learn the truth, he must get her talking; and not just in monosyllables.

Melissa gave a wry smile. 'More fuel for the flames.'

On top of the heap was an old green Penguin, a copy of a book by a lawyer who had been dead for forty years. Harry picked it up.

'*Tragedy at Law*. The story of my life.' She didn't smile again, so he added, 'Actually, it's one of my favourites.'

'Ashley's too.'

'Did he ever tell you the final line? The detective says that he supposes it's the first case of someone being driven to suicide by a quotation from the law reports.'

She took the book from him and glanced without seeing at the last page. 'So many things can drive people to suicide.'

'You were right, by the way. Luke killed himself.'

'Yes, I know. Not that it matters. Nothing matters.'

'That's not true.' He paused. 'Why are you burning the books?'

Her voice breaking, she said, 'I hate them, didn't you realise that? Bloody mysteries. I've lived with them all my married life. I'm sick of them. I want to rid myself of them. For ever.'

As she tore the title page out of the book, he said, 'Yet you provided the money to let Ashley run this shop, indulge his hobby to his heart's content.'

She gave a mocking laugh. 'Soft, wasn't I? I felt I owed him something – for his kindness when we first got together after my father died. And because I was less than a proper wife to him. But now that's all done with. And there are books to be burned.'

She squatted in front of the fire. Seemingly oblivious of his presence, she ripped out a dozen more pages, tossing them into the greedy flames.

He took a deep breath and, crossing his fingers behind his back, sat down beside her. 'I know what happened, Melissa.' Well, it was partly true.

She turned her white face to him. 'You don't know the half of it...'

'Ashley killed Roy, didn't he?'

'But do you know why?'

'To keep Roy quiet.' He paused. 'What I'm not sure about is the reason he wanted to keep Roy quiet.'

She closed her eyes and bit her teeth into her pale pink lips so hard that even as Harry watched, a trace of blood appeared.

'Because he'd asked Roy to kill my father.'

Chapter 23

'He was too ingenious for his own good,' Harry said, half to himself. His mind was racing. 'He had what seemed like a smart idea and then couldn't resist temptation. It was over-elaborate. Once I realised he was trying to misdirect me, I began to understand what he was trying to do.'

She gave an absent-minded nod. Still she was tearing pages and feeding them to the fire. 'He would always get carried away. This place, for instance, he was like a child in a sweetshop when he was here. I couldn't deny him.'

'He wanted to convince me – and the police – that there was something strange and sinister about the death of Luke Dessaur. If Luke had been murdered, then Ashley had a watertight alibi because he was with you in Toronto at the time.'

'Just as he was in France when my father was killed,' she said. 'He was repeating an old trick.'

Harry was thinking aloud. 'The next step was to link Roy's death with Luke's. If Roy's death was regarded as an accident, fine. But even better if people thought he'd murdered Luke and then committed suicide. Poetic justice of a sort. Either way, Ashley was safe from suspicion. Before you left for Canada, Luke told Ashley that one of the Kavanaugh trustees was on the take. He was too discreet to name the person he had in mind, either to Ashley or me. Ashley assumed that Roy must be the culprit. It was a logical mistake. He knew Roy was greedy...'

'Roy was blackmailing Ashley,' Melissa said wearily. 'That's why Ashley killed him. Roy had no need to steal from the Trust.'

'Ashley won't have seen it like that. He knew Roy of old, he didn't put anything past him. Besides, Roy was the obvious suspect. Frances, Tim and Matthew Cullinan seemed beyond reproach.'

'Ashley was supposed to be Roy's oldest friend,' she said, 'but the truth is that he'd always envied Roy,' she said. 'Feared him, too. Ashley lived in a fantasy world. Roy was a doer.'

'Once I learned that Luke had confronted Cullinan about the missing money, I started to question everything Ashley had told me. If Roy had no motive, then either Luke had been murdered by someone else – or not been murdered at all. This evening I finally made sure Luke did kill himself.'

'You know about Bruce Carpenter?'

He was surprised. 'Yes. Do you?'

She sighed. 'The last time we spoke, Ashley told me the whole story.'

'Would you tell me? Please?'

She swallowed before saying, 'Luke was drunk and desperate. He tried to ring Ashley in Toronto. He trusted Ashley, had no-one else he felt he could confide in. When he couldn't get through, he decided it was Fate. He was meant to die. He scribbled a note to Ashley and went downstairs and put it in the hotel postbox. It was waiting for us when we got back to Britain, but Ashley told no-one. He wanted to make use of it. He was fond of Luke, but he wasn't above exploiting his godfather's death for his own purposes.'

'The way I picture it, Luke went up to his room and drank too much whisky. Then he wriggled through the window and chucked himself out. Messy, but quick.'

'That's what he said he was going to do in the note. It was maudlin stuff, Ashley said. He'd been heartbroken when we got the news that Luke was dead. He had no idea that Luke was gay.'

'Ashley portrayed himself as Roy's loyal friend,' Harry said. 'But when I remembered what he had said to me, I realised he'd done nothing to dispel the suggestion that Roy was on the fiddle from the Trust. I found myself wondering if Ashley had concocted an elaborate scheme to frame Roy – and then kill him. Neat: he transformed a suicide into a murder and dressed up a murder of his own as suicide.'

'He'd read too many books,' Melissa said sourly. The last of the Hare novel was curled and browning on the fire. She took the next book from the pile. *After the Funeral.*

'I suppose that once he hit upon the idea, he found it irresistible. After all, he'd spent a lifetime soaked in mystery fiction – why not create a puzzle of his own? Ashley's never had to fight to earn a living. He's been able to indulge himself on your father's fortune ever since leaving university. To someone out of touch with reality, the plot must have seemed attractive. Especially when he was the only person who had proof that Luke committed suicide. Presumably he destroyed the letter?'

She nodded and kept tearing pages as he continued: 'I suppose he arranged to call on Roy at the flat and got him so pissed that Roy didn't have the faintest idea he was being fed a lethal dose of pain-killers.'

'Roy was meant to be going out that night. To see a show the Trust had supported. But Ashley persuaded him to stay in. Roy had been pressing for more money and Ashley said I was asking questions, starting to get suspicious. He'd rung Roy in the morning and spun some line about needing to talk. I'd had a migraine that day, I couldn't care less what Ashley was up to. I think he came back in the early hours.'

'The way I've imagined it, after he was satisfied that Roy was out for the count and never going to come round again, he left via the roof, with the door closing itself behind him. All he had to do then was to clamber back down the fire escape and then over the gate which led back to the street so that the main door of the building remained locked from the inside. He also had a stroke of luck. He found something in Roy's flat which he thought would help him in creating the impression of suicide.'

The heat from the fire was so fierce that he had to move back as he described Roy's cartoon of himself on the gallows. But Melissa seemed oblivious to it. Her dull eyes gazed at him.

'The Hanging Man. Like the Tarot card.'

'What?'

'Oh, that woman who buys all the books. Juliet May. She gave Ashley a Tarot reading, you know and turned up the Hanging Man card. He wasn't too happy. He seemed to think it was more alarming than she was prepared to admit. She said he had no need to worry.' Melissa laughed harshly. 'What do you think the cartoon meant?'

'I guess Roy had been thinking a great deal lately about the time he killed your father. Perhaps he wasn't totally devoid of conscience after all.'

She hissed, 'He was a monster.'

'But the cartoon did reinforce the idea of the remorseful suicide, which suited Ashley down to the ground.' He studied Melissa. 'Will you tell me your side of the story?'

She put down the book and shrugged. 'Not much to tell. You know how wives usually discover their husbands' infidelities by chance – when they empty their jackets before sending them off to the dry cleaners or something? I found out my husband was a murderer in much the same way. He was in his study at home when the phone rang. I picked up the extension to hear Roy talking to Ashley – about killing my father.'

He stared at her, horrified, trying to imagine what must have gone through her mind.

She ran her teeth along her lip and said, 'It seemed my husband was being bled dry by his old pal – an ex-boyfriend of mine. As far as I could gather, he'd paid Roy to mow down my father in a supposed hit-and-run accident. He was trying to wriggle out of it, pretend it was nothing to do with him, but he was no match for Roy. Roy even teased him about his love for stories about unbreakable alibis.'

'Oh God,' Harry said softly. And to think people said Freeman Wills Crofts was a humdrum writer.

'The three of us hung around together at uni. Ashley was crazy about me, it was almost embarrassing. I liked him, but he didn't excite me. I suppose I was just a spoiled little daddy's girl, having a good time. In those days I enjoyed men dancing attendance. As long as it didn't go too far. Roy and I went out for a while, but his sheer selfishness began to bore me. Besides, he was pestering me for sex all the time.'

Tears were beginning to fill her eyes and she had to wipe them away before continuing. 'My father was a marvellous man. Tough, handsome, successful. None of the boys I knew began to compare with him. I worshipped Daddy – and he worshipped me. He used to say that I was the only thing that mattered to him once my mother was gone. I could tell he didn't think much of my boyfriends. So I dropped them. That's what happened with Roy.'

'And Roy bore a grudge?'

'Perhaps. He didn't like it when I said I didn't want to see him again. Ashley asked me for a date and I did let him take me to the cinema. He behaved beautifully, but I thought it only fair to say that I wasn't interested in a relationship.'

'And then your father was killed?'

'It was the worst time of my life,' she said. 'Even now there are days when I think about him and...'

Her voice trailed away and Harry found himself saying, 'You told me Ashley was kind to you.'

'I needed him then. It is pathetic, I know, but getting married seemed a natural thing to do. I felt so grateful.'

'But when you overheard the conversation on the phone, you realised Ashley and Roy had planned it all?'

'That's right. I didn't listen to the details – I didn't want to.'

'You might have been jumping to conclusions. Why not talk to Ashley and find out...?'

'Oh, for God's sake stop sounding like a lawyer,' she snapped. 'What matters is that those two bastards conspired to take my father away from me. The only man I've ever really loved. I told you before – whoever killed Daddy deserved to be punished. I'd always longed for the chance to find the bastard. Longed for it. I just never realised I'd been living with him all these years. For Daddy's sake, I wanted justice. I suppose you'd call it taking revenge.'

For all the heat in the room, he felt suddenly cold. 'You mean – by burning Ashley's books?'

She brushed a stray blonde hair out of her face. 'It's worse than that. Much worse.'

Trying to keep his voice calm, he said, 'Where is he, Melissa?'

'Downstairs. In the cellar.'

'What did you do?' he asked, fearing the answer.

She stared at the pile of books, shifted it nearer to the fire. 'In many ways, Ashley has been a wonderful husband. He's stayed in love with me. Even though he had my father murdered, and I hate him for it, it was because of how he felt about me. The truth is, I've never given him much encouragement, in bed or out of it. But there were these things he wanted to do...'

'Yes?' Harry's throat was dry.

'He had endless fantasies. Bondage sex, things I wouldn't even want to describe. The thought of it turned my stomach. I always used to say no and he put up with it. But when I wanted to hurt him, I knew what I had to do to get him at my mercy. I said I'd decided to give him everything he wanted. The Tarot reading gave me the idea.' She paused. 'He was so excited when I lifted his wrists above his head and chained them to the rings in the cellar wall. I waited until he'd realised that he was playing in my game, and not the other way round, before I came back and told him I knew the truth. He denied it, of course. He told me it was Roy's idea and

Roy's alone. But he would say that, wouldn't he? I scarcely listened. In the end he was screaming for mercy.'

'What did you do?'

'I've never had much time for mercy.'

Harry's heart was thudding inside his chest. 'When was this?'

She stretched her arms out. 'I've rather lost track of the days. This was just after Ashley killed Roy, I suppose. I was so glad he'd done half my job for me. He told me the whole story. It was as you described. Not as foolproof as he thought, eh?'

He could feel his gorge rising. 'I – I need to see for myself, Melissa. I must look inside the cellar.'

She nodded in the direction of the door. 'After you.'

His hands were trembling, but he stood up and moved out into the passageway. Without turning round, he asked, 'Is he still alive?'

He held his breath until she answered hoarsely. 'I don't think so, Harry. I didn't let him drink anything, you see.'

Pushing open the door which led to the cellar, he peered into the subterranean blackness. The steps were stone and rough-hewn. He began to edge down them. His skin was prickling, his palms were wet. At the bottom, he screwed his eyes up until they hurt as he tried to adjust to the lack of light.

He could see a cracked mirror which bore a smudged message in lipstick. Reflected in the glass was a dark figure suspended from the opposite wall. The naked body of a man Harry had once counted as a friend. A phrase at the end of a thirties detective story filled his mind. *And he was duly hanged.* But for all that Harry could tell, as waves of sickness convulsed him, Ashley might have been crucified.

The smell of death was suffocating. Harry bent over and retched once, twice. This was no place for the living. Unable to stand any longer, he began to crawl back up the steps. As he reached the top he heard a crash and knew that he had another cause for fear.

Flames were slapping around the shop door at the end of the passageway. To his right lay the way out to the cold city streets and safety. He summoned up all his strength and took the three steps to his left that took him to the room where he had left Melissa.

The fire had driven her behind the counter. Her face wore a look of infinite sadness and in her hand was a burning paperback. The tower of books had become a pyre. As he watched, paralysed, she touched the nearest shelves with her torch.

'Melissa! For God's sake!'

She said, so calmly that he could barely hear the words above the noise of the raging flames, 'There is no God, you ought to know that.'

As she spoke, her shirt caught fire. She let the book fall but did not flinch. Instead, she smiled.

He could scarcely breathe, but he tore off his jacket and slapped it against her burning clothes. Then he caught her wrist and dragged her off her feet and through the door. He could think of nothing but the need to get them both out of the building. His eyes were watering; he could hardly see out of them but it did not matter. She was heavier than he would have thought, but gasping with the effort he pulled her along the passageway.

She began to claw at him. 'No! Leave me!'

Her fingernails cut into his hand but he did not feel pain. It was as if he were in a stupor, drunk with despair at the evil that men do. They were five strides from the door that led outside. He sucked the foul air into his lungs and tightened his grip on her narrow wrist. Four strides more. Three. Two. One.

A last heave and they were over the threshold. It was raining hard and the smack of the downpour roused him from his daze. She had stopped fighting and he hauled her limp body across the yard into the back street beyond. Then he released his hold and stared at the building from which they had escaped. Far above the cellar that had become a tomb, the fire had lit the night sky. He could hear people calling and footsteps pounding along the pavement.

Melissa lay at his feet. He found it impossible to recall the beauty of the red and ravaged face gazing up at him.

'Why?' she whispered.

A vision came into his mind of a high priest wielding a wicked blade. He wanted to say something about blood and sacrifice and the need to believe in something.

But there were too many mysteries and the words refused to come.

'You said yourself, if only her father wasn't around...'

'But I never wished him harm.'

'Too late now. The deed is done.'

Ashley stared at his friend, appalled. They were in the corner of the bar at the students' union. Roy had already been drinking for a couple of hours. His face was flushed with booze and excitement.

'How – how could you have done it?'

'You'd be surprised, actually. I had a few jars beforehand, of course. But really, it was like the title of that book you were reading at the back of the lecture theatre a couple of months back. Murder is Easy.'

'I can't believe it. I simply can't believe you...'

'You ought to believe it. I owed you a favour. The money that godfather of yours lent me was a big help, just when I needed it. You know, if I didn't know better, I'd swear that he fancied me.'

'You – you're sick. You disgust me.'

'Listen.' Roy's voice hardened. 'Don't get the idea you can rat on me. Don't ever think that. We're in this together. If anyone ever tries to pin anything on me, I'll say it was your idea. I was helping you out.'

'But I never wanted you to do anything. I never wanted him dead.'

'Who's to know that?' Roy smiled and put his arm round Ashley's shoulder. 'But play your cards right now and she'll be yours for life. And that is what you wanted, isn't it? It's a good bargain.' Roy paused. 'It's worth selling your soul to make your dreams come true.'

Excerpt from *First Cut is the Deepest*

Prologue

How long have you been afraid of me? Last night I noticed your glance in my direction when you thought I wasn't looking - and I saw the dread deep in your eyes. I kept my secret for so long, but in the end you were sure to learn the truth. Perhaps you guessed sooner than I realised. After all, it's simple when you know: you recognise the clues which were there all the time, make sense at last of so many oddities, things that didn't quite add up. And now that you know, you are being eaten away by fear.

Do you remember telling me once why the law drew you like a moth to the flame? All of us need rules, you said, and we must believe in rules. Rules which draw a line between right and wrong. What is left for us if we don't have faith, if we can't cling to the belief that life is more than chance and accident? Without justice, the world is wild and dangerous. But the law's a lousy mistress, we should have learned that by now. She's fickle and shameless. Each time you put your trust in her, she lets you down.

So let's forget the law; it can't deliver us from evil. The time has come to face reality. Inside your heart, you know I'm killing you.

No more deceit: the choice is simple. One of us has to die. And I'll be honest with you, I'm scared too. Yet there's no escaping our destiny. My flesh tingles as I close my eyes and picture in my mind the darkness that lies ahead of us.

Chapter One

'Forget it, it's too risky.'

'That's half the fun, isn't it?' asked the voice at the other end of the line.

'What if he finds out?'

'No-one need ever know,' Juliet May whispered, 'apart from you and me.'

Outside in the corridor, someone banged on Harry Devlin's door, made him jump. 'The last client who said that to me,' he muttered, 'finished up with five years for money laundering.'

'Then thank God it's your body I'm after, not your legal advice.'

Harry tightened his grip on the receiver. 'Hey, whatever happened to safe sex?'

'Overrated, don't you agree? Listen, there's nothing to worry about.' She was amused, her tone persuasive. She'd have made a good advocate, he thought, could have persuaded a hanging judge to let her off with a neck massage. 'Casper is in London until tomorrow evening. Everything's perfect. The house is in the middle of nowhere. This may be the best chance we ever get.'

The door rocked on its hinges. Jim Crusoe was standing outside, hand on hips, forearm raised to show the face of his wristwatch. Harry saw the time and gave his partner a caught-in-the-act grin. He could feel his cheeks burning. Cupping his hand over the mouthpiece, he said, 'Sorry, I forgot. With you in half a minute.'

Jim grunted and slammed the door. Harry said into the phone, 'I'm late for a meeting at our bank. A date with the Loan Arranger.'

A giggle. 'Don't tell me, he's got a sidekick called Tonto. Does this mean you have to take out an overdraft to buy the champagne for tonight?'

It was a bitter day in November. The morning news had warned of gales and now he could hear them roaring in from the waterfront.

The office heating had broken down at lunch-time and the cold was seeping into his room through cracks in the window frames. Yet his palms were damp and anticipatory lust wasn't entirely to blame.

'I haven't said I can make it tonight.'

'Don't play hard to get,' Juliet said. 'You want what I want.'

Was that true? He was breathing hard, conscious of the pounding of his heart. 'Adultery isn't good for your health.'

'You're not commiting adultery. It's years since your wife died.'

This wasn't the time to quibble about matrimonial law or the proper interpretation of the Book of Leviticus. He didn't want to finish up like a discredited politician, arguing that his deceits were 'legally accurate'. 'If Casper hears about this,' he said, 'we'll both finish up in intensive care. Maybe worse.'

'Forget him. You ought to relax. The trouble is, you're too uptight.'

'He's dangerous. You've said so yourself.'

'I can picture you tensing up,' she said softly. 'Don't worry, we can have a nice soothing bath together.'

He couldn't help imagining her arms as they stretched around him, her long fingers probing the cavities beneath his shoulder blades, the sharp red nails starting to dig into his back. Closing his eyes, he could smell her perfume, taste the champagne on her lips, feel the thick mass of her hair brush against his cheeks, then his chest.

'But...'

'No buts, Harry. Remember the Tarot reading I gave you? You're in for a life-changing experience.'

That's what I'm afraid of. He sucked air into his lungs. It was supposed to be an aid to rational thought.

'Seven thirty,' she said, filling the silence. 'It's less than four hours away. I can hardly wait, can you?'

Another angry knock at the door. Harry let out a breath. So much for rational thought. Well, whoever chose as an epitaph - 'he was always sensible'?

'No,' he said. 'I can't.'

Carl Symons swallowed the last loop of spaghetti and wiped his mouth clean with his sleeve. He turned up the volume on the portable television on his kitchen table. The bellow of the wind outside was drowning out even the determined cheeriness of the weather forecaster.

'Not a night to be out and about, with storms across the region and the likelihood of damage to property. And a word for all drivers from our motoring unit: don't travel unless your journey is absolutely essential.'

Carl belched. The wind and rain didn't bother him: he wasn't going anywhere tonight. He'd left work at five sharp so as to get home before the weather worsened, the first time in months that he hadn't worked late. Even so, it had seemed like a long day. Unsatisfactory, too. He'd emailed Suki Anwar, asking her to come to his office at four, and the bitch had sent an insolent reply, refusing on the pretext that she had an urgent case to prepare. As if that wasn't enough, on his way to the car park, he'd caught sight of Brett Young behind the wheel of his clapped-out Sierra. For a moment he'd thought Brett was putting his foot down, trying to run him down as he was crossing Water Street. He'd had to skip through the traffic to gain the safety of the pavement on the other side. He'd felt himself flushing and he could picture Brett giving a grim smile at his alarm. *Bastard*. A lying bastard, too, one who had got what he deserved. Carl wasn't sorry about what he'd done.

He laughed out loud and sang in a rumpled baritone, '*Je ne regrette rien.*'

It made him feel better. He'd forget about Suki and Brett. Better to spend a couple of hours working on his report for tomorrow's meeting. It would assuage his conscience for that prompt departure from the office. And he did have a conscience about it. His parents were long dead, but they had inculcated in him the puritan work ethic; he prized diligence above all things. Not even his worst enemy - whoever that might be; he suspected that he was spoiled for choice - could accuse him of laziness. Later, he might relax with a film. Channel 4 was showing an old black and white movie called *Nosferatu*.

He wondered whether to have a Mars bar and decided against it. The lager had better stay in the fridge as well. Tomorrow he intended to wear his best suit and he'd noticed that the trousers were getting tight. He'd always nourished a deep contempt for people with pretty faces, people like Suki and Brett. Only fools judged by appearances: good looks were a mask for weakness. Yet he'd always secretly prided himself on his flat belly. He'd lost his hair young and he'd never been a Robert Redford, but at least he wasn't overweight. Truth was, he needed to look the part at the meeting: nowadays presentation mattered in everything, including the prosecution service. So - how best to present the latest conviction rates? The figures were looking good; the trick was to make sure everyone got the message that the credit belonged to him. No-one could deny he'd justified his promotion. A Principal Crown Prosecutor owed a duty to the taxpayer. He'd told the appointment board that it was vital to be selective. No point in pursuing the ones who were sure to get away. The secret was to target cases where the evidence was cast-iron so that not even a Liverpool jury could fail to bring in a verdict of guilty.

A deafening crash outside almost knocked him off his feet. He swore loudly. A roof tile gone, by the sound of it. He'd already spent a fortune renovating this place. Trouble was, it was too exposed. He'd bought it after receiving confirmation of his promotion in the summer, intrigued by its setting on the bank of the Dee, looking across to the Welsh hills. Once upon a time, before the silting of the river had destroyed the old Dee ports forever, there had been a small anchorage here. This house had once belonged to the harbour master. Now its isolation was part of its charm to Carl; he liked his own company best. Over the years, he'd realised that he didn't have much time for his fellow human beings. So often they whined about being used, when in truth they had asked for it. The prospect of evenings alone held no terrors for him: he was no longer his own boss during the working day, but still he preferred to do as he pleased. But if the cost of maintaining the house continued to rise, rising further in the hierarchy would no longer be merely an ambition. It would be a necessity.

He turned on the outside light and opened the door which gave on to a York stone courtyard at the side of the house. The wind stung his cheeks and blew the rain into his eyes as he stood on the threshold. Shivering, he blinked hard and finally made out the fragments of slate scattered across the paving and the grass beyond. On the other side of the low wall, the waves were lashing the shore like flails on the back of a galley slave. He had never seen the Dee so wild. A sudden gust caught the wooden door and almost snapped it off its hinges. He swore, then heaved the handle and shut out the night.

Why did I say yes?

Harry killed the engine of his MG and sat hunched over the steering wheel, staring through the rain-streaked windscreen into blackness. On his way over here, radio reports had told of the gales leaving a trail of destruction from the mountains of Snowdonia all along the north coast of Wales. A woman swept away in a swollen river, a dozen caravans tossed into the sea. Now the storm was ripping through Wirral. He couldn't help shivering, but it had nothing to do with the elements.

He should not be here. Not so much because of guilt, more because he was sure that one day his affair with Juliet would end in tears. Perhaps worse. Casper May had betrayed his wife a hundred times, or so she reckoned. He beat her too: Harry had seen the bruises and his tears of rage had trickled over them. Casper had, it was true, come a long way since his days as loan shark, charging rates of interest that would have made Shylock's eyes water. His security firm was due to go public soon and nowadays he saw more of government ministers than pleading debtors. The politicians were keen to build bridges with business and to wine and dine an entrepreneur famed for his charitable fund-raising: he might be persuaded to volunteer a donation to party funds. But respectability was only skin deep. If he realised he'd been cuckolded by a small-time solicitor, honour would need to be satisfied.

Harry had heard the story of a rival security boss who had undercut Casper for a contract to look after a dockside container terminal. A week after he'd gone missing, he'd been found inside one of the containers with a hood over his head and a gag in his mouth. The body was discovered on the same day that Casper was lunching with a task force from the Regional Development Agency, sharing ideas on how to make the north-west a better place to live in. He'd sent flowers to the widow, a woman he'd slept with in his younger days. The names of the scallies who had kidnapped the man and left him to die were common knowledge in the pubs of Dingle, but no-one had ever been charged. When Casper May was involved, it made sense to look the other way.

It still wasn't too late. He could turn the MG round now and set off for home. Why not settle for beer rather than the bottle of Mouton Cadet he'd stashed in the boot, maybe watch the late vampire film on Channel 4 and admire Max Schreck's uncanny impersonation of an inspector from the Inland Revenue? He could call Juliet tomorrow and make an excuse. Even if he said something about seeing her around, she'd guess that it was over. No great loss for her: she would soon find someone else to amuse herself with.

But as he buttoned his coat up to the neck to keep out the cold, he realised that for him it was too late after all. No longer was it a matter of choice. She was waiting for him in the lonely cottage. He could not help but seize the chance to be with her again.

Carl turned the key in the mortice lock, but there was no escape from the wind in the living-room chimney. A frantic sound, he thought, the sort a beast might make if caught in a trap. He shook his head, surprised at himself. He wasn't given to flights of fancy. Imagination was a nuisance. It played no part in the preparation of a case for court, in the effective prosecution of criminal offenders.

He cursed as the picture on his television began to flicker and the actor's voices in the Fiat commercial became garbled and discordant. Suddenly the programme cut off and the fluorescent overhead light went out.

Blindly, he stumbled towards the hall, cracking his knee against a cabinet as he crossed the uneven floor. He had to remember to duck his head under the low beams as he went through the doorway. Everything seemed unfamiliar in the dark. He tried the light switch next to the stairs. Nothing. A power line must have been brought down in the storm.

Shit, shit, shit.

At least he was prepared for a black-out. He prided himself on his organisational abilities and he always had supplies to enable him to cope with a crisis. Experiences like this, he told himself, proved the wisdom of such foresight. He crept back into the kitchen and found a packet of candles and a box of matches in a drawer. The flame was weak and the room was full of shadows, but anything was better than pitch darkness.

He tried the transistor radio. The Meteorological Office was issuing another warning of severe gales. *Tell me something I don't know.* He retuned to Radio 3 for a bit of background Beethoven whilst he pulled the paperwork for tomorrow's meeting out of his briefcase. Perhaps if the power didn't come back on, he would only work for an hour or so. He'd already done the hard graft. It wouldn't do any harm to turn in early and make sure he was fresh and ready for the meeting. If all went well, he could hope for another promotion marking at his next performance appraisal. His sights were set high. A move to another office wasn't impossible if no vacancy cropped up in Liverpool. He wasn't prepared to waste his life away, waiting to step into dead men's shoes.

A knock at the front door. For an instant he confused the noise with the rage of the storm. After all, no-one in their right mind would be out on a night like this. But it came again, the sound of the heavy brass knocker hammering against oak.

It must be one of the Blackwells. Either the mother who lived at the cottage up the slope, the only person he could possibly describe as a neighbour, or her drink-sodden son if he happened to be around. Perhaps they weren't equipped to deal with a power cut. He toyed for a moment with the idea of driving a ruthless bargain for a candle and a couple of vestas. The mother looked as if she had a decent body, considering her age. She hadn't let herself go, he liked that in a woman. The thought made him smile as, carrying the candle in its holder, he unlocked the door.

It was freezing outside and so dark that it took him a moment to focus. Then he saw the light glinting on the blade of the axe in his visitor's hand.

The cottage belonged to Linda Blackwell, personal assistant to Juliet in her public relations business. Harry couldn't face the prospect of sleeping in Casper's bed and his own flat was out of bounds because one of his neighbours was a client of Juliet's and they couldn't run the risk that she'd be recognised. In the past, their trysts had taken place in anonymous hotels in places like Runcorn and Frodsham, where they could be confident they wouldn't bump into anyone they knew. Tonight was supposed to be different. Special. She had given him directions, detailed and specific, warning him that the place would be difficult to find in the dark.

'It's called the Customs House, but it's only tiny and you could easily miss it. She bought it after her husband died. Once you've branched off the main road, ignore the signs to the country park. Carry on for half a mile past the nursery and the tumbledown cottage until you come to the end of the lane. Tucked away underneath the trees are a couple of lock-up garages. The one on the left is Linda's. She's let me have the key, so I'll park my Alfa inside there. You leave your car in front of the door. For God's sake don't block her neighbour's access. She can't bear him. I don't know why, but I can guess.' A laugh. 'He's a lawyer and you know how difficult they can be.'

Harry wished now that he'd asked the neighbour's name. The last thing he wanted was to bump into someone he knew. What could he say? 'Can't stop, I'm just off for a tryst with the wife of a gangster'? In theory, it might do wonders for his image - as long as Casper May never got to hear of it. He checked again to make sure that even the most pedantic conveyancer could not complain that his right of way had been obstructed and set off down the path which led into the spinney which bordered the lane.

'For God's sake, don't forget to bring a torch,' she'd instructed him. 'There are no lights and the path twists and turns on its way through the wood.'

Good advice, he reflected, as he shone the pencil beam through the darkness. Without the help of a light, he would soon be hopelessly lost amongst the trees. Juliet obviously knew her way here of old. Had she explained this route before, to a previous lover he'd heard nothing about? If so, was it any of his business?

The path was muddy underfoot and he found himself wondering why anyone would want to live here, in the back of beyond. The city he had left behind twenty minutes earlier seemed already to belong to a different world. He could imagine that in the height of summer this wooded walk might be idyllic, but only a fool would trade the warmth of home on the wildest night of winter for the rain drenching his hair and the wind stinging his cheeks.

The gale dropped for a moment and he heard a rustling amongst the trees. He shone his torch and could dimly perceive dark shapes above his head. What sound did bats make? He was a townie; natural history had never been a strongpoint. To think he might have been in his flat this evening, watching a vampire film on the box, rather than experiencing the Grand Guignol of a date with a murderer's wife. If ever there was a night for the un-dead to rise, this was it.

He tripped over a tree stump but somehow managed to keep his grip upon the holdall which contained the champagne and a few overnight things. The torch slipped from his other hand and rolled away. He scrabbled around in the darkness and when he picked it up, found that the bulb was smashed. In a fit of temper, he hurled the thing away into the undergrowth before squatting on his haunches and cradling the bag with the bottle whilst he told himself to calm down. Pity it wasn't full of whisky; he'd have brought a hip flask if he'd realised the scale of this endurance test. Perhaps Juliet had dreamed up the assignation as a challenge, a measure of the scale of his obsession with her. When he arrived at the Customs House, he'd probably find that there was a dual carriageway running straight past the front door. He inched forward and realised that the path was beginning to fall away beneath his feet.

'When you reach the edge of the cliff, the track starts to wind down. There's a hand-rail and you'd better cling on. It will be slippery with all this rain.'

She was a mistress of understatement, he decided. Unable to see where he was going, he clamped his left hand around the wet wooden railing and put one foot gingerly in front of another. He knew that, ahead and below, flowed the river that divided England from Wales, but he could see nothing of it. On either side of him, trees swayed like monstrous exotic dancers mocking his timidity.

'Soon the path forks. Make sure you follow the left branch. Steps lead down to the Customs House. The other way takes you to the lawyer's cottage.'

He missed his footing and almost fell again. These must be the steps. He told himself that he was almost there. Inching down the pathway, he saw the dark outlines of a house loom in front of him: it must be the place. Yet why were there no lights? He felt suddenly sick and wondered if, for some unknowable reason, she had betrayed him. If he walked in, would he find himself greeted by Casper May, rather than his wife?

'I'll leave the door ajar. You won't need to ring the bell.'

He found himself on a cinder path running up to a small porch. As he moved forward, he saw the front door open, framing the slender figure he couldn't stop thinking about.

'Come in, quick,' she urged. 'You'll catch your death out there.'

As consciousness returned, Carl Symons became fuzzily aware that his head was hurting. Hurting as it had never hurt before. The haft of the axe must have struck him on the temple, a blow so sudden that he'd not even had time to raise his hands in an attempt at self-defence. He forced his eyes open, trying to blink away the tears of pain. The skin of his cheeks and hands was grazed and sore. He'd been dragged inside and laid out on the floor of the kitchen.

The stone was cold against his flesh. By the flickering light of the candle, he could see a pool of blood. It had leaked from the wound in his temple and on to the ground.

The candle wavered. With a desperate effort, Carl tried to shift his head so that he could follow the pool of light. Even the slight movement made him want to squeal.

A face emerged from the shadows and bent down towards him, as if to judge the extent of his suffering. Carl could see two hands as well. One held the axe, the other a sharpened stave.

The face was familiar to Carl but there was a strange light in the eyes that he had never seen before. The face came closer still but did not answer. Hypnotised, he watched as a tongue appeared and began to lick the pale lips. The axe was held aloft. White teeth bared in a savage smile.

Carl tried to form a single word and heard his own voice, croaky and pleading.

'*Please.*'

But even as he spoke, the axe began to move towards him. Carl knew it was too late to beg for mercy. His bowels loosened.

The Making of *The Devil in Disguise*

My first five books, set in Liverpool and featuring Harry Devlin, were often described by reviewers as "gritty urban thrillers". However, that phrase did not quite capture the type of books I set out to write. My aim was to create entertaining mysteries which updated the traditions of the classic detective novel in the context of a modern city background, while offering (for those readers who wanted something more than just entertainment, important though entertainment is in genre fiction) some exploration of aspects of character and society.

Because Harry was a rather down at heel individual, with a client base that was scarcely blue-chip, I'd found myself writing about the seamier side of life in Liverpool - especially in the first book, *All the Lonely People*, but to some extent in its successors as well. Prostitutes, gangsters and seedy nightclubs all featured from time to time. As I'd grown in confidence, I'd tried out different approaches in the way I plotted, and told my stories, and when I started thinking about the sixth novel in the series, it seemed perfectly natural to me to set it in a middle class milieu, with less focus on the mean streets than before.

I was also interested in writing a story that was a more explicit homage to Golden Age detective fiction than my earlier books. I've come to the genre as a child by reading the books of Agatha Christie, and although I also delight in the more sophisticated writing of crime novelists such as Patricia Highsmith, Ruth Rendell and Frances Fyfield, I continue to enjoy the work of the Queen of Crime. The idea of producing a mystery that was a modern riff on a Christie theme was very appealing. But I didn't want simply to write a pastiche. I thought it should be possible to write a book that combined the ingenuity of Christie's best work with an interesting depiction of people and place that met the expectations and demands of a contemporary readership.

It is a truism that there is only a finite number of plot ideas, even though people disagree about what the precise number is. My first Harry Devlin short story, "The Boxer", gave a fresh twist to the plot of the Sherlock Holmes story, and this experience prompted me to try to do something similar, but much more elaborate, with the plot of an Agatha Christie novel. The book I chose was one of the very first adult mysteries that I read, the Hercule Poirot classic, *After the Funeral* (also known by the less subtle title of *Funerals Are Fatal*). It's a story which has a simple yet brilliant deception at its heart; having admired the trick for so long, I wondered how to give it a fresh, and different, life, and finally came up with a variation on Christie's theme that I like to think she would have approved. I've never come across anyone who has spotted the connection without my drawing it to their attention, but I did give the Poirot story, as well as Christie herself, name checks in the novel.

I also seized the opportunity to create, as one of my key settings, a Liverpudlian bookshop specialising in crime fiction. How I wish The Speckled Band had really existed! Like Harry, I'd have loved to flip through the battered rarities, and I included mention of the work of some of my favourite Golden Age authors, such as John Dickson Carr, Philip MacDonald, and the largely forgotten Richard Hull, one of the few accountants to write mysteries. As usual in the Devlin books, there are also references to movies that appeal to me, notably *Night Moves* and *Vertigo*.

I also indulged myself by integrating into the story-line a performance in Liverpool of the Bacharach and David musical *Promises, Promises*, Neil Simon's book for which was based on the screenplay of another classic film, *The Apartment*. The show was a huge hit on Broadway and in the West End in the late 60s, but then disappeared from view. However, it enjoyed a revival at the Bridewell Theatre in London while I was writing the book, and my agent Mandy Little and I found that the music and the jokes had stood the test of time well, even though more than another decade was to pass before the show returned to Broadway for another successful run. The Bridewell Theatre was an intriguing and unusual venue which I reinvented and relocated to Merseyside as The Pool Theatre.

Writing a book that is part of a series of mysteries is - or, at least, can be - different in some ways writing a stand-alone novel. Undeniably, there are drawbacks. One snag is that the reader can be pretty confident that the series detective will survive to fight another day, so it is important to find creative ways of building up the tension. Another is that the main characters' backstories need to be explained to readers who are not familiar with them, without boring those readers who are. And there is always the risk of slipping into the formula of the tried-and-tested, potentially with damaging results.

Yet there are very real compensating advantages, which to my mind make writing a series a joy. For instance, minor characters can come and go as the needs of the individual story dictate. Here, I enjoyed bringing back Jonah Deegan, the grumpy old gumshoe, as well as introducing a new and contrasting character to support him. Stephanie Hall, his niece and business partner, was someone I thought of as possible future love interest for Harry, but in this book the fun lay in portraying her relationship with Jonah and in establishing her as someone Harry could trust. With this groundwork laid, who knows what might happen between them one of these days?

But in the short-term, I decided to switch Harry's personal focus from Kim Lawrence to Juliet May. My original plan with Kim has been to contrast her crisp feminism and crusading zeal with Harry's rather crumpled yet enduring passion for justice. I felt, however, that I'd taken their relationship as *far* as I could, but I want to match Harry with someone who spelt danger - the glamorous wife of a murderous villain. His risky affair with Juliet created the set-up for the next book I wrote, *First Cut Is the Deepest*, and even after a long gap in time, their relationship so continued to fascinate me that, a decade after it came into being, it again formed a significant element of the storyline in *Waterloo Sunset*. Of course, I had no way of foreseeing this when I created Juliet - it just illustrates the point about the benefits and pleasures of series writing.

The sub-plot about Davey Damnation that began in *Eve of Destruction* was resolved in this book. I like the idea of extending a sub-plot over more than one book in a series, and I returned to this way of writing later, in the first couple of Lake District Mysteries. My aim always, though, is to make sure that the books can be read in any order without any significant reduction in enjoyment.

In trying to give a perspective on areas of Liverpool life different from those in the first five books, I made use of a variety of settings. Not just obvious scenes, like the Albert Dock, but the tunnel lined with tombstones in the grounds of the Anglican Cathedral. To capture the atmosphere of the rooftop above Roy Milburn's studio, I went on to the roof of the seven-storey office building where I worked from 1980 until moving in 2011. Very windy up there it was, too. Like Harry, I wondered if a sudden gust from the river might pick me up and throw me on to the street far below. The Piquet Club was my own invention; over the years I've spent a bit of time in two of Liverpool's famous private members' clubs, the Lyceum (which now no longer exists) and the Racquets Club, but rather more as a proprietor (that is, member) of the Athenaeum, a delightful oasis in the midst of the city's shopping area, and possessing an impressive library. But as far as I know, none of those venerable institutions ever boasted a collection of erotica similar to that with which I endowed the Piquet.

Names of characters in a novel do matter, partly for artistic reasons and also because of the need to minimise the risk of accidental libel. Yet conjuring names up is quite a challenge. The names have to "feel right". I use various methods for naming characters, but my favourite is to use the names of Derbyshire county cricketers, past and present. When I went to watch the team play a game at Derby not long before I started *The Devil in Disguise*, I was introduced by a friend to a number of the players, including the South African Test batsman Darryll Cullinan. He expressed enthusiasm for having a character named after him - hence Matthew Cullinan. Some time after the book was published, I received an email from one Anthony Dessaur, who was researching his family's unusual name. He'd come across the book and wanted to know what had prompted me to invent the name of Luke Dessaur. I explained how I used Derbyshire cricketers' names, and that Wayne Dessaur had had a spell as one of the county's batsmen. Wayne turned out to be Anthony's son, and duly acquired a copy of the book, suitably inscribed. A strangely unexpected but, to me, enjoyable contact.

When I was writing the book, I discussed the work in progress with my editor, Kate Callaghan. She was keen on the story, but felt it needed a dramatic opening, and on reflection, I agreed. So I introduced the prologue, which was not there in the first version. Unfortunately, to my extreme disappointment - and bafflement-Kate's boss Judy Piatkus, who had taken me on as an unpublished author, and given me much support, really did not care for the book. The less "gritty" style and story-line didn't appeal to her. I still keep a copy of a letter she wrote to Mandy expressing her concerns - a reminder to myself that opinions about literature are always subjective (and that publishers certainly don't always get their own judgments right!)

Of course, one has to take criticisms from sensible and experienced judges seriously, but I was convinced Judy was wrong about *The Devil in Disguise*. She wanted me to put it to one side and write a new Devlin, but I had faith in the book and so did Mandy. Happily, Hodder & Stoughton agreed that the story worked well, and offered to take on the whole Devlin series, starting with this book (they later reprinted the earlier books in paperback for good measure.) So it all worked out for the best in the end. And at least I'd gained experience of the ups and downs of a writer's career - an experience that has helped sustain me ever since. I still have a soft spot for *The Devil in Disguise* and it's a joy to see it enjoy a fresh lease of life.

Martin Edwards: an Appreciation

by Michael Jecks

Both as a crime writer and as a keen exponent of the genre, Martin Edwards has long been sought out by his peers, and is now becoming recognised as a contemporary crime author at the top of his form.

Born in Knutsford, Cheshire, Martin went to school in Northwich before taking a first class honours degree in law at Balliol College, Oxford. From there he went on to join a law firm and is now a highly respected lawyer specializing in employment law. He is the author of Tottel's *Equal Opportunities Handbook*, 4th edition, 2007.

Early in his career, he began writing professional articles and completed his first book at 27, covering the purchase of business computers. His non-fiction work continues with over 1000 articles in newspapers and magazines, and seven books dedicated to the law (two of which were co-authored).

His life of crime began a little later with the Harry Devlin series, set in Liverpool. The first of his series, *All The Lonely People* (1991), was shortlisted for the CWA John Creasey Memorial Dagger for the first work of crime fiction by a new writer. With the advent of his second novel, Martin Edwards was becoming recognised as a writer of imagination and flair. This and subsequent books also referenced song titles from his youth.

The Harry Devlin books demonstrate a great sympathy for Liverpool, past and present, with gritty, realistic stories. 'Liverpool is a city with a tremendous resilience of spirit and character,' he says in *Scene of the Crime,* (2002). Although his protagonist is a self-effacing Scousers with a dry wit, Edwards is not a writer for the faint-hearted. 'His gifts are of the more classical variety - there are points in his novels when I think I'm reading Graham Greene,' wrote Ed Gorman, while *Crime Time* magazine said 'The novels successfully combine the style of the traditional English detective story with a darker noir sensibility.'

More recently Martin Edwards has moved into the Lake District with mystery stories featuring an historian, Daniel Kind, and DCI Hannah Scarlett. The first of these, *The Coffin Trail*, was short listed for the Theakston's Old Peculier Crime Novel of the year 2006.

In this book Martin Edwards made good use of his legal knowledge. DCI Hannah Scarlett is in charge of a cold case review unit, attempting to solve old crimes, and when Daniel Kind moves into a new house, seeking a fresh start in the idyllic setting of the Lake District, he and she are drawn together by the murder of a young woman. The killer, who died before he could be convicted, used to live in Kind's new cottage.

Not only does Edwards manage to demonstrate a detailed knowledge of the law (which he is careful never to force upon the reader), with the Lake District mysteries he has managed to bring the locations to vivid life. He has a skill for acute description which is rare - especially amongst those who are more commonly used to writing about city life.

More recently Edwards has published *Take My Breath Away*, a stand-alone psychological suspense novel, which offers a satiric portrait of an upmarket London law firm eerily reminiscent of Tony Blair's New Labour government.

Utilising his legal experience, he has written articles about actual crimes. *Catching Killers* was an illustrated book describing how police officers work on a homicide case all the way from the crime scene itself to presenting evidence in court.

When the writer Bill Knox died, Edwards was asked by his publisher to help complete his final manuscript, on which Knox had been working until days before his death. Bill Knox's method of writing was to hone each separate section of his books before moving on to the next, so Martin was left with the main thrust of the story, together with some jotted notes and newspaper clippings. From these he managed to complete *The Lazarus Widow* in an unusal departure for him.

More conventionally, Martin Edwards is a prolific writer of short stories. He has published the anthology *Where Do You Find Your Ideas?* which offers a mix of Harry Devlin tales mingled with historical and psychological short stories. His *Test Drive* was short listed for the CWA Short Story Dagger.

Edwards edits the regular CWA anthologies of short stories. These works have included *Green for Danger*, and *I.D. Crimes of Identity*, which included his own unusual and notable story *InDex*. In 2003 he also edited the CWA's *Mysterious Pleasures* anthology, which was a collection of the Golden Dagger winners' short stories to celebrate the CWA's Golden Jubilee.

A founder member of the performance and writing group, Murder Squad, Martin Edwards has found the time to edit their two anthologies.

When not writing and editing, Edwards is an enthusiastic reader and collector of crime fiction. He reviews for magazines, books and websites, and his essays have appeared in many collections.

He is the chairman of the CWA's nominations sub-committee for the Cartier Diamond Dagger Award, the world's most prestigious award for crime writing.

Martin Edwards is one of those rare creatures, a crime-writer's crime-writer. His plotting is as subtle as any, his writing deft and fluid, his characterisation precise, and his descriptions of the locations give the reader the impression that they could almost walk along the land blindfolded. He brings them all to life.

(An earlier version of this article appeared in *British Crime Writing: An Encyclopaedia,* edited by Barry Forshaw)

Meet Martin Edwards

Martin Edwards is an award-winning crime writer whose fifth and most recent Lake District Mystery, featuring DCI Hannah Scarlett and Daniel Kind, is *The Hanging Wood*, published in 2011. Earlier books in the series are *The Coffin Trail* (short-listed for the Theakston's prize for best British crime novel of 2006), *The Cipher Garden*, *The Arsenic Labyrinth* (short-listed for the Lakeland Book of the Year award in 2008) and *The Serpent Pool*.

Martin has written eight novels about lawyer Harry Devlin, the first of which, *All the Lonely People*, was short-listed for the CWA John Creasey Memorial Dagger for the best first crime novel of the year. In addition he has published a stand-alone novel of psychological suspense, *Take My Breath Away*, and a much acclaimed novel featuring Dr Crippen, *Dancing for the Hangman*. The latest Devlin novel, *Waterloo Sunset*, appeared in 2008.

Martin completed Bill Knox's last book, *The Lazarus Widow*, and has published a collection of short stories, *Where Do You Find Your Ideas? and other stories*; 'Test Drive' was short-listed for the CWA Short Story Dagger in 2006, while 'The Bookbinder's Apprentice' won the same Dagger in 2008.

A well-known commentator on crime fiction, he has edited 20 anthologies and published eight non-fiction books, including a study of homicide investigation, *Urge to Kill* .In 2008 he was elected to membership of the prestigious Detection Club. He was subsequently appointed Archivist to the Detection Club, and is also Archivist to the Crime Writers' Association. He received the Red Herring Award for services to the CWA in 2011.

In his spare time Martin is a partner in a national law firm, Weightmans LLP. His website is www.martinedwardsbooks.com and his blog www.doyouwriteunderyourownname.blogspot.com

Also Available from Martin Edwards

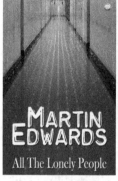

All the Lonely People

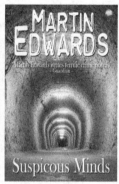

Suspicious Minds

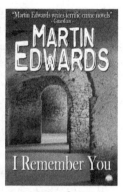

I Remember You

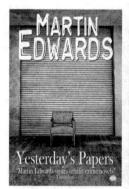

Yesterday's Papers

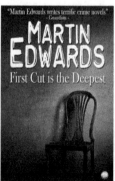

First Cut is the Deepest

CPSIA information can be obtained
at www.ICGtesting.com
Printed in the USA
BVHW091912270319
543880BV00012B/284/P